THE BILLION DOLLAR BRAIN

A NOVEL BY *Len Deighton*

By the author of FUNERAL IN BERLIN

THE
BILLION DOLLAR
BRAIN

G. P. Putnam's Sons New York

Library of Congress Catalog Card Number: 66-10466

Fourth impression

3957
2-28-66

Spring is a virgin, summer a mother, autumn a widow, winter a stepmother.

—RUSSIAN PROVERB

Two mythical countries (Kalevala and Pohjola) fight a perpetual war. They both want a magic mill that grinds endless salt, corn and money. The most important figure in this conflict is an old man named Vainamoinen. He is a wizard and wise-man. He is also a musician and plays tunes upon the bones of a pike. Vainamoinen woos a lovely young girl Aino but she drowns herself rather than marry an old man.

—KALEVALA: *a Finnish folk epic*

Mr. Paul Getty . . . is quoted as having said that a billion dollars is not worth what it used to be.

—NUBAR GULBENKIAN

Contents

THE BILLION DOLLAR BRAIN

| *London—Helsinki*

CHAPTER 1

IT was the morning of my hundredth birthday. I shaved the final mirror-disk of old tired face under the merciless glare of the bathroom lighting. It was all very well telling oneself that Humphrey Bogart had that sort of face; but he also had a hairpiece, half a million dollars a year and a stand-in for the rough bits. I dabbed a styptic pencil at the razor nicks. In the magnifying mirror it looked like a white rocket landing on the uncharted side of the moon.

Outside was February and the first snow of the year. At first it was the sort of snow that a sharp PR man would make available to journalists. It sparkled and floated. It was soft yet crisp like some new, sugar-coated breakfast cereal. Girls wore it in their hair and the *Telegraph* ran a picture of a statue wearing some. It was hard to reconcile this benign snow with the stuff that caused paranoia among British Railways officials. That Monday morning it was building-up in crunchy wedges under the heels of shoes and falling in dry white pyramids along the

11

front hall of the Charlotte Street office where I worked. I said "Good morning" to Alice and she said "Don't tread it in" to me, which summed up our relationship nicely.

The Charlotte Street building was an ancient creaking slum. The wallpaper had great boils full of loose plaster and there were metal patches in the floor where the boards were too rotten to repair. On the first-floor landing was a painted sign that said ACME FILMS—CUTTING ROOMS and under that a drawing of a globe that made Africa too thin. From behind the doors came the noise of a movie projector and a strong smell of film cement. The next landing was painted with fresh green paint. On one door a dog-eared piece of headed notepaper said *B. Isaacs Theatrical Tailor* which at one time I had considered very funny. Behind me I heard Alice puffing up the stairs with a catering-size tin of Nescafé. Someone in the dispatch department put a brass band record on the gramophone. Dawlish, my boss, was always complaining about that gramophone but even Alice couldn't really control the dispatch department.

My secretary said, "Good morning." Jean was a tall girl in her middle twenties. Her face was as calm as Nembutal and with her high cheekbones and tightly drawn black hair she was beautiful without working at it. There were times when I thought that I was in love with Jean and there were times when I thought that she was in love with me, but somehow these times never coincided.

"Good party?" I asked.

"You seemed to enjoy it. When I left, you were drinking a pint of bitter while standing on your head."

"You do exaggerate. Why did you go home alone?"

"I have two hungry cats to support. Two thirty is definitely my bedtime."

"I'm sorry," I said.

"Don't be."

"Truly."

"Going with you to a party is to be there alone. You plant me down, go around chatting with everyone, then wonder why I haven't met them all."

"Tonight," I said, "We'll go to some quiet place for dinner. Just us."

"I'm taking no chances. Tonight I'm cooking a birthday feast at the flat. I'll give you all your favorite things."

"You will?"

"To eat."

"I'll be there," I said.

"You'd better be." She gave me a perfunctory kiss, "Happy birthday," and leaned across and put a glass of water and two Alka-Seltzer tablets on my blotter.

"Why not put the tablets into the water?" I asked.

"I wasn't sure if you could bear the noise." She unlocked my trays and began to work steadily through the great pile of paper work. By midday we hadn't made much impression upon it. I said, "We aren't even keeping up with the incoming."

"We can start a 'pending' tray."

"Don't be so female," I said. "All that does is call some of it another name. Why can't you go through it and handle some of it without me?"

"I already did."

"Then sort out the 'information onlys,' mark them for return to us and pass them on. That would give us a breathing space."

"Now who's kidding himself?"

"Can you think of something better?"

"Yes. I think we should get a written directive from Organization to be sure we're handling only files that we should handle. There may be things in this tray that have nothing to do with us."

"There are times, my love, when I think none of it has anything to do with us."

Jean stared at me in an expressionless way that might have indicated disapproval. Maybe she was thinking about her hair.

"Birthday lunch at the Trat," I said.

"But I look awful."

"Yes," I said.

"I must do my hair. Give me five minutes."

"I'll give you six," I said. She *had* been thinking about her hair.

We lunched at the Trattoria Terrazza: Tagliatelle atta Carbonara, ossobuco, coffee. Pol Roger throughout. Mario complimented me on having a birthday and kissed Jean to celebrate it. He snapped his fingers and up came Strega. I snapped my fingers and up came more Pol Roger. We sat there, drinking champagne with Strega chasers, talking, snapping fingers and discovering ultimate truth and our own infinite wisdom. We got back to the office at three forty-five and I realized for the first time how dangerous that loose lino on the stairs can be.

As I entered my office the intercom was buzzing like a trapped bluebottle. "Yes?" I said.

"Right away," said Dawlish, my boss.

"Right away, sir," I said slowly and carefully.

Dawlish had the only room in the building with two windows. It was a comfortable room although overcrowded with pieces of not very valuable antique furniture. There was a smell of wet overcoat. Dawlish was a meticulous man who looked like an Edwardian coroner. His hair was gray moving toward white and his hands long and thin. When he read he moved his fingertips across the page as though getting a finer understanding from the sense of touch. He looked up from his desk.

"Was that you falling down the stairs?"

"I stumbled," I said. "It's the snow on my shoes."

"Of course it is, my boy," said Dawlish. We both stared out of the window; the snow was falling faster and great white snakes of it were wriggling along the gutter, for it was still dry enough to be lifted by the wind.

"I'm just sending another 378 file to the PM. I hate this clearance business. It's so easy to slip up."

"That's true," I said and was pleased that I didn't have to sign that file.

"What do you think?" asked Dawlish. "Do you think that boy is a security risk?"

The 378 file was a periodic review of the loyalty of S.1's— important chemists, engineers, etc.—but I knew that Dawlish just wanted to think aloud so I grunted.

"You know the one I'm worried about. You know him."

"I've never handled his file," and as long as choice was concerned I'd make damned certain I didn't. I knew that Dawlish had another nasty little bomb called the 378 file subsection 14, which was a file about trade union officials. At the slightest show of intelligent interest I would find that file on my desk. "Personally. What do you feel about him personally?" asked Dawlish.

"Brilliant young student. Socialist. Pleased with himself for getting an honors degree. Wakes up one morning with a suede waistcoat, two kids, job in advertising and a ten-thousand-quid mortgage in Hampstead. Sends for a subscription to the *Daily Worker* just so that he can read the *Statesman* with a clear conscience. Harmless." I hoped that reply carried the right blend of inefficient glibness.

"Very good," said Dawlish, turning the pages of the file. "We should give you a job here."

"I'd never get on with the boss."

Dawlish initialed a chit at the front of the file and tossed it into the Out tray. "We have another problem," he said, "that won't be solved as easily as that," Dawlish reached for a slim file, opened it and read a name. "Olaf Kaarna: you know him?"

"No."

"Journalists who have well-placed, indiscreet friends call themselves political commentators. Kaarna is one of the more responsible ones. He's Finnish. Comfortable." (Dawlish's word for a private income.) "He spends a great deal of time and money collecting his information. Two days ago he spoke to one of our embassy people in Helsinki. Asked him to confirm a couple of small technical points before an article is published next month. He's thinking of sending it to *Kansan Uutiset,* which is the left-wing newspaper. If it was something harmful to us, that would be a good place to set the fuses. Of course we don't know what Kaarna has up his sleeve but he says he can show that there is a vast British Military Intelligence operation covering northern Europe and centered in Finland." Dawlish smiled as he said this and so did I. The thought of Ross at the War Office masterminding a global network was a little unreal.

"And the clever answer is . . . ?"

"Heaven knows," said Dawlish, "but one must follow it up. Ross will no doubt send someone. The Foreign Office have been told; O'Brien can hardly ignore the situation."

"It's like one of those parties where the first girl to leave will have everyone talking about her."

"Quite so," said Dawlish, "that's why I want you to go tomorrow morning."

"Wait a minute," I said. I knew there were all kinds of reasons why it was impossible, but the alcohol blurred my mind. "A passport. Whether we get a good one from the Foreign Office or a quick job from the War Office we will tip our hand and they will delay us if they want to."

"See our friend in Aldgate," said Dawlish.

"But it's 4:30 now."

"Exactly," said Dawlish. "Your plane leaves at 09:50 A.M. That gives you well over sixteen hours to arrange it."

"I'm overworked already."

"Being overworked is just a state of mind. You do far more work than you need on some jobs, less than you need on others. You should be more impersonal."

"I don't even know what I'm supposed to do if I go to Helsinki."

"See Kaarna. Ask him about this article he's preparing. He's been silly in the past, show him a couple of pages of his dossier. He'll be sensible."

"You want me to threaten him?"

"Good heavens, no. Carrot first; stick last. *Buy* this article he's written if necessary. He'll be sensible."

"So you keep saying." I knew it was no good betraying even the slightest amount of excitement. Patiently I said, "There are at least six men in this building who could do this job, even if it's not as simple as you describe. I speak no Finnish. I have no close friends there, I'm not familiar with the country nor have I been handling any file that might have a bearing on this job. Why do I have to go?"

"You," said Dawlish, removing his spectacles and ending the discussion, "are the one best protected against cold."

Old Montagu Street is a grimy slice of Jack the Ripper real estate in Whitechapel. Dark grocers' shops, barrels of salt herring. A ruin. A kosher poultry shop. Jewelers. More ruins. Here and there tiny groups of newly painted shops carry Arabic signs as a fresh wave of underprivileged immigrants probes into the ghetto. Three dark-skinned children on old bicycles pedaled away quickly, circled and stopped. Beyond the tenements the shops began again. One, a printer's, had fly-specked business cards in the window. The printed lettering had faded to pale pastel colors and the cards were writhing and twisting with bygone sunlight. The children made another sudden sortie on their bicycles, leaving arabesques in the thin skin of snow.

The door was stiff and warped. Above my head a small bell jangled and shed dust. The children watched me enter the shop. Inside the small front office there was an ancient counter, topped with a slab of glass. Under the glass were examples of invoices and business cards; faded ghosts of failed businesses. On a shelf there were boxes of paper clips, office sundries, a notice that said *We take orders for rubber stamps* and a greasy catalogue.

As the bell echoes faded, a voice from the back room called, "You the one that phoned?"

"That's right."

"Go on up, luv." Then very loudly in a different sort of voice she screamed, "He's here, Sonny." I opened the counter flap and felt my way up the narrow stairs.

At the rear, gray windows looked down upon yards cluttered with broken bicycles and rusty hip baths all painted with a thin film of snow. The scale of the place seemed too small for me. I'd wandered into a house built for gnomes.

Sonny Sontag worked at the top of the building. This room was cleaner than any of the others but the clutter was worse. A table with a white plastic surface occupied much of the room. On the table there were jam jars crammed with punches, needles and scrapers, graving tools with wooden mushroom heads that fit into the palm of the hand, and two shiny oil-stones. Most of the wall space was filled with numbered brown cardboard boxes.

"Mr. Jolly," said Sonny Sontag, extending a soft white hand that gripped like a Stillson wrench. The first time I ever met Sonny he forged a Ministry of Works pass for me in the name of Peter Jolly. Since that day, with a faith in his own handi-work that typified him, he always called me Mr. Jolly.

Sonny Sontag was an untidy man of medium height. He wore a black suit, black tie and a black rolled-brim hat which he seldom removed. Under his open jacket there was a hand-knitted gray cardigan from which hung a loose thread. When he stood up he tugged at the cardigan and came a little more unraveled.

"Hello, Sonny," I said. "Sorry about this rush."

"No. A regular customer should expect special consider-ation."

"I need a passport," I said. "For Finland."

Looking like a hamster dressed in a business suit, he lifted his chin and twitched his nose while saying "Finland" two or three times. He said, "Mustn't be Scandinavian, too easy to check the registration. Mustn't be a country that needs a visa for Finland because I haven't time to do a visa for you." He wiped his whiskers with a quick movement. "West Germany; no." He went humming and twitching around the shelves until he found a large cardboard box. He cleared a space with his elbows, then just as I thought he was going to start nibbling at the box he tipped its contents across the table. There were a couple of dozen mixed battered passports. Some of them were torn or had corners cut and some were just bunches of loose pages held together with a rubber band. "These are for can-nibalizing," explained Sonny. "I take out pages with visas I need and doctor them. For cheap jobs—the hoop game *—no good for you, but somewhere here I have a lovely little Republic of Ireland. I'd have it ready in a couple of hours if you fancy it." He scuffed through the mangled documents and produced an Irish passport. He gave it to me to look at and I gave him three blurred photos. Sonny studied the photos carefully and then brought a notebook from his pocket and read the microscopic writing at close range.

"Dempsey or Brody," he said, "which do you prefer?"

"I don't mind."

He tugged at his cardigan, a long strand of wool fell away. Sonny wound it quickly around his finger and broke it free.

"Dempsey then, I like Dempsey. How about Liam Dempsey?"

"He's a darling man."

"I wouldn't attempt an Irish accent, Mr. Jolly," said Sonny, "it's very difficult the Irish."

"I'm joking," I said. "A man with a name like Liam Dempsey and a stage-Irish accent would deserve all he got."

"That's right, Mr. Jolly," said Sonny.

I got him to pronounce it a couple of times. He was good with names and I didn't want to go around mispronouncing my own name. I stood against the measure on the wall and Sonny wrote down *5'11", blue eyes, dark brown hair, dark complexion, no visible scars.*

"Place of birth?" inquired Sonny.

"Kinsale?"

Sonny sucked in a breath in noisy disagreement. "Never. Tiny place like that. Too risky." He sucked his teeth again "Cork," he said grudgingly. I was driving a hard bargain.

"O.K. Cork," I said.

---

* Hoop game—using a worthless thing as security when passing a check or taking a car, etc., on approval.

He walked back around the desk, making little disapproving sounds with his lips and saying, "Too risky Kinsale," as if I had tried to outsmart him. He pulled the Irish passport toward him and then turned up the cuffs of his shirt over his jacket. He put a watchmaker's glass into his eye and peered closely at the ink entries. Then he stood up and stared at me as though comparing.

I said, "Do you believe in reincarnation, Sonny?" He wet his lips and smiled, his eyes shining at me as though seeing me for the first time. Perhaps he was, perhaps he was discreet enough to let his clientele pass unseen and unremembered.

He said, "Mr. Jolly, I see men of all kinds in my trade. Men to whom the world has been unkind and men who have been unkind to the world, and believe me they are seldom the same men. But men do not escape the world except by death. We all have our appointments in Samarra. That great writer Anton Chekhov tells us, 'When a man is born he can choose one of three roads. There are no others. If he takes the road to the right, the wolves will eat him up. If he takes the road to the left, he will eat up the wolves. And if he takes the road straight ahead of him, he'll eat himself up.' That's what Chekhov tells us, Mr. Jolly, and when you leave here tonight you'll be Liam Dempsey but you won't discard anything in this room. Destiny has given all her clients a number," he swept a hand across the numbered cardboard boxes, "and no matter how many changes we make she knows which number is ours."

"You're right, Sonny," I said, surprised at mining a rich vein of philosophy.

"I am, Mr. Jolly, believe me, I am."

CHAPTER 2

FINLAND is not a Communist satellite, it is a part of western Europe and shares its prosperity. The shops are jammed full of beefsteaks and LP records, frozen food and TV sets.

Helsinki airport is not a good place from which to make a confidential phone call. Airports seldom are, they use rural exchanges, record calls and have too many cops with time on their hands. So I took a taxi to the railway station.

Helsinki is a well-ordered provincial town where it never ceases to be winter. It smells of wood sap and oil heating like a village shop. Fancy restaurants put smoked reindeer tongue on the menu next to the tournedos Rossini and pretend that they have come to terms with the endless lakes and forests that are buried silent and deep out there under the snow and ice. But Helsinki is just the appendix of Finland, an urban afterthought where half a million people try to forget that thousands upon thousands of square miles of desolation and arctic wasteland begin only a bus stop away.

The taxi pulled into the main entrance of the railway station. It was a huge brown building that looked like a 1930 radio set. Sauna-pink men hurried down the long lines of mud-spattered buses and every now and again there would be a violent grinding of gears as one struck out toward the long country roads.

I changed a five-pound note in the money exchange, then used a call box. I put a twenty-penni piece into the slot and dialed. The phone was answered very promptly as though they were sitting on it at the other end.

I said, "Stockmann?" It was the largest department store in Helsinki and a name that even I could pronounce.

"Ei," said the man at the other end. *Ei* means no.

I said *"Hyvää iltaa,"* having practiced the words for "good evening" and the man at the other end said, *"Kiitos"*—thank you—twice. I hung up. I hailed another cab in the forecourt. I tapped the street map and the driver nodded. We pulled away into the afternoon traffic of the Aleksanterinkatu and finally stopped at the waterfront.

It was mild in Helsinki for that time of year. Mild enough for the ducks in the harbor to have a couple of man-made breaks in the ice to swim on but not so mild that you could go around without a fur hat unless you wanted your ears to fall off and shatter into a thousand pieces.

One or two tarpaulin-covered carts marked the site of the morning market. The great curve of the harbor was white, the churned water frozen into dirty boulders of ice. A small knot of soldiers and an army lorry were also waiting for the ferry. Now and again they laughed and punched each other playfully and their breath rose like Indian signals.

The ferry arrived following the clear channel of broken ice which grudgingly permitted its passage. The boat hooted and the freezing air formed new scar tissue over the wet wound of its path. I lit a Gaulois under cover of the bulkhead and watched the army lorry crawl up the loading ramp. Standing in the marketplace beyond there was a man with a tall column of hydrogen-filled balloons. The wind caught them and they wavered over him like a brightly colored totem that he couldn't quite balance. A gray-haired businessman in an astrakhan hat spoke briefly with the balloon seller. The balloon seller nodded toward the ferry. The gray-haired man didn't buy. I felt the roll of the boat under the weight of the lorry. There was a hoot to warn the last passengers and a thrash of water before the stubby bow chopped back into the dense floating ice.

The gray-haired man joined me on the deck. He was big, and made even bigger by his heavy overcoat. The gray astrakhan hat and the fur collar exactly matched his hair and got mixed into it when he turned his head toward the sea. He was smoking a pipe and the wind blew sparks from it as he came through the door. He leaned over the rail beside me and we both watched the great heaving slabs of ice. It looked like every cabaret act of the thirties had tipped its white grand piano into this harbor.

"Pardon me," said the gray-haired man. "Do you happen to know the phone number of Stockmann's Department Store?"

"It's 12-181," I said, "unless you want the restaurant."

"The restaurant number I know," said the man. "It's 37-350."

I nodded.

"Why have they started all this?"

I shrugged. "Someone in the Organization Department read one of those spy books." The man flinched a bit at the word "spy." It was one of those words to avoid, like the word "artist" is avoided by painters. He said, "It takes me all my time to remember which bits you say and which bits I say."

"Me too," I said. "Perhaps we've both been saying it the wrong way round." The man in the fur collar laughed and more sparks flew from his pipe bowl. "There are two of them as your message said. They are both in Hotel Helsinki and I think they know each other even though they're not talking."

"Why?"

"Well, last night they were the only two people in the dining room. They both ordered in English loud enough for the other to hear and yet they didn't introduce themselves. I mean, two Englishmen in a foreign country dining alone and not even exchanging a greeting. I mean, is it natural?"

"Yes," I said.

The gray-haired man puffed at his pipe and nodded, carefully noting my reply and adding it to his experience. "One is about your height, leaner—perhaps 75 kilos, clean shaven, clear voice, walks and talks like an army officer; about thirty-two. The other is even taller, talks very loudly in an exaggerated English accent, very white face, ill at ease, about twenty-seven years old, thin, maybe weighs—"

"O.K.," I said. "I've got the picture. The first will be Ross's man that the War Office has sent, the other from F.O."

"I would think that too. The first one, who is registered as Seager, had a drink with your military attaché early yesterday evening. The other calls himself Bentley!"

"You've really been thorough," I said.

"It's the least we can do." He suddenly pointed across the frozen sea as someone walked out onto the deck behind us. We stared at one of the ice-locked islands as if we had just exchanged a juicy piece of information about it. The newcomer stamped his feet, "One finnmark," he said. He collected the fare hastily and turned back into the warm cabin.

I said, "Apart from these public-school punters are there other foreign contacts with Kaarna?"

"It's hard to say. The town is full of strange people; Americans, Germans, even Finns who dabble a little in"—he wriggled his fingers to find a word—"informations."

Across the ice I could see the island of Suomenlinna and a group of people waiting for the boat. "My two haven't visited Kaarna?" The man shook his head. "Then it's time someone did," I said.

"Will there be trouble?" We were nearly there now. I heard

the driver starting the lorry. "Don't worry," I said. "This isn't that sort of job."

I woke up in the Hotel Helsinki at seven A.M. the next morning. Someone was coming into my room. The waitress put the tray down beside my bed. Two cups, two saucers, two pots of coffee, two of everything. I tried to look like a man with a friend in the bathroom. The waitress opened the shutters and let the cold northern light fall across my bed. When she had gone I dissolved half a packet of laxative chocolate into each pot of coffee. I rang for room service. A man came. I explained that there was some mistake. The coffee was for two men down the hall, Mr. Seager and Mr. Bentley. I gave him their room numbers and a one-mark note. Then I showered, shaved, dressed and checked out of the hotel.

I walked across the street to the first-floor shopping promenade where the charladies were flicking a final mop across the shiny floors of unopened shops. Two fur-hatted cops were eating breakfast in the Columbia Café. I took a seat near the window and stared across the square to the Saarinen railway station which dominated the town. More snow had fallen during the night and a small army of shovelers were clearing the bus stop.

I ate my breakfast. Kellogg's Riisi Muroja went "snap, crackle pop," the eggs were fine and so was the orange juice, but I didn't fancy coffee that morning.

Helsinki is only a kilometer wide at the end of the peninsula. Here in the south part of the town where the diplomats live and work, the old-fashioned granite buildings are quiet and parking is easy. Kaarna lived in a broody block of apartments that still bore the scars of Russian attacks. Inside the foyer the furnishings had that restrained colorless elegance that steel, glass and granite invariably produce. Kaarna's apartment was on the fourth floor; No. 44. A small light behind the bell push said Dr. Olaf Kaarna. I rang the bell three times. I had no appointment with Kaarna but I knew that he worked at home and seldom left his apartment before lunchtime. I hit the buzzer again and wondered if he was struggling into his bathrobe and cursing. There was still no reply and looking through the letter box I could see only a dark hallstand piled high with mail and three closed doors. I felt the cold metal of the letter box against my forehead slide gently forward with a click. The heavy door swung open and almost toppled me across the welcome mat. I pushed the buzzer again, holding the door open with my toe as though I wasn't really doing it. When it became evident that no one was going to come I moved quickly. I flipped through the pile of mail, and then into all the rooms. A kitchen. As tidy as you can get without dismantling the furniture. The lounge like the Scandinavian-Modern department of a big store. Only the study looked lived-in. Books covered the walls and papers were untidily heaped across the pine desk. Bottles of ink and wire staplers were used as paperweights. Behind the desk was a glass-fronted bookcase; inside it were rows of expanding files neatly titled in Finnish. There was a rack of test tubes, clean and unused, on the windowsill, and under the window a secretary's desk with a sheet of −.20 finnmark stamps, a letter opener, a balance, a bottle of gum, an empty bottle of nail varnish and a trace of spilled face powder. I found Kaarna in the bedroom.

Kaarna was a smaller man than his photos suggested and upside down, the globular head was far too large for his body. The top of his bald head brushed lightly upon the superb carpet. His mouth was open enough to reveal his uneven upper teeth and from it blood had run along his nose and into his eyes, ending in a sort of Rorschach caste mark in the center of his forehead. His body was sprawled across the unmade bed with one shoe trapped in the headboard, which prevented him from sliding to the floor. Kaarna was fully dressed. His polka-dot bow tie was twisted up under his collar and his white nylon laboratory coat was smothered in raw egg, still slimy and fresh. Kaarna was dead.

There was blood low down on the left side of his back. It looked dark, like a blood blister under the nonporous nylon coat. The window was wide open and, though the room was freezing cold, the blood was still hemoglobin fresh. I inspected his short clean fingernails where the lecturers tell us we'll find all sorts of clues but there was nothing there that could be seen without an electron microscope. If he had been shot through the open window it would account for his being thrown back across the bed. I decided to look for bruising around the wound but as I gripped him by the shoulder he began to slide—he hadn't even begun to stiffen—falling into a twisted heap on the floor. He made quite a noise and I listened for any movement from the apartment below. I heard the elevator moving.

Logically my best plan would have been to remain there, but I was in the hall, wiping doorknobs and worrying whether to steal the mail before you could say "scientific investigator."

The elevator stopped at Kaarna's floor. A young girl got out of it, closing the gate with care before looking toward me. She wore a white trench coat and a fur hat. She carried a briefcase that appeared to be heavy. She came up to the locked door of No. 44 and we both looked at it for a moment in silence.

"Have you rung the bell?" she said in excellent English. I suppose I didn't look much like a Finn. I nodded and she pressed the bell a long time. We waited. She removed her shoe and rapped on the door with the heel. "He'll be at his office," she pronounced with certainty. "Would you like to see him there?"

London said he didn't have an office and that wasn't the sort of thing that London got wrong. "I certainly would," I said.

"Do you have papers or a message?"

"Both," I said. "Papers and a message." She began to walk back toward the elevator, half-turning toward me to continue the conversation. "You work for Professor Kaarna?"

"Not full time," I said. We went down in the elevator in silence. The girl had a clear, placid face with the sort of flawless complexion that responds to cold air. She wore no lipstick, a light dusting of powder and a touch of black on the eyes. Her hair was blond but not very light and she'd tucked it up inside her fur hat. Here and there a strand hung down to her shoulder. In the foyer she looked at the man's wristwatch she was wearing.

"It's nearly noon," she said. "We would do better to wait till after lunch."

I said, "Let's try his office first. If he's not there we'll have lunch nearby."

"It's not possible. His office is in a poor district alongside highway five, the Lahti road. There is nowhere to eat around there."

"Speaking for myself . . ."

"You are not hungry." She smiled. "But I am, so please take me to lunch." She gripped my arm expectantly. I shrugged and began to walk back toward the center of town. I glanced up at the open window of Kaarna's flat; there were plenty of places in the building opposite where a rifleman could have sat waiting. But in this sort of climate where the double-glazed windows are sealed with tape a man could wait all winter.

We walked up the wide street on pavements that were brushed in patterns around humps of recalcitrant ice like a

Japanese sand garden. The signs were incomprehensible and consonant-heavy except for words like *Esso, Coca-Cola* and *Kodak* sandwiched between the Finnish. The sky was getting grayer and lower every moment and as we entered the Kaartingrilli Café small businesslike flakes began to fall.

The Kaartingrilli is a long narrow place full of heated air that smells of coffee. Half of the wall space is painted black and the other half is large picture windows. The décor is all natural wood and copper and the place was crowded with young people shouting, flirting and drinking Coca-Cola.

We sat down in the farthest corner, overlooking a crowded parking lot where every car was white with snow. With her heavy coat off the girl was much younger than I thought. Helsinki teems with fresh-faced girls born when the soldiers returned home. Nineteen forty-five was a boom year for gorgeous Finns. I wondered whether this girl was one of them. "I am Liam Dempsey, a citizen of Eire," I said. "I have been gathering material for Professor Kaarna in connection with a transfer of funds between London and Helsinki. I live in London most of the year."

She presented her hand across the table and I shook it. She said, "My name is Signe Laine. I am a Finn. You work for Professor Kaarna, then we shall get along swell because Professor Kaarna works for me."

"For you," I said without making it a question.

"Not for me personally." She smiled at the thought. "For the organization that employs me."

She held her hands as though she'd seen too many copies of *Vogue*, picking up one hand with the other and holding it against her face and nursing it like it was a sick canary.

"What organization is that?" I asked. The waitress came to our table. Signe ordered in Finnish without consulting me.

"All in good time," she said. Outside in the parking lot the wind was carrying the snow in horizontal streaks and a man in a bright woolen hat with a bobble on it was struggling along with a car battery, leaning into the wind and trying not to slip on the hard, shiny gray ice.

Lunch was open cold-beef sandwiches, soup, cream cake, coffee and a glass of cold milk, which is practically the national drink. Signe bit into it all like a buzz saw. Now and again she asked me questions about where I was born and how much I earned and whether I was married. She put the questions in the offhand preoccupied way that women have when they are very interested in the answers.

"Where are you staying, you're not eating your cream cake."

"I'm not staying anywhere and I'm not allowed cream cake."

"It's good," she said. She dipped her little finger into the chocolate cream and held it to my lips. She put her head on one side so that her long golden hair fell across her face. I licked the cream from her fingertip.

"Did you like that?"

"Very much."

"Then eat it."

"With a spoon it's not the same."

She smiled and looped a long strand of hair around her fingers, then asked me a lot of questions about where I was going to stay. She said that she would like to take the documents intended for Kaarna. I refused to part with them. Finally we agreed that I would bring the documents to a meeting the next day and that meanwhile I wouldn't recontact Kaarna. She gave me five one-hundred-mark notes—over fifty-five pounds sterling—as immediate expenses, then we got down to serious conversation.

"Do you realize," she said, "that if the material you are carrying got into wrong hands it could do a great deal of harm to your country?" Signe didn't fully understand the distinction between Eire and the United Kingdom.

"Really?" I said.

"I take it"—she pretended to be very occupied with the lock of her briefcase—"that you wouldn't want to harm your own country."

"Certainly not," I said anxiously.

She looked up and gave me a sincere look. "We need you," she said. "We need you to work for us."

I nodded. "Who exactly is 'us'?"

"British Military Intelligence," said Signe. She wound a great skein of golden hair around her fingers and secured it with a wicked-looking pin. She got to her feet. "See you tomorrow," she said and pushed the bill across to me before leaving the restaurant.

I checked into the Marski that afternoon. It's a tasteful piece of restrained Scandinavian on Mannerheim. The lights are just bright enough to glint on the stainless steel, and sitting on the black leather at the bar is like being at controls of a Boeing 707. I drank vodka and wondered why Kaarna had been smeared with raw egg and what had happened to the eggshells. I had a quiet little laugh about being recruited in British Intelligence but not a big laugh for two reasons.

First, it's the usual practice of all intelligence organizations to tell their operatives that they are working for someone whom they will be happy to work for. A Francophile is told that his reports go to Quai d'Orsay, a Communist is told that his orders come from Moscow. Few agents can be quite sure whom they work for because the nature of the work precludes their being able to check back.

The second reason that I wasn't getting a big laugh was because Signe just might be working for Ross's department at the War Office. Unlikely but possible.

As a general rule—and all general rules are dangerous—agents are natives of the country in which they operate. I wasn't an agent nor was I likely ever to be one. I delivered, evaluated and handled information that our agents obtained but I seldom met one except a cutout, or go-between, like the Finn I had spoken with on the ferry. I was in Helsinki to do a simple task and now it was becoming very complex. I should follow up this strange opportunity but I was not prepared. I had no communication arranged with London except an emergency contact that I dared not use unless world war were imminent. I had no system of contacts, for not only was I forbidden to interrupt the work of our resident people but, judging by the speed with which the gray-haired man answered the phone, that was a public call-box number.

So I had another vodka and slowly read the expensive menu and felt in my pocket the five hundred marks the girl with the wide mouth had given me. Easy come; easy go.

CHAPTER 3

THE next morning was blue and sunny but still a couple of degrees below zero. The birds were singing in the trees of the esplanade and I walked through the center of town. I walked up the steep hill where the University buildings are painted bright yellow like boardinghouse custard and down onto Unioninkatu and the shop full of ankle-length leather coats.

The girl Signe was standing outside the leather shop. She

said good morning and fell into step beside me. At Long-Bridge we cut off to the left without crossing it and walked alongside the frozen inlet. Under the bridge, ducks were probing around among the debris that was scattered across the ice, soggy old cardboard cartons and dented cans. The bridge itself was pockmarked with bomb-splinter scars.

"The Russians," said Signe. I looked at her.

"Bombed Helsinki; damaged the bridge."

We stood there watching the lorries coming into the city.

"My father was a trade unionist, he used to look at that damaged bridge and say to me, 'Those bombs were made by Soviet workers in Soviet factories in the land of Lenin, remember that.' My father had devoted all his life to the trade union movement. In 1944 he died broken-hearted." She walked ahead rather quickly and I saw the quick flash of a pocket handkerchief as she dabbed at her eyes. I followed her and she climbed down toward the frozen surface of the water and began to walk out on the ice. Other tiny figures were taking the same shortcut across the inlet farther to the west. Ahead of us an old woman was tugging a small sled full of groceries. I planted my feet carefully, for the ice was worn smooth by a winter of heavy use. I came alongside Signe and she took my arm gratefully.

"Do you like champagne?" she asked.

"Are you offering some?"

"No," she said. "I just wondered. I'd never had champagne until three months ago. I like it very much. It's almost my very favorite drink."

"I'm pleased," I said.

"Do you like whisky?"

"I like whisky very much."

"I like all alcohol. I expect one day I shall become an alcoholic." She picked up a handful of snow, compressed it into a snowball and threw it with great energy a hundred yards along the ice. "Do you like snow? Do you like ice?"

"Only in whisky and champagne."

"Can you have ice in champagne? I thought that was wrong."

"I was just kidding," I said.

"I know you were," she said.

We came to the other side of the frozen water and I walked up the embankment. Signe stayed on the ice and fanned her eyelashes.

"What's the matter?"

She said, "I don't think I can make it. Could you help me?"

"Stop fooling about, there's a good girl."

"O.K.," she said cheerfully and climbed up beside me.

The city changes slightly on the north side of Long-Bridge. Not in the sudden dramatic way that London changes south of the river or Istanbul changes across the Galata Bridge; but on the north side of Long-Bridge, Helsinki becomes duller, the people are not so smartly dressed and lorries outnumber the cars. Signe took me to a block of flats near Helsinginkatu. She pressed a bell push in the foyer to announce our arrival but produced a key to let us in. Few of Helsinki's buildings have the bright newly minted shine that is associated with Finnish design; instead they are like well-weathered Victorian hotels. This block was no exception but inside, the air was warm and the carpets soft. The apartment we entered was on the sixth floor. There were lithographs on the walls and Artie Shaw on the turntable. The main room was light and large enough to hold a few examples of superb Finnish furniture and still leave room to practice dancing the rumba.

The man practicing the rumba was a short thickset man with thinning brown hair. One hand he held in the air beating time to the music. The other hand held a tall drink. His footwork was adequate and while we stood in the doorway he treated us to an extra few moments of expertise before looking up and saying, "Well, you old Limey sonuvabitch. I knew it was you." He took Signe into his arms with an easy movement and they began to dance. I noticed that Signe's feet were actually standing on his toes, and he waltzed around the floor taking her weight upon his feet as though she were a rag dummy tied to his feet and wrists. The dance ended and he said, "I knew it was you" again. I said nothing and he swallowed the remainder of his drink and said to Signe, "Oh boy, buttercup, did you let your pants down for the wrong guy." *

Harvey Newbegin was a neatly dressed man: gray flannel suit, initialed handkerchief in top pocket, gold watch, and a relaxed smile. I had known him for a number of years. He had been with the U. S. Defense Department for four years before transferring to the State Department. I had tried to get him working for us at one time but Dawlish had failed to obtain authority to do it. Under those droopy eyelids Harvey had quick intelligent eyes. He used them to study me while going to get us all a drink. The music was still thumping out of the record player. Harvey poured three glasses of whisky and soda, dropped ice into two of them, then walked across to me and Signe. Halfway across the floor he picked up the beat of the music and did a brief sequence of steps the rest of the way.

"Don't be such a fool," Signe said to him. "He's such a fool," she added. Harvey gave her the glass of whisky, let go of it before she grasped it, and in mid-fall caught it with the other hand and handed it to her without spilling it. "He's such

---

* Like many modern espionage terms this comes from the German: *"die Hosen herunterlassen"*—take one's trousers off. This means to reveal that you are an agent and attempt to recruit someone into your organization. The older term for this was "moment of truth."

a fool," she said again with admiration. She shook little drop-
lets of melted snow from her hair. Her hair was much shorter
and even more golden today.

When we were all seated, Harvey said to Signe, "Let me
tell you something, doll—this guy is a hot tamale. He works
for a very smart little British Intelligence outfit. He's not as
dopey as he looks." Harvey turned to me. "You've been tan-
gling with this guy Kaarna."

"Well . . ."

"O.K., O.K., O.K., you don't have to tell me. Kaarna is
dead."

"Dead?"

"D.E.D. dead. It's here in the newspaper. You found him
dead. You know it, pal."

"I give you my word I didn't," I said.

We looked at each other for a minute, then Harvey said,
"Well anyway, he's joined the major leagues, there's nothing
we can do about that. But when Signe was hustling you yesterday it was because we urgently need someone to carry between
here and London. Could you take on a part-time job for the
Yanks? The pay is good."

"I'll ask the office," I said.

"Ask the office," he said scornfully. He tapped his toe on
the carpet. "You're a big boy with a mind of your own. Why
ask anyone?"

"Because your smart organization might just let the word
slip, that's why." Harvey put a finger across his throat. "So
help me God, they won't. We are a very neat, tight-fitting
department. Guaranteed no snafus. Cash on the barrelhead.
What sort of deal have you with your London setup, anyway?"

I said, "I work on a free-lance basis. They pay me a fee
per assignment; it's a part-time job." I paused. "I could handle
some extra tasks if the money was right and if you're quite

sure London won't find out from your people. . . ." It wasn't
true but it seemed a suitable answer.

Harvey said, "You'd like working with us and we'd be
tickled to have you."

"Then it's a deal," I said. "Explain my duties, as they say in
domestic circles."

"Nothing to it. You'll be carrying materials between here
and London. It'll seldom be anything you can't declare."

"So what's the catch?"

"Valuables. We must have someone who won't walk off
with the consignment. You'll have your first-class air-fare paid.
Hotel and expenses. A retainer and a fee per trip. As one pro
to another I'll tell you it's a good deal." Signe gave us drinks
and as she turned toward the kitchen Harvey gave her an affec-
tionate pat on the bottom. "The fat of the land," he said. "I'm
living on the fat of the land."

Signe wrenched Harvey's hand away from her, snorted and
walked out with a beguiling movement of the *gluteus maximus*.

Harvey moved his armchair nearer to me. "We don't nor-
mally tell our operatives anything about the organization but
I'll make an exception for you under the old pals act. This is
a private intelligence unit financed by an old man named Mid-
winter. Calls himself General Midwinter. He's from one of
those old Texan families that have a lot of German blood.
Originally the family came from one of the Baltic states—
Latvia or Lithuania—that the Russians now have and hold.
This old guy Midwinter has dreams of liberating the territory.
I guess he'd like to install himself as a king or something."

"Sounds great," I said. "It's a long time since I worked for
a megalomaniac."

"Hell. I'm exaggerating but he has got an oversimplified
mind. Brilliant men often have. He likes to hear that those
poor bastards across there are all set to start a revolution."

"And you help his illusions," I supplied.

"Look, the guy's a multimillionaire, a multibillionaire maybe. This is his toy. Why should I spoil his fun? He made his money from canned food and insurance, that's a dull way to make a million, so he needs a little fun. The CIA siphon a little money to him—"

"The CIA?"

"Oh, they don't take us seriously but you know how their minds work—stealing hubcaps in Moscow is the CIA's idea of a blow for freedom. And some of the stunts we pull are pretty good. He has four radio stations on ships that beam into the Baltic states. You know the sort of thing; 'stand by for freedom and Coke.' They have a mass of computer equipment and a training school back in the States. Maybe they will send you for training, but if they do I'll make sure it's kept plushy for you. And the money!" Harvey poured me a huge drink to demonstrate that aspect of my new employer. "When do you plan to return to London?"

"Tomorrow."

"That's great. This is your first task; stay to lunch." Harvey Newbegin laughed. "When you get to London go to the phone booth at Trinity Church Square, Southeast one, take the L to R book and make a small pencil dot beside the Pan-American entry. Go back next day and on the same page margin there will be a phone number written in pencil. Phone that number. Say you are a friend of the people at the antique shop and you have something you would like to show them. If anyone at the other end asks who you want to speak to, you don't know, you were given this number and told there was someone there interested in buying antiques. When the people at the other end make an appointment, be there twenty hours later than that time. Got that?"

"Yes," I said.

"If there is any kind of snarl up, ring off. Standard control meeting procedure; that is to say, return and do the whole thing again twenty-four hours later. O.K.?" Harvey held up his glass of vodka and said, "This is something those Russkies do damn well. Pip pip down the hatch." He swallowed the rest of the vodka in one gulp, then clutched at his heart and pulled a pained face. "I have heartburn," he explained. He took his wallet out and removed a five-mark note and ripped it into two pieces in a very irregular tear. He gave half of it to me. "The man you meet will want your half of this before he parts with his package, so look after it."

"Yes," I said. "Perhaps you will explain what it is I have to collect."

"It's simple," said Harvey Newbegin. "You go empty-handed. You bring back half a dozen eggs."

| *London*

A master I have, and I am his man,
Gallopy dreary dun.

—Nursery Rhyme

CHAPTER 4

WHEN I got back to London I put spots in telephone directories and went through the rest of Harvey Newbegin's party games for the under-fives. A stuffy voice on the phone said, "Don't worry about that twenty hours nonsense they told you at the other end. You get along here now. I'm waiting to go down to my boat for a couple of days."

So I went to King's Cross: BED AND BREAKFAST cards jammed into grimy windows and novelty shops that sell plastic feces and musical toilet-roll holders. There was a brass plate outside number fifty-three. SURGERY. *Dr. Pike.* The plate was garnished with qualifications. Near the front door there were two dented dustbins and about thirty old milk bottles. A cold wet sleet was beginning to fall.

The door was unlocked but a small buzzer sounded as I pushed it open. The waiting room was a large Victorian room with a decorated ceiling. There was a wide selection of slightly broken furniture with disemboweled copies of *Woman's Own* strategically placed under notices about antenatal clinics and repeat prescriptions. The notices were penned in strange angular lettering and held in place by crisp pieces of ancient sticking plaster.

In one corner of the waiting room, painted white with the word "surgery" on it, was a hardboard box. It was large enough to contain a desk and two chairs. One chair was large, leather covered and swiveled smoothly on ball bearings; the other chair was narrow, sickly and lame in one leg. Dr. Pike counted his fingertips methodically and revolved toward me. He was a large, impeccably groomed man of about fifty-two. His hair was like a black plastic swimming cap. His suit was made of thin uncreasable blue steel and so was his smile.

"Where's the pain?" he said. It was a joke. He smiled again to put me at my ease.

"In my hand."

"Really? You really have a pain in your hand?"

"Just when I put it in my pocket."

Pike looked at me carefully and remembered that there are some people who mistake a friendly word for an invitation to be familiar. "I'm sure you were the life and soul of the sergeants' mess."

"Let's not exchange war experiences," I said.

"Let's not," he agreed.

On Pike's desk there was a pen set, a large dog-eared desk-diary, a stethoscope, three prescription pads and a shiny brown ball about as big as a golf ball. He fingered the shiny sphere.

I said, "We will be working together for a long time so why don't we decide to get along with each other?"

"That's a remarkably intelligent idea."

Pike and I loathed each other on sight but he had the advantage of breeding and education so he swallowed hard and went out of his way to be nice to me.

"This package of . . ." He waited for me to finish the sentence.

"Eggs," I said. "Package of eggs."

"It may take a day or so to come through."

"That doesn't tally with my instructions," I said.

"Perhaps not," he said in a restrained way, "but there are complex reasons why the timing is unpredictable. The people involved are not the sort to whom one can give a direct order." He had the precise accentless English that only a diligent foreigner can produce.

"Oh," I said, "and why not?"

Pike smiled while keeping his lips pressed together. "We are professional men. Our livelihood depends upon a code of conduct, it's essential that we do nothing unethical."

"Are discovered doing nothing unethical, you mean," I said.

Pike did that tricky smile again. "Have it your way," he said.

"I will," I said. "When will the package be ready?"

"Not today certainly. There are some benches near the children's sandpit in St. James Park. Meet me there at four forty-five P.M. Saturday. Ask me if my paper has the stock market prices and I'll have a *Financial Times*. I'll say, 'You can read this for a few minutes.' If I'm carrying a copy of *Life* magazine don't make contact, it will indicate danger." Pike fingered his yellow bow tie and nodded my dismissal.

My God, I thought, what have these boys been smoking? They're all doing it. I nodded as though these charades were a regular part of my working day and opened the door.

Pike said, ". . . carry on with the tablets and come back and see me in about a week," for the benefit of a couple of old flower pots who were sitting in the waiting room. He needn't have bothered because he was shouting at the top of his voice as I left, trying to get them to look up.

In view of the razzle-dazzle these boys were going through it was reasonable to suppose they were having me followed, so I took a cab and waited till we got into a traffic jam, paid off the driver quickly and hailed a cab moving in the opposite direction. This tactic, well handled, can throw off the average tail if it's using a private car. I was back in the office before lunchtime.

I reported to Dawlish. Dawlish had that timeless, ageless quality that British civil servants develop to spread confidence among the natives. His only interest in life, apart from the antiques which littered the office and the department which he controlled, was the study and cultivation of garden weeds; perhaps they weren't unrelated interests.

Dawlish had sandwiches sent up from Wally's Delicatessen and asked me lots of questions about Pike and Harvey Newbegin. I thought Dawlish was taking it much too seriously but he's a cunning old devil; he's apt to base his hunches upon information he hasn't given me access to. When I said I'd told Harvey Newbegin that I only worked for WOOC(P) part-time, Dawlish said, "Well, you certainly weren't lying about that, were you?" He munched into one of Wally's corned-beef sandwiches and said, "You know what they'll do next?"

"No, sir," I said and really meant it.

"They will send you to school." He nodded to reinforce his theory. "When they do, accept. It's got seeds in," he said. Dawlish was staring at me in a horrified, faintly maniacal way. I nodded. Dawlish said, "If I've told him once, I've told him a thousand times."

"Yes, sir," I said.

Dawlish flipped the switch on his intercom. "If I've told him once I've told him a thousand times. I don't like that bread with seeds in."

Alice's voice came through the box with all the unbiased

dignity of a recording. "One round on white, one round on rye with seeds. You have eaten the wrong ones."

I said, "I don't like caraway seeds either." Dawlish nodded at me so I said it again at the squawk-box, louder and more defiantly this time.

"Neither of us likes bread with seeds," Dawlish said to Alice in a voice of sweet reasonableness. "How can I get this fact promulgated?"

"Well, I can't be expected to know that," said Alice.

"I suppose," said Dawlish, "that my best plan would be to file it in a cosmic clearance file." He smiled at me and nodded approval at his own witticism.

"No, sir, put it into the non-secret waste bin. I'll have someone take it away. Would you like something else instead?"

"No thank you, Alice," said Dawlish and released the switch.

I could have told him that he'd never win an argument with Alice. No one ever had.

But it would have taken more than that to upset Dawlish. He had done well that year. The January estimates had been submitted to Treasury and Dawlish had just about doubled our appropriation at a time when many people were predicting our closedown. I'd spent long enough in both the Army and the Civil Service to know that I didn't like working in either; but working with Dawlish was an education, perhaps the only part of my education that I had ever enjoyed.

"Pike." Dawlish said. "They never get tired of recruiting doctors, do they?"

"I can see the advantage," I said. "The waiting room full of people, the contact has complete privacy when talking to the doctor; very tricky to detect."

Dawlish had second thoughts about the sandwich. He picked the seeds out of the bread with a paper knife, then took a bite. "What was that? I wasn't listening."

"They are tricky to detect."

"Not if you get them in your teeth they're not, beastly little things. I can't think who likes them in bread. By the way, you were followed when you left that doctor's surgery." Dawlish made a deprecating gesture with the palm of his hand. "But of course you know that or you wouldn't have taken evasive action."

"Who followed me?"

"We are not sure yet. I put young Chilcott-Oates onto it, but apparently our quarry is shopping in Finchley Road and keeping the boy on his toes, he hardly had time to dial the number Alice says." I nodded. Dawlish said, "You are making those scornful noises with your teeth. One wishes you wouldn't do that."

"Chico," I said.

"It's essential he learns," said Dawlish. "You won't let him do anything and that way he will never improve. It will be a splendid success."

I said, "I'll go downstairs and try to get a little work done."

Dawlish said, "Very well, but this business with Newbegin is top priority, don't let anything interfere with that."

"I'll remind you of that remark next month when the Organization Department is making itself unpleasant." I went downstairs and watched Jean touching up the paint on her finger-nails. She looked up and said hello, using the warm breath to dry the paint.

"Busy?" I said. I settled down behind the desk and began to go through the trays.

"There's no need to be sarcastic. I spent all day Saturday going through the 'information onlys' and making a précis on tape."

"I'm sorry, love. This Newbegin business has come up just

at the wrong time. Without that we could probably have brought all the desk work up to date. Have you checked out that all these files are ours, as you so cleverly suggested?"

"Forget the flattery," Jean said. "Yes, we've got rid of some of them but a lot of it comes up here because of your high security clearance. I have a new idea for that."

"Give."

"Well, some of these files marked with secret codings are not really even confidential but they originated in a secret file so everything subsequently bearing that file number is automatically secret. If you will authorize me to break some of these omnibus files into sub-files with separate numbers, a lot of them will no longer be secret and can be handled downstairs. What's more, it's much more efficient to have sub-files, because two departments can work on two aspects of the same problem at the same time if they each have a sub-file."

"Genius," I said. "Now I know why I love you."

"You don't love anyone. Not even yourself."

"You know I couldn't help it. I had to wait until the passport was ready."

"I spent hours cooking all your favorite things; you arrive at one A.M."

"I had all my favorite things at one A.M."

She didn't answer.

"I'm forgiven?"

"We can't go on like this indefinitely."

"I know," I said. Neither of us spoke for ages.

Jean finally said, "I know that this sort of work . . . Well, I wouldn't want you to stop. Even when it's dangerous."

"It's nothing like that, lover. I'm not going to get myself hurt. I'm a cautious coward with too much survival training."

Jean said, "Even good drivers get killed when amateurs

ram them; I think Harvey Newbegin is a clumsy amateur. You must be very careful."

"Don't make me even more neurotic. Newbegin has a good record with the Defense Department and the State Department. The Americans don't hang on to a man that long unless he's worth his money."

"I just don't trust him," said Jean with that stubborn feminine intuition. She came close and I put an arm around her.

"Just because he pinched your bottom at the White Elephant Club," I said.

"And a lot of help you were. You did nothing."

"That's my specialty," I said, "I always do nothing."

CHAPTER 5

I LEFT the office at seven that night. Jean's brother was on one of his rare visits to London and they were going out to dinner, but Dawlish thought I should stay available. So I went back to my flat and cooked bacon and eggs and sat in front of the fire with Vol. 2 of *Fuller's Decisive Battles* and read about the siege of Yorktown. It was a pleasant evening until 8:15 P.M. when the phone rang.

The Charlotte Street operator said, "Scramble please." Before I had a scrambler fitted I had to do standby duties at the office. I pressed the button. Dawlish said, "The boy has turned up trumps apparently."

"Why apparently?" I said.

"The fellow who followed you is down on the river," said Dawlish, ignoring my question. "We shall have to pass your way. We will pick you up in fifteen minutes." Dawlish rang off abruptly. I knew he had the same doubts about Chico's abilities as I had but he was determined to demonstrate to me the proper loyal attitude to one's subordinates.

Dawlish arrived at 8:37. He was in a black Wolseley driven by one of our ex-police drivers. With Dawlish there was Bernard, one of the brighter of the public school boys we had recruited of late, and a man named Harriman.

Harriman was a big, hard man who looked more like a doorman than a lieutenant colonel from Special Field Intelligence. His hair was black and tight against his bony skull. His skin was wrinkled and leatherlike, and his teeth were large and uneven. He was intellectual in a way that might be considered suspect in a regular officer. I guessed that the man we were after was going to be taken into custody because Harriman had special authorization from the Home Office to execute a warrant with minimum fuss and paperwork.

They wouldn't have a drink so I climbed into a raincoat and we drove off toward the docks.

Dawlish said, "Young Chico has done quite a good job here."

"Yes," I said. Harriman and I exchanged a grimace. I heard the car radio-phone say, "O.K., switch to Channel Six for a car-to-car with Thames five." Then Bernard in the front seat said, "Are you receiving me, Thames five?" and the police boat said it was receiving us loud and clear. Then we said we were receiving the police boat loud and clear and then Bernard asked them to report their position and they said, "Tower Bridge, Pickle Herring Street side."

Bernard said, "Come up to Wapping Police Station, Thames five, to take up passengers."

Thames five said, "No one in small boat answering description you gave but we'll have another look at Lavender Wharf on the way back."

Information room said, "Have you finished your car-to-car?" in a voice that suggested we had and added, "I'll show you still dealing, Thames five," and Dawlish said, "What are those chaps doing out there, playing cards?" He smiled.

"This chap went all around Finchley," Dawlish continued imperturbably. "Chico kept on his tail, then about six-thirty he wound up at The Prospect of Whitby. Chico has him bottled up there, so we'll take a look at him."

"With all this entourage, I thought you were going to cordon off the area."

Dawlish gave me a twitch of a smile. "Bernard here is night duty officer. Harriman is handling a river-traffic job. We all have good reasons for being here," Dawlish said.

I said, "And I have some great reasons for staying home but no one will listen to them."

As we crossed Tower Bridge I saw the police boat heading downriver through the gray choppy water. We passed the Tower of London, went around the one-way traffic system as far as the Mint, then turned into Thomas More Street: twenty-feet high walls that twist and turn relentlessly. Each turn of the road fails to reveal the end of the street and the walls seem to get higher; it was the last reel of *Dr. Caligari*.

Along Wapping High Street and Wapping Wall the wharves and cranes were high, dirty, and silent. The car headlights ignited the green flickering eyes of stray cats and shiny cobblestones. The Wolseley bounced over the tiny bridges of the dock entrances and under the grimy catwalks. Just behind the fences there were sudden expanses of dark water where passenger boats were twinkling with yellow lights and white-coated waiters, like the Hilton laid on its side, carved into sections and ready to tow out to sea. We dropped Bernard off at Wapping Police Station where two policemen in waterproofs and waders were waiting for him.

Chico was standing outside the pub. The Prospect of Whitby is a bow-fronted tourist attraction. In summer they throng here like harbor rats. But this was winter and the window was opaque with condensation and the door shut tight against the cold. We tumbled out like the Keystone Cops. Anxious excitement plastered Chico's hair against his damp pink forehead.

"Hello, sir," he greeted each of us in turn. Chico led the three of us inside the pub and made a big operation of buying us drinks as if he was a sixth-form boy with three housemasters. He got so excited that he was calling the barman "sir."

The interior of the Prospect is dark with artful knickknacks and inglenooks and the big kick is that the customers leave thousands of visiting cards, theatre tickets and associated paper pinned to the antlers so that you feel like a bug in a litter basket. I walked right through the bar and out to the balcony that overlooks the Pool of London. The water was as turbid as oil. The waterfront was still and deserted. I heard Dawlish trying to prevent Chico from sending down to the cellar for the type of sherry that Dawlish liked. Finally, to ease the agony of the whole thing, Harriman said, "Four big bitters" to the barman, who was as relieved as anyone. They followed me onto the balcony. When we were finally standing in a small Druidian circle with ritualistic foaming glasses Chico said, "He's away across the river."

I said nothing. Harriman said nothing, so finally Dawlish said, "Tell them how you know."

Chico said, "I proceeded as instructed—"

Dawlish said, "Just explain."

Chico said, "I watched him go inside. I followed him through to this balcony but by that time he had gone down this iron ladder to a rowboat and rowed toward the far bank. I phoned the office and suggested that they alert the river police. My informant says that he was making for a large gray boat standing off Lavender Wharf. I have identified it as a Polish vessel."

Dawlish and Harriman looked at me, but I wasn't keen to make a fool of myself so I looked at Chico and wondered why he was wearing a tie with fox heads on it.

Dawlish and Harriman looked across the water toward the Polish ship and Dawlish said they would leave Chico with me. They took the car and visited the Port of London Authority Police.

Chico produced a large leather cigar case. "Do you mind if I smoke?" he said.

"As long as you don't tell me about an amusing little claret you discovered last night."

"I won't, sir," Chico agreed.

The sky was as red as an upturned hull and propping it up were great forests of cranes. From Lavender Wharf came the oily smell that pilots are said to navigate by on foggy days. Chico said, "You don't believe me?"

"It's nothing to do with me," I said. "Grannie has come along to show us how to do our job, so let him handle it." We drank beer and watched the slow movement of the water. A police launch came around the bend and turned toward the Rotherhithe side. I could see Bernard, Dawlish and Harriman in the rear talking to a policeman and being careful not to point at the Polish boat.

"What do you think?" Chico asked.

"Let's take it very slowly," I said. "You followed this man here. How were you traveling?"

"We were each in separate taxis."

"You saw this man enter by the bar entrance?"

"Yes."

"How far behind him were you?"

"My cab gave his cab space to turn round, then I paid my cab and told him to wait. I was a minute behind him."

"A full minute?"

"Yes, at least," Chico agreed.

"You followed him right through the pub out to this balcony?"

"Well, I couldn't see him at the bar so the only explanation was that he walked right through and onto the balcony here."

"So that's what you think?"

"Well, I wasn't sure until I spoke to the witness on the balcony."

"And he said?"

"He said that a man had walked through and down the ladder and rowed away."

"Now tell me what he really said."

"That's what he said."

"What did you ask him?" I said wearily.

"I asked him if a man had done that and he said, 'Yes, there he is across the river. There.' "

"But you couldn't see him?"

"No, I just missed seeing him."

"Go and find this joker who saw him."

"Yes, sir," said Chico.

He came back with a potbellied man in a brown whipcord suit and a matching flat cap. He had a large nose and heavy lips and his complexion was raw and pink. He spoke with the hoarse, full-chested voice men acquire when they address small crowds. I guessed him to be a bookie or a ticktack man especially since whipcord—which doesn't attract animal hair—is favored by racetrack men. He extended a large hand and shook mine in overhearty friendliness.

"Tell me what you told him," I said.

"About the feller climbing down the ladder and rowing off out to sea?" He had a loud beery voice and was delighted with any opportunity for using it. "I could see he was up to no good right from—"

"I've got a hot meal waiting," I said, "so let's make it quick. This man went down onto the mud. How deep into it did he sink?"

The big-nosed man thought for a moment. "No, he had the boat under the foot of the ladder."

"So his shoes didn't get dirty?"

"That's right," he boomed. "Hand the gentleman a coconut Bert. Ha-ha."

"So he sat in the rowboat while it traversed twenty feet of mud, to the river. Would you care to explain that a little more fully?"

He grinned a great ugly gap-toothed grin. "Well, Squire—"

"Look. Having a joke with little Lord Fauntleroy here is one thing but making a false statement to a police officer is a criminal offense punishable by . . ." I paused.

"You mean?" He pushed a large thumb toward Chico. "And you?"

I nodded. I guessed he had a license to lose. I was glad he had interrupted because I didn't know what it was punishable by.

"I was just sending him up. No harm meant, Squire." He turned to Chico. "Nor to you, Squire. Just my fun. Just my fun."

A little gray corrugated woman behind him said, "Just his fun, sir." The big-nosed man turned to her and said, "All right, Florrie, I'll handle this."

"I understand the temptation involved," I said. Big-nose nodded solemnly. I tapped Chico's shoulder. "This young man," I said to big-nose, "will be back in a moment or so to buy you some beer until a couple of other gentlemen arrive. Then if you will be kind enough to explain your joke to them . . ."

"Certainly. Certainly," said big-nose.

I walked back through the bar to the street. Chico said, "What do you think happened?"

"There's no thinking involved. You followed this man here. He isn't inside the bar, therefore he either went upstairs—unlikely—or he left. There is no evidence that he left via the balcony as your funster friend suggested so it seems likely that he turned around at the rear of the bar and walked down that alley and out of the side entrance. If I had been him I would have had my own taxi waiting—I remember you said it was turning around—but before driving away I would have given the driver of your cab a quid and told him that you wouldn't need him anymore."

"That's right," said Chico. "My taxi wasn't here when I came out again. I thought it was odd."

"Good," I said. "Well, when Mr. Dawlish and Mr. Harriman have completed their activities perhaps you would explain those details to them."

I beckoned the driver of the Wolseley and he drove over to me. I got in. "I'll go back to my flat now," I said to the driver.

The police radio was still tuned in and it was saying, ". . . he's a flasher Gulf one-one. Ends. Origin Information Room. Message timed at two-one-one-seven."

"How will Mr. Dawlish and the rest of us get back?" asked Chico. The driver turned the volume down but it was still audible, like the voices of a gang of midgets jammed somewhere in the engine. I said, "You see, Chico, Mr. Dawlish likes these opportunities for a little vicarious high living; I personally prefer an evening by the fire. So next time you feel like creating an international incident complete with night boat trips and Polish ships, try to give me advance warning. To make me even happier, next time you are given a surveillance task"—heaven forbid I thought—"just take a short length of movie that I can view in comfort."

"I will, sir."

"Splendid," I said in reasonable likeness of Dawlish's voice. The car moved slowly forward.

"It was good practice, anyway," said Chico.

" 'A' for effort," I said and went home.

CHAPTER 6

SATURDAY. Dr. Pike was in St. James Park before me. He was sitting on the bench near the lake reading the *Financial Times* exactly as arranged. So not to spoil the fun I asked him about the stock exchange and he lent me his paper. He was dressed more prosperously than he had been at the surgery; Saxony suit, tweed fisher hat and a short reversible raincoat with knitted collar. He flipped his cuff upon a gold wristwatch as I took his newspaper.

"It's incredibly cold," Pike said.

"I didn't come a thousand miles to discuss the weather. Where's the package?"

"Steady on," said Pike. "It will be ready today, don't fret."

"Did you have me followed yesterday, Pike?" I asked.

"Nigel, don't put your new shoe in the water, there's a good boy. No, certainly not. Why should I?"

Nigel stopped putting his new shoe in the water and began to poke a large Labrador with his toy whistle.

"Someone did."

"Not me. The doggie doesn't like that, Nigel."

"So you won't mind if I have him laid out?"

"Couldn't care less. He's growling to tell you he doesn't like it, Nigel. Have him killed for all I care."

"And you still say you don't know who it is?"

"Mr. Dempsey, or whoever you are. I do a job and keep my nose clean. If the people for whom we work send someone to follow you and you decide to brain the fellow, good luck. He thinks you are giving him the whistle to play with, Nigel. Good doggie, give Nigel his whistle back; good doggie. Stroke him, Nigel, show you want to be friends. Anything the fellow gets will serve him right for being inefficient. Too much inefficiency in this country at the moment. People are damned slack. Brain him by all means. It might teach the top people to keep me informed."

Dr. Pike went and retrieved Nigel's whistle and brought Nigel back to where we were sitting.

"Look at your hands." Pike produced a large handkerchief, held it for the child to spit on, then wiped his hands with the damp cloth. It seemed unhygienic.

"Where is the package now?"

"At my brother's, I think." He looked at his watch again and did some sort of calculation. "At my brother's. It's tar, Nigel. I told you not to touch the fence. Tuck your scarf in; don't want to catch cold."

"How far is that?"

"There you are. A nice clean boy. Besterton, a village near Buckingham."

"Let's go," I said.

"I'd like to drop young Nigel first," Pike said. Me too, I thought.

"They think you want to give them bread, Nigel. I'll take him to his riding school. Then we'll go on from there. It's not far out of our way. They won't hurt you, Nigel, nice kind ducks. Don't be frightened, they won't hurt you. Shall we go in my car?"

"Suits me."

"They think you want to give them bread. Well, we'll walk that way. No; they never hurt nice little boys. My Jaguar's the red one. Don't kick gravel at the ducks, Nigel, you'll spoil your shoes."

Doctor Felix Pike and his brother Ralph both lived in a small village. There was a sharp frontier between the houses of the natives—plaster gnomes, nylon curtains, metal-frame windows and prefab garages—and the houses of the invaders—modern sculpture, whitewash, antique gates, brown wainscoting, grandfather clocks. Pike drove up to a modern version of a Georgian house. In the drive there was a silver Porsche convertible. "My brother's car," Pike said. "He's not married," as though the car was an automatic reward for a remarkable feat; which I suppose in a way it was. "My younger brother, Ralph, lives there," Felix Pike said, pointing to a converted limestone barn adjacent to his house. The driveway was full of bronze urns and the house was full of Regency stripes, illuminated niches, wall-to-wall Wilton and furniture with bobbles on. There was a sweet smell of lavender polish as we walked through a couple of rooms that were just for walking through, into what Mrs. Pike—a tightly scripted woman with mauve hair—called the small lounge. There was a quartet of Queen Anne chairs arranged around a late medieval electric fire. We sat down.

Through the French windows the lawn was the size of a small landing strip. Beyond it six bonfires built tall columns of smoke on flickering bases of flame as though a besieging army were encamped there among the bare foggy trees.

The woman with mauve hair waved to the nearest fire and a man threw a final shovel-load of something onto it and walked to the patio. He wiped the blade of the shovel clean with a wire brush and placed it into a wooden box. He brushed his boots upon the mat, then entered through the French windows. He wore those sort of worn-out ancient clothes that the English upper classes wear on Sundays to distinguish them from the people who wear their best clothes on that day. He adjusted the silk choker at his throat as though it was a mosquito net, and I was a mosquito.

"This is my younger brother Ralph," said Dr. Felix Pike. "He lives next door."

"Hello," I said. We shook hands and Ralph said, "Good man" in the low sincere voice they use in films just before they do something dangerous. Then, in case the old clothes and choker should have misled me, he produced a hide case containing six Cristo No. 2's. He offered them around but I preferred my Gaulois.

This man Ralph was younger than the first Pike; perhaps not even forty in spite of his pure white hair. He was slightly flushed and shiny with the exertions of gardening and although at least twenty pounds heavier than his brother he either had it well strapped-up or did thirty push-ups before breakfast. He smiled that same tricky smile that his brother Felix had. He fished a gold cigar cutter from his gardening waistcoat and circumcised his cigar.

"Things at the surgery," said Ralph, the one in gardening clothes, as if he was offering them with the cigars. His foreign accent was a trace heavier than his elder brother's.

"Fine," said Felix Pike. "Fine."

"I do the honors?" Ralph asked and without pausing poured us all brandy and soda into heavy cut-glass goblets.

Dr. Felix Pike said, "And I trust all your . . ." His voice trailed away.

"Fine," said the man in gardening clothes. He lit his cigar with care and sat down on a hard chair to avoid soiling the chintz.

Dr. Felix Pike said, "I see our Corrugated Holdings dropped a packet, Ralph."

Ralph exhaled without haste. "Sold Thursday. Sell while they're rising; don't I always tell you that? *Certum voto pete finem,* as Horace says." Ralph Pike turned to me and said, *"Certum voto pete finem;* set a limit to your desire." I nodded and Dr. Felix Pike nodded and Ralph smiled kindly.

Ralph said, "When I go public I'll look after you, never fear. I'll give you a green form, Felix. And hold on to them this time. Don't do an in-and-out as you did with the Waldner shares. If you want a word of advice, unload your coppers and tins; they're going to take a nasty drop; mark my advice, a nasty drop."

Dr. Felix Pike didn't like taking advice from his younger brother. He stared at him and moistened his lips with the tip of his tongue.

Ralph said, "You should remember that, Felix."

"Yes," said Dr. Felix Pike. His mouth slammed down like a guillotine blade. It was a nasty mouth, an all-or-nothing device that closed like a trap and when it opened you expected a greyhound to leap out.

Ralph smiled. "Been down to the boat lately?"

"Was going today." He stabbed a thumb at me as though soliciting a ride on a lorry. "Then this came up."

"Bad luck," said Ralph. He pinged my empty goblet with his fingernail. "Another?"

"No thanks."

"Felix?"

"No," said Dr. Felix Pike.

"Did Nigel like the submachine gun?"

"Loved it. He wakes us up every morning. I'm not supposed to thank you because he's writing to you himself; with chalk on brown paper."

"Ha-ha," said Ralph. *"Arma virumque cano."* He turned to me and said, "Of arms and the man I sing. Virgil."

I said, *"Adeo in teneris consuescere multum est.* As the twig is bent the tree inclines. Also Virgil." There was a silence, then Dr. Pike said, "Nigel loved it" again, and they both stared at the garden. "Do have another," Ralph offered.

"No," said Dr. Felix Pike. "I must change, we have people coming."

"Mr. Dempsey will be wanting the package," said Ralph as if I wasn't listening.

"That's right," I said to prove I was.

"Good man." He kissed the cigar affectionately but fearfully, as if there was a good chance it might explode. "I brought it today," he said, "it's switched on."

"Good," I said.

I reached into my back pocket and produced my torn half of the five-mark note. Dr. Felix Pike walked across to one of the illuminated nooks. He moved two soft-focus portraits of his wife, another of those shiny brown spheres that I'd seen at the surgery—and finally found his half of the note under one of the Staffordshire figures that were drawn up in ranks along the glass shelves. He passed the half banknote to his brother Ralph who fitted the two halves together in the same casual but careful way that he had handled the spade and cigar.

"Right," he said and went to get my half dozen eggs for

Helsinki. The package was wrapped in that plain discreet green paper that Harrods use. It was tied with a little loop to carry it. Before we left, Ralph said that coppers would take a nasty drop again.

Dr. Pike would like very much to have given me a lift back to the center of town but . . . I understood, didn't I? Yes. I took a bus.

The fog had become thicker and was that sort of green they call a "pea souper." The shoe shops were prisms of yellow light and past them, buses were ambling; trumpeting aimlessly like a herd of dirty red elephants looking for a place to die.

I held the green wrapped package on my knees and developed a distinct impression that it was ticking. I wondered why the second Mr. Pike had said it was switched on but I didn't intend to find out the hard way.

Waiting for me at Charlotte Street was one of the "bombers."

"Here it is," I said. "Easy does it, I'd like to deliver it in one piece."

"I'm not taking chances today," said the duty bomber. "I've got a steak and kidney pudding waiting for me tonight."

"Take your time," I said. "It's the long slow simmering that produces the flavor."

"You got a little huffy last night," Dawlish said.

I said, "I'm sorry."

"Don't be," said Dawlish. "You were right. You have instinct that comes from training and experience. I won't interfere again." I made noises like a man who doesn't want compliments.

Dawlish smiled. "I don't say I won't have you fired or transferred, but I won't interfere." He toyed with his fountain pen as though uncertain how to break the news. "They don't like it," he said finally. "The written memo went to the Minister this morning."

"What did the memo say?"

"Precious little," said Dawlish. "One sheet of foolscap double-spaced. I pretended it was a précis." He smiled again. "We've known about this organization run by Midwinter but we've never had it linked to this country before. Both these Pike brothers are Latvian, they hold extreme right political views and the one named Ralph is a top biochemist. That's what the memo said and it worried the Minister sick. I've been over there twice today and neither time did I have to wait longer than three minutes. It's a sure sign. Worried sick." Dawlish tutted and I tutted in sympathy. "Stick close to your friend Newbegin," said Dawlish. "Get into this Midwinter organization and take a good look at it. I only hope yesterday won't make it dangerous for you."

"I don't think so," I said. "The Americans are not spiteful whatever other faults they have."

"Good," said Dawlish. He poured me a glass of port and talked about the set of six-dram glasses he had bought in Portobello Road.

"Might be eighteenth century. They call that trumpet-bowled, see?"

"Great," I said. "But aren't there only five glasses?"

"Ahh! Set of six with one missing."

"Ahh," I said.

Dawlish's squawk-box buzzed and the bomber's voice said, "Can I talk, Mr. D?"

"Go ahead," Dawlish said.

"I've got it on the X-ray. It's got electrical wiring in it so I want to go slowly, Mr. Dawlish."

"Good heavens yes," said Dawlish. "One doesn't want the building blown to smithereens."

"Two doesn't," said the duty bomber and then he laughed and said it again, "two doesn't."

The small metal box that the Pike brothers had given me contained six fertile eggs and an electrical device that kept them at a constant temperature of 37° C. Each egg shell had a wax-penciled number, a filed notch and a puncture. Through the hyaline membrane of each egg a hypodermic needle had inserted a living virus. The eggs had been stolen from the Microbiological Research Establishment at Porton. The duty driver took them back to that quiet and picturesque corner of old England at five o'clock that morning, using a blanket and hot water bottle to keep them warm and alive.

For my trip to Helsinki, Dawlish and I put six medium-grade new-laid eggs into the metal box. We got them from the canteen but had a terrible job removing the little lion stamp marks that guarantee purity.

CHAPTER 7

THE West London Air Terminal is stainless steel and glass, like a modern corned-beef factory. Passengers are felled, bled, eviscerated and packed firmly into buses watched by men with wheelbarrows and dirty boots and red-eyed girls who pat their hairdos and tear up colored pieces of paper.

A resonant female voice began the countdown on the bus departure and at the last moment Jean decided to ride out to the airport with me. The airport bus contained the driver, Jean, myself and nine other passengers, all but one being male. In the bus baggage compartment were twelve cases of medium size, one hatbox, three paper-wrapped parcels, one Hessian-wrapped box, one document case, three sets of skis (in presses and complete with sticks), one set of which were slalom skis, and a small hamper containing samples of ladies' shoes.

It was a good haul for the thief who hijacked the whole lot of it. In my case was the electrically heated box of eggs.

The morning flight to Stockholm and Helsinki was delayed by ninety-seven minutes. By that time the skis and two bags were recovered but neither were mine. Because I thought I might be under surveillance by parties unknown, LAP Special Branch questioned the only witness of the theft that could be found—a LAP police constable named Blair—and delivered this transcript of his account to me on the airplane.

| Special Branch | *Confidential* |
| London Air Port | *Copy 2 of 2* |

Transcript from tape-band. Police Constable Blair in conversation with Det. Sgt. Smith. Special Branch LAP.

Det. Sgt. Smith: We are particularly interested in the man you saw this morning and so I am recording now in order to make a transcript that will keep your descriptions on record. Don't give your answers in a formal way, don't hesitate to correct anything after you have said it and don't hurry; we have plenty of tape. Tell me first what drew your attention to this particular man.

PC Blair: He seemed very strong. He was working harder than I've seen any of the porters ever work (*laughter*). He sort of um lifted the um cases over into the van one in each hand. He did the whole load in about six journeys across the pavement.

Det. Sgt. Smith: Tell me what he said when he saw you watching.

PC Blair: Well er like I told you he er I didn't don't er remember exactly the words he used but it was something like "How's about a go at the old winter sporting" but it was more American than that.

DET. SGT. SMITH: Did you take him for an American?

PC BLAIR: No, I told you I didn't.

(*4 seconds silence*)

DET. SGT. SMITH: (*indistinguishable*) . . . the tape.

PC BLAIR: He had a cockney accent but he tried to talk with an American accent.

DET. SGT. SMITH: And the words?

PC BLAIR: And the words he used were an American expression. Yes. I can't . . .

DET. SGT. SMITH: No matter. Go on about his appearance.

PC BLAIR: He was about medium height. Five ten, nine, about.

DET. SGT. SMITH: Clothes?

PC BLAIR: He wore white overalls with a red badge here.

DET. SGT. SMITH: (*indistinguishable*)

PC BLAIR: White overalls with a red badge on his left breast pocket. The overalls were dirty and so were his other clothes and that.

DET. SGT. SMITH: Describe his other clothes.

PC BLAIR: He had a striped tie with a tinny sort of er cheap pin thing pinned into it like er pin. He er (*4 seconds silence*).

DET. SGT. SMITH: Don't hurry.

PC BLAIR: Had this funny hair, funny mousy-colored hair.

DET. SGT. SMITH: How was it funny do you mean?

PC BLAIR: It wasn't a wig or anything but it was funny and after he had leaned over the van he touched his hair like er women do when they look into a glass er.

DET. SGT. SMITH: How do you know it wasn't false?

PC BLAIR: Well, there's a man who goes to a pub I know who has false hair and you can tell here (*pause*) where his hair sprouts (*laughter*) at his forehead.

DET. SGT. SMITH: You decided that he wasn't wearing false hair after looking at his hairline front and neck.

PC BLAIR: Yes. (*long pause*) I think. I think he was just a bit er vain about his hair. I think that's all it was.

DET. SGT. SMITH: Would you tell me about his face again?

PC BLAIR: Well, he was a bit pale and he had these sort of er terrible sort of bad teeth and that. And a pair of black rim National Health type glasses.

DET. SGT. SMITH: Tell me as you told me before.

PC BLAIR: His breath smelling?

DET. SGT. SMITH: Yes.

PC BLAIR: Well, that's right. He had bad breath and these bad teeth. Black teeth. (*7 seconds pause*)

DET. SGT. SMITH: Is there anything you would like to add to that description? There's no rush.

PC BLAIR: No, there's nothing. I can't think of anything except (*3 seconds pause*) well, just to say he wasn't a freak or anything. He was pretty normal-looking I mean er I wouldn't want to harp on anything of the things I've mentioned they I mean er he looked pretty ordinary I mean. *End of transcript from tape-band.*

Top copy of transcript to be signed by Det. Sgt. Smith and PC Blair.

I read that transcript on the plane to Helsinki. It was more interesting than the pamphlet about inflating dinghies but only just.

| *Helsinki*

Pit, pat, well-a-day,
Little Robin flew away;
Where can little Robin be?
Gone into the cherry tree.

—Nursery Rhyme

CHAPTER 8

UNDER the armpit of Scandinavia, Finland fits like a gusset; and if this gusset were a piece of rotten calico then it would rip in the ragged shredded way that Finland has done. The rips are lakes. They are large and numerous and they contain islands that contain lakes that contain islands until the tatters of the coastline fray into the cold northern sea. But at this time of year there is no sea. For miles and miles the shadow of the airplane has flitted across hard shiny ice. It is only when a glimpse of brown forest is seen through the snow that one can be sure that the coast has been crossed.

I saw Signe standing among the red-roofed airport huts even before we landed and while we taxied in she was running and waving and smiling a gigantic smile. As we walked toward an ancient Volkswagen she took my arm and rested too heavily upon it and asked if I'd brought her anything from London.

"Only trouble," I said. She made me get in the driver's side and we followed a Volga police car and did a careful legal speed all the way into town.

"Did Harvey tell you to meet me?" I asked.

"Certainly not," said Signe. "He doesn't tell me whether to go to meet my friends. Anyway, he is in America. Conferring."

"Conferring about what?"

"I don't know. That's what he said. Conferring." She grinned.

"Turn left here and pull up."

We entered that same comfortable flat off Siltasaarenk where I had met Harvey the previous week. Signe stood behind me and helped me off with my coat.

"Is this Harvey Newbegin's place?"

"It is an apartment house that my father bought. He installed a mistress here. The girl was a white Russian of an aristocratic family. My father loved my mother but this girl Katya he loved foolishly; as she indeed loved him. Last year my father . . ."

"How many fathers do you have?" I said. "I thought he died of a broken heart when the Russians bombed Long-Bridge."

"That wasn't true about him dying." She ran the tip of her tongue along her upper lip as she concentrated. "He asked me to circulate the story of his death. Really, he and Katya . . . You're not listening."

"I can listen and pour a drink at the same time."

"He went with this girl Katya who is so beautiful that it would hurt you to touch her . . ."

"It wouldn't hurt me to touch her."

"You must listen more seriously. They are living at an address that only I know. Even my mother thinks they are dead. They were in a train crash, you see . . ."

"It's a little early in the day for a train crash," I said. "Why don't you take off your coat and relax?"

"You don't believe me."

"I do," I said. "I am your credulous court buffoon and I hang upon every syllable, but I listen even better with a cup of coffee."

When she brought the coffee, elegant little cups on an embroidered tray cloth, she knelt on the floor and put the cups upon the low coffee table. She was wearing a man's sweater back to front, and under her hair—cut high and short now at the back—there was a triangle of white skin as soft and fresh as a newly broken bread-roll.

I fought down an impulse to kiss it. "You have a lovely trapezius," I said.

"Have I? How nice." She said it automatically. She poured out the coffee and presented it to me like John the Baptist's head. "I have a flat in New York," she said. "It's much nicer than this. I spend a lot of time in New York."

"Really," I said.

"Well, this flat's not mine."

"No," I said. "When your old man and Katya come back—"

"No, no, no."

"You'll spill the coffee," I said.

"You are just being nasty."

"I'm sorry."

"All right," she said. "If we are telling stories, we are telling stories. If we are not telling stories, we tell the truth."

"That's a good arrangement."

"Do you think a woman should be able to smile with her eyes?"

"I don't know," I said. "I've never thought about it."

"I think she should." She covered her mouth with her hand. "You tell me when I'm smiling just from watching my eyes."

It's not easy to describe Signe for she left you with a memory out of all relation to her true appearance. She was strikingly pretty but her features were not regular. Her nose was too small to balance her high flat cheekbones and her mouth was made for a face at least two sizes larger. When she laughed and giggled it stretched from ear to ear, but half an hour after leaving her you found yourself remembering Harvey's claim that she was the most beautiful girl in the world.

"Now?" she said.

"Now what?" I said.

"Am I smiling with my eyes?"

"To play this game fairly," I said, "you would need to have a hand that was bigger than your mouth."

"Stop it, you are spoiling it."

"Don't hit me," I said.

For two days Signe and I waited for Harvey Newbegin to return. We saw a gangster film of New York during which Signe kept saying "That's near where I live." We had dinner on top of a tall building in Tapiola and looked out across the ice-locked offshore islands. I almost learned to ski at the cost of a torn jacket and a twisted elbow.

On the evening of the second day we were back in the flat near Long-Bridge. Signe had cooked a fish with a sloppy skill which enabled her to read a pulp magazine and prepare dinner simultaneously without having anything burn or boil over. When dinner was over she brought a plate of petits fours in silver wrappers and a bottle of schnapps.

"Have you known Harvey a long time?"

"I've seen him on and off over the years."

"He runs things here, you know."

"I didn't know."

"Yes. He's in sole charge in this part of Europe. He's gone back to New York for a conference."

"So you said."

"I don't think he's the sort of man who is good at controlling a whole . . ."

"Network?"

"Yes, network. He's too . . . emotional."

"Really?"

"Yes." She bit into one of the little cakes with her ice-white teeth. "He's madly in love with me. Do you think that's good?"

"It's O.K. as far as I'm concerned."

"He wants to marry me."

I remembered all kinds of girls whom Harvey has wanted to marry at some time or other. "Well, you're young yet. I imagine you'll want to think about that for a little while."

"He's going to divorce his present wife."

"He said that?"

"No, his analyst told me at a party in New York." She folded the silver square of wrapping paper in half and made it into a little boat.

"Then he's going to marry you?"

"I don't know," she said. "There are lots of men in love with me. I don't think a girl should be rushed into bedding down."

"I think they should," I said.

"You're wicked." She put the little silver-paper boat onto her fingertip like a hat and wiggled it. "He's wicked," she said to the finger and the finger nodded. "Harvey's wife is awful."

"You are probably a little biased."

"No, I'm not biased. I know her. We were all at a party at Mr. Midwinter's. You don't know Mr. Midwinter, do you?"

"No."

"He's a dear. You'll meet him. He's Harvey's boss." She fingered a coffee mark on my shirt. "I'll remove that before it stains. Give me the shirt. You can borrow one of Harvey's."

"O.K.," I said.

"At this party everyone was wearing really pretty dresses.

You know, with jewels and silver things in their hair and some really great shoes. All the women had really smart shoes. Sort of *that* shape." She took off her shoe and put it on the table and modified it with her two index fingers. "You can get them in Helsinki now, but at that time . . . Anyway I had only been in New York for a couple of days and I only had the clothes I had taken with me. You understand?"

"Sure, it's a real problem."

"No, it really is a problem if you are a woman. Men can have one dark suit and wear it all day and no one will even notice, but women are expected to have the right clothes for lunch and afternoon tea and working in and then have some stunning outfit for evening. Then next day people think you should have things they haven't seen before. If you . . ."

"You were telling me about a party."

"Yes. Well, I'm telling you. I went to this party at Mr. Midwinter's and it's a wonderful house with footmen and things and I went just in the sort of clothes I'd wear for a party here in Helsinki. I mean just a friendly little party. So there in the middle of all these men in tuxedoes and women in three-hundred-dollar dresses . . ."

"Didn't Harvey tell you what they would be wearing?"

"No. You know what he's like. He daren't go near me when his wife's around. Anyway, I'm standing there like a creep . . . Creep?"

"Creep, yes. That will do."

"Well, I'm standing there like a creep in this dress with dots on it. Dots. Can you imagine?"

"Yes."

"Mrs. Newbegin comes over to me. She looks like this." Signe narrowed her eyes to slits and sucked her cheeks in a grotesque imitation of a girl in a fashion magazine. "She's wearing a fabulous black silk sheath dress and satin shoes.

Satin shoes. She looks me up and down and says, 'I'm Mr. Newbegin's wife.' Mr. Newbegin. She turns to her friend and says, 'It's just terrible that Harvey didn't tell her it was formal. I'm sure she has a dozen really pretty little formals she could have worn.' She's so patronizing you've no idea. She's horrid." Signe produced a little box and began applying bright green shadow to her eyelids. She finished, fluttered her lashes at me and smoothed the corduroy dress over her wide hips. She rested the side of her face against my legs. "She's horrid," she repeated. "Terrible life she leads."

"She sounds a bit fierce," I said.

"She's a Leo; fire sign, sun sign. Lightning and domination. Pushing. It's a masculine sign of driving force. Men Leos are O.K., but women Leos tend to push their husbands. Harvey Newbegin is the same sign as me; Gemini. Air. Mercury. Split twins, passionate, dramatic, vicious, intelligent. Lots of movement, darting around to avoid trouble. Terrible with Leo. Geminis and Leo have an evasive relationship. It's a bad combination."

"But you get on well with Harvey?"

"Wonderfully. You've got nice brown arms. You're an Aquarian."

"Have they all got brown arms?"

"Air sign. Spirit and mystery. Always keep a part of themselves back. They have a high wall around them, more profound than most people, more detached and scientific. It's my favorite sign, goes well with Gemini." She grasped my arm to demonstrate. Her fingers were slim and feather-light. She ran them down my arm lightly enough to make me shiver. She picked up my hand, put my fingertips into her open mouth, twisted my hand and kissed my palm noisily.

"Do you like that?" I didn't answer.

She grinned and dropped my hand.

"When I get married I'm going to keep my name. What's your name? I never can remember."

"Dempsey," I said. "Liam Dempsey."

"Well, if I married you I would want to have the name Signe Laine-Dempsey."

"You were just about to tell me what sort of terrible life Mrs. Newbegin has."

Signe pulled a face of distaste. "Businessmen. Horrid wives talking about their husbands' cars. Big business, you know. It's the women I hate, I quite like older men."

"Well, that gives me a chance," I said. "I'm old enough to be your father."

"You are not old enough to be my father," she said while tracing a pattern with her thumbnail into the knee of my trousers.

"Don't do that, there's a good girl."

"Why?"

"Well, this is one of my better suits for one thing."

"And also it's rather disturbing?"

"Yes and also it's rather disturbing."

"There you are; Geminis do affect Aquarians."

"I am old enough to be your father," I said to myself as much as to her.

"I wish you wouldn't keep saying that. I'm nearly eighteen."

"Well, in September eighteen and a half years ago," I thought for a moment, "I had just finished my exams. I went to Ipswich for a holiday. There was a company of ATS girls billeted in the same street." I paused to think hard. "Is your mother a blond ATS girl with a mole on her right shoulder and a slight lisp?"

Signe giggled. "Yes. I swear it's true."

She lifted my vest at the back of my trousers. "You have a very nice back," she said. She ran a finger along the vertebrae appreciatively. "A very nice back. That's important in a man."

"I thought you were going to remove that spot from my shirt," I said. "That's why I'm sitting here in my vest, remember?"

"A very nice back," she said. "I should know; after all, my father was one of the most famous osteopaths in the whole of Sweden."

"It's a good shirt," I said. "You needn't wash it, leave it to soak."

"Until he was called to set a bone in the back of the Queen of Denmark," she said. "That's how it all began."

She squirmed against me and suddenly we were kissing. Her mouth was clumsy and awkward like a child's good night, and when she spoke the words vibrated inside my mouth. "Passionate, dramatic and vicious," she said. "Gemini and Aquarius are good in conjunction." She was still kissing me and kneading my leg skillfully.

Oh well, I thought. I might as well see if there's anything in this astrology lark.

CHAPTER 9

HARVEY flew in the next day. We went out to meet him at the airport and Signe hugged him and told him how much she'd missed him and how she had cooked all his favorite foods for one vast homecoming meal but she had had an urgent phone call about sickness in the family and the dinner had all burned up so now we must eat in a restaurant.

The story about the dinner was a fantasy but I envied Harvey his welcome just the same. She ran across the airport like a newly born antelope unsteady on its legs, and stood with elbows bent and legs apart as though afraid of toppling through her fantasies into womanhood.

The first thing I did was tell Harvey that the eggs and all my baggage had been stolen at the airport but Harvey Newbegin was in one of his rich-busy-man moods and went bustling around making tutting noises for a couple of days. He took the idea of the package being stolen with studied anger and said the people concerned "really took a flyer. It was booby-trapped like crazy."

"Thanks," I said. "That would have been nice if the customs had asked me to open it."

Harvey gave me a heavy-lidded glance. "Customs was fixed."

Then he slammed off into his office. Any room into which Harvey put his typewriter he called his office.

Harvey spent a lot of time in the office and apart from asking me if I'd spoken to Dawlish—a suggestion which I impassively denied—he didn't say much to me until the morning of the third day, which was a Tuesday. Harvey took me out to a sauna club he belonged to. It was a short drive from the city. Harvey had always had a mania for showers and baths and he had taken to the sauna ritual with great enthusiasm. This club was on a small island off the coast and it was reached by a causeway. There was little to show that we were on an island, for the snow covered everything from horizon to horizon. The clubhouse was tucked into a line of fir trees, a low building rich with the reds and browns of natural wood. The snow made horizontal lines of white where it had lodged between the timbers.

We undressed and walked right through the shiny white-tiled shower room where a woman attendant was scrubbing someone with a loofah. Harvey opened a heavy door. "This is the smoke room," Harvey said. "Typically Finnish."

"Good," I said. I don't know why I said that.

Inside it was the size and shape of a cattle truck. Two slatted benches occupied most of the space and they were high up so that you had to sit with neck bent or smash your head against the ceiling. All the inside surfaces were wood, the fire smoke had blackened them and the heat produced a rich, resinous smell of burning pine.

We sat on the bench looking out of a window that was the size of a very large letter box. The thermometer was reading over 100° C but Harvey had fiddled with the stove and said it would get hot in a moment. "That's nice," I said. I felt as if someone was pressing my lungs with a steam iron. Through the double-glazing the trees were heavy with snow and when the wind blew handfuls of it away it looked as though the trees were breathing on the cold air.

Harvey said, "You've got to understand that we are a very special little outfit. That's why I wanted to make sure you didn't say anything about it to Dawlish."

I nodded.

"You didn't say anything to him? On your honor?"

What a strange medieval mind you have, I thought. On your honor is calculated to make me break down and confess.

"On my honor," I said.

"Good," said Harvey. "Because New York was giving me hell about employing you and I've gone out on a limb. You see, we have a special operation coming our way tomorrow."

It was getting very hot in the room. Even Harvey—who had a dark complexion—had gone the color of a boiled lobster. Outside in the snow two men had climbed out of a Renault van with saws and ropes and were tapping one of the trees.

"I didn't want to handle it," Harvey said. "Are you getting too hot?"

"No, I'm fine. Why didn't you?"

"Wrong time of year, for one thing." He smacked his legs with a birch branch. The smell of the leaves was suddenly very strong. I wondered how they preserved branches complete with leaves until this time of year. "Oh, there are a thousand reasons why I wanted them to wait."

"They wouldn't?"

"They have their reasons. They want him in and out within a month at the very outside. He's a technician taking a look at some technical stuff. Machinery or something. It's Pike's brother—you met him?"

"I see," I said. I didn't see anything except a man tying a rope around the large upper branch of a tree.

"It's dangerous," Harvey said. Even Harvey was feeling a little discomfort now. He was sitting very still and his breathing was shallow.

"In what way?"

"These drops. I hate them."

"Drops?" I said. I had a nasty little feeling in my inside that had nothing to do with the sauna. I hoped very much Harvey didn't mean what I thought he might. He stood up and went across to the stove. I watched him dip into a bucket and throw a scoopful of water onto the hot stones of the fire. He looked up at me. "Drop from a plane," he said.

"Parachute into the Soviet Union?" The man at the base of the tree had begun to operate the electric felling-saw even before the other one began to descend.

"They don't use a chute. They drop them from a light plane into snowdrifts."

"You had me worried for a minute."

"I'm not kidding. I'm serious," Harvey said, and I could see that he was.

The bottom end of the rope was fixed to the back of the van and it took up the slack and held the tree in tension to give the saw ease of movement. Suddenly I felt the change of temperature. A thousand pinpricks of scalding steam grew to knife points and the knives twisted. I opened my mouth and felt the scalds on the mucous membrane inside my throat. I closed my mouth and felt as though I had gargled with barbed wire. Harvey watched me closely. He said, "It's only fifty miles to the coast of the USSR. If we went high enough to use a chute we'd be picked up on radar immediately after takeoff."

It was still hot but the pinpoints of scalding water had changed to steam. My skin was burning. I avoided looking at the thermometer.

"What's the difference?" I asked. "If you are really dropping anywhere along that coast I wouldn't give them forty-eight hours before they are signing a statement for the public prosecutor. That's the Baltic Military District * over there. One of the most sensitive areas in the world. It's full of missiles, airfields, sub-bases, the lot; and what's more, it's full of guards and patrols."

Harvey squeegeed the sweat from his face with the edge of his hand and then he looked at his hand as though trying to tell his own fortune. He stood up. "You're probably right," he said. "Maybe I've been too long with this screwy outfit; I'm beginning to believe that stuff they are handing out from the New York office. Let's get out of here, huh?" But neither of us moved. Outside, the van revved up. The spine of the tree curved like a man stretching tall after a heavy sleep. Its arms

* See Appendix 1.

flicked snow loose in a final fastidious gesture of contempt, and then the whole thing began to tilt. It was a slow graceful fall. There was no sound through the double-glazing. I watched the tree hit the ground in a cloud of snow. "Just like that," said Harvey. "You're right. Just like that." And I knew that he had been watching the death of the tree too.

Harvey opened the heavy door of the smoke room. The central room was urgent and noisy like a front-line dressing station. Old women in white coats were clattering around with loofahs and stainless-steel buckets and throwing water over motionless pink men on slabs.

I followed Harvey outdoors into the snowscape. We walked naked along the path that led across the ice-covered sea. Harvey walked along in an envelope of white steam. I suppose I did too for I didn't feel even slightly cold. Harvey dropped through a large hole in the ice. I followed and tasted the salty sweet taste of the Baltic.

I opened my eyes underwater and saw the ghostlike shape of Harvey against the darkness all around. For one terrifying moment I fancied what would happen to someone carried under the ice by the current. Perhaps not another break in the ice for what? One hundred miles? Two hundred miles?

My head bobbed out into the cold dry air. Harvey's face was near, his fair hair plastered close to the skull by the sea water. I noticed a small bald patch on the crown of his head. I still didn't feel the cold.

"You're right," Harvey said. "Right about this hunky we're dropping tomorrow. The poor bastard is a write-off."

"Can't you . . ."

"No no," said Harvey. "Not even if I wanted to. Just make sure he doesn't get too close a look at me, that's all I can do. Self-preservation; the first law of intelligence."

Harvey swam toward the ladder. On the shore one of the men was tying a rope to another tree.

I was keen to stay close to Harvey while he made preparations for the dispatch of this agent, but Harvey left the flat before breakfast. Signe brought me coffee in a pot with a felt cover that had eyes and a nose, then she sat on the edge of my bed holding a silly conversation with the felt cover while I drank my coffee.

"Harvey's given me a job to do," she said, tiring of her game.

"Really?"

"Rilly. All Englishmen say rilly like that."

"Give me a break. I've only been awake three minutes."

"Harvey's jealous of us."

"Did he find out?"

"No, it's his Slavic melancholy."

It was true that Harvey Newbegin's family had come from Russia but there was nothing Slavic about him that anyone but Signe could detect.

"Did Harvey tell you he was Slavic?"

"He didn't have to, he has a typical Moujik face. A Finn can recognize a Russian at a thousand meters across open sights. That faint reddish tinge in his fair hair, did you notice that? And those orange-brown eyes. Beer-colored we say. Look at my face. I am a typical Tavastian. Broad head, broad face, fair complexion, blond hair, bluish-gray eyes and this funny concave nose I have." She stood up. "Look at my structure. Big bones, wide hips. We are Tavastian people from the south and center of Finland. You will see no one like Harvey among us."

"It's a great structure."

"You say things like that and Harvey will guess."

"I don't give a damn what he guesses," I said.

She poured me a second cup of coffee. "Today he told me to deliver a packet and I was not to tell you. *Pooooofffff*. I'll tell you if I want to, he thinks I am a child. When you have showered and shaved we shall deliver it together."

Signe drove the old VW carefully—she was a good driver—and insisted upon taking me the prettiest way to Inkeroinen which meant through the little side roads around Kouvola. It was a sunny day and the sky was like a new sheet of blotting paper with blue ink tipped into the middle of it. The road curved and climbed and went through all the antics of a mountain pass to persuade you that the land wasn't rather flat, and small clumps of trees and farmhouses aided the illusion. It was lonely and small groups of children going to school on skis waved to us as we passed.

I had the feeling that Signe hadn't dismissed Harvey's words of caution about me as completely as she professed and I carefully refrained from asking about the parcel. At Kouvola where the railway line divides we took the southern road, which still follows the railway. A long train of timber wagons and oil tanks was being shunted around a siding and the locomotive laid a coil of black smoke across the white landscape.

Signe said, "What do you think's in the parcel? It's in the glove compartment."

"Hell," I said, "let's not waste a wonderful trip talking business."

"I want to know. Tell me what you think."

I took a small brown paper parcel from the glove compartment. "This?"

"Money, eh?"

"It's not the shape of any money I ever saw."

"But if I told you that Harvey borrowed two paperback books from me last night?"

"Got you," I said. If you allowed for the shape of two paperbacks, between them and jutting from the end was a two-inch pack of what could be paper money.

"Dollar bills."

"Could be."

"What do you mean could be? You know it is."

"Yes."

"I've got to leave them in a taxicab in Inkeroinen."

Inkeroinen is a scattering of shops and houses clustered around a small railway junction. The main street looks like the approach to a village. In the shops there are refrigerators from West Germany, jazz records and detergents. Across the road is a small wooden kiosk selling cigarettes and newspapers; the back portion of it is a taxi drivers' den. Outside there were three bright new taxis. Signe stopped the VW on the far side of the road and killed the motor. "Hand me the packet," she said.

"What will you give me for it?" I asked.

She looked at her watch for the fourth time in two minutes. "My virtue," she said.

"None of us has that anymore," I said.

She smiled tightly and took the packet. I watched her walk across the road to the Ford taxi. She opened the rear door and looked in as though looking for something she had mislaid. When she closed the door again the packet wasn't in her hand. A white Porsche came along the road from the direction of Kotka. It was traveling fast and wobbled as it hit that bumpy piece of road under the railway bridge. It lost speed and pulled up outside the kiosk with a squeal of brakes. The police highway patrols use white Porsche cars.

I moved into the driving seat and started up the motor of Signe's VW. It was warm and sprang to life immediately. A policeman got out of the Porsche, putting on his peaked cap as he did so. Signe saw the policeman just as I pulled away from the curb. He touched his peaked hat and began to say something to her. Along the road behind me came the country bus from Kouvola. I drove twenty yards ahead so that the bus would not be blocking my way when it stopped at the bus stop, then I stopped and looked back. On the window of the cabmen's room a hand was wiping clear a small area of condensation.

The police driver of the Porsche got out of the car and went around Signe to the kiosk. Signe was not looking toward me. By all the normal rules I should have pulled away before that, but if the road was clear I could let things get more serious before doing anything and if it was blocked it was already too late. A familiar figure got out of the bus and walked straight to the cab rank. I had no doubt that he was going to pick up the package. He walked past Signe and both cops. He climbed into the rear seat of the Ford. The driver of the police car purchased two packets of Kent and threw one pack to his friend, who caught it without a pause in his speech to Signe, then saluted, and both policemen got into the Porsche. The man in the rear seat of the taxi showed no sign of finding the package but now he leaned across the driver's seat and sounded the horn. The police car revved up and roared away. I turned the VW around and pulled up to where Signe was standing. She climbed in.

"Glad you stayed?" She smirked.

"No," I said. "It was sloppy and unprofessional. I should have moved away immediately."

"You are a coward," she said mockingly as she got in beside me.

"You're right," I said. "If they ever have a coward's trade union, I'll be the man representing England at the World Congress."

"Yes," said Signe. She was still at the age when honor,

bravery and loyalty outweigh result. I wished I hadn't said England since I was carrying the Irish passport, but Signe gave no sign of noticing the error.

I drove slowly up the road, not wishing to overtake the white police car. In my mirror I saw the Ford taxi moving up on me fast. The snow was banked in humps at the roadside but I pulled in as much as I could to let him pass. The man in the rear of the car wore a roll-brim hat and smoked a cigar. He was leaning comfortably into the corner of his seat reading the unmistakable pages of the London *Financial Times*. It was Ralph Pike. I suppose he was worrying whether coppers were taking a nasty drop.

I wondered why Ralph Pike hadn't brought his own packet of eggs to Helsinki and whether by tomorrow night he wouldn't have another kind of drop to be worried about.

I left Signe and the car at Stockmann's Department Store. I wanted to buy some blades and socks but most of all I wanted to avoid arriving back at the flat at the exact time she did, just in case Harvey should be angry at her disobeying him.

Harvey was at the flat when I got back. He was kneeling in the middle of the lounge fixing small bulbs to the roof rack of Signe's VW.

"It's damn cold," I said. "What about some coffee?"

"Given reasonable luck it will drop even lower by midnight. We'll need all the cold we can get if the ice is to be firm enough for the plane to land." He expected me to ask questions but I carefully refrained from showing interest. I wandered into the kitchen and made some coffee. The blue patch of sky had long since disappeared and as the light faded the snow took on a fluorescent glow.

"It's not snowing?" Harvey called.

"No, not yet."

"That's all we need," Harvey said.

"A delay?"

"This pilot won't delay. He'll fly through a dish of corned-beef hash. It's a crackup out there on the ice that I'm most afraid of. Sweating it out trying to repair the plane with the dawn creeping up like thunder—boy, that's no way to earn a living."

"You don't have to talk me round," I said. "I believe you."

"The passenger arrived—*owwww*." Harvey had jabbed his finger with a screwdriver. He put the finger into his mouth, sucked at it and then waved it around in the air. "Wanted to rest up somewhere."

"What did you say?"

"What did I say? Listen, you talked me into realizing what's going to happen to that cat twenty-four hours from now. I told him to keep walking till sundown."

"He's going to be tired by the time the plane comes."

"What do you want me to do?" Harvey said, making it a one-word question. I pulled a face.

"Don't go limp on me, boy," said Harvey. "You are my flavor of the month. I needed you to point out the facts of life."

"Thanks," I said. "But don't foul it up just to prove I'm right."

"Hell. The guy's got enough dough to buy himself a hotel room to rest up in."

"What time does he call here?"

"Have you got crepe-de-chine ears? He doesn't call here. When the Russkies dig him out of the snow tomorrow he'll say he knows nothing about our operations in Helsinki and I'm going to make sure he's not lying. He meets us over on the far side of town at nine-thirty P.M."

"Supposing he's tired by then? Supposing he ducks out?"

"Then I won't be sobbing, buster; that will be just dandy."

He fixed the last lamp holder to the roof rack and inspected his wiring.

"Help me carry this into the hall. Then we sit and watch TV till nine P.M."

"Suits me," I said. "I can use a little vicarious excitement."

CHAPTER 10

IT'S a weird feeling to have only a layer of ice between you and the sea. Weirder still to drive out across the Baltic in a Volkswagen. Even Signe had been a little nervous about that, especially with the four of us inside it, for the ice would not last a lot longer. When we had driven off the land, Signe and Harvey had studied the shrinkage and cracking of the ice at the water's edge and pronounced it safe.

We were four because Ralph Pike was with us now. He had said hardly anything since we had picked him up at a draughty street corner where the Hanko road leaves Helsinki. He was wearing a peaked cap of brown leather and a long black overcoat. He loosened his scarf when he got into the car and I could see the collar of his overalls under the coat.

When we had driven for ten minutes or so across the plain of frozen sea Harvey said, "All out." It was a dark night. The ice glowed and the air smelled of putrefaction. Harvey connected the roof rack to two batteries. He tested the circuit. The lights fixed to the roof rack came on but paper cones prevented them from being visible from the shoreline. I fancied that I could see the lights of Porkkala to the southwest—for the coast bends south along here—but Signe said that it would be too far away. Harvey took a measure of the wind with a little spinner and then reparked the VW so that the lights would show the pilot the direction of the wind. He switched off two of the lights to indicate the wind speed.

Ralph Pike asked Harvey if he could smoke. I knew how he felt, for in an operation like this nerves take over and you rest so heavily upon the skill of the dispatcher that you ask his permission to even breathe.

"One last good cigar," Ralph Pike said to no one and no one answered. Harvey looked at his watch and said, "Time to get ready." I noticed that Harvey had forgotten his resolve not to let Pike get a good look at him and stayed close to him all the time. Harvey got a piece of canvas out of the front of the car and then Pike took his overcoat off and they wrapped the coat into the canvas and strapped it up very tight on a long strap, the other end of which they fixed to the belt of Ralph Pike's overalls. The overalls were very complicated with lots of zip fasteners and under the arm there was a leather piece that held a long-bladed knife. Pike took off the peaked cap and tucked it inside his overalls which he then zipped up tight to the neck. Harvey gave him one of those rubber helmets that paratroopers wear on practice drops. Then Harvey walked around Pike, tugging and patting and saying "You'll be all right" as though to convince himself. When he was sure everything was exactly as prescribed he got a Pan-Am bag from inside the car. He rummaged around inside it. "I'm ordered to give you these things," Harvey said, as though he didn't want to really, but I don't think he meant that, he was just over-keen to do everything by the book.

First he handed over a bundle of Russian paper money that was little bigger than a wad of visiting cards and some coins jangled. I heard Harvey say, "Gold Louis, don't flash them around."

"I won't be flashing anything around," Pike said angrily.

Harvey just nodded and twisted a silk scarf inside out to demonstrate the map that was printed on the silk lining. I would have thought silk a little ostentatious for Russia but nobody asked my opinion. Then Harvey gave him a prismatic compass that was designed like an old-fashioned turnip watch (complete with a chain that was used as a measure for distance judging). Then they did a countdown on his papers—"army service card," "check," "former residence card," "check," "passport," "check," "working paper," "check." Then Harvey produced two items from his own pocket. The first was a plastic ball-point pen. Harvey held it up for Pike to see.

"You know what this is?" Harvey said.

Ralph Pike said, "It's the poison needle."

Harvey said, "Yes," very briefly, and handed it over before giving him the little 6.35mm Tula-Korovin automatic that the Russians used to call "the nurses' gun."

"Correct and complete?" Harvey asked.

"Correct and complete," said Ralph Pike, fulfilling some strange ritual.

Signe said, "I think I hear it coming."

We all listened but it was two full minutes before we heard it. Suddenly its noise was distinct and loud like a tractor coming over the western horizon. The low-flying plane stretched its sound full-length across the hard ice. The navigation lights were switched off but I could see the Cessna Skywagon flying steadily in the cold air. As it got nearer, the white face of the pilot shone in the glow from his instruments and he waggled the wings in greeting. It climbed slightly as it neared us—so that he could see the indicator lights on the roof rack of the car, I suppose—then it dipped a wing and dropped abruptly to the ice. Its long skis struck the ice flat-on and the fuselage rocked on the heavy springs. The pilot cut the motor and the plane slid toward us with a curious hissing sound. Harvey said,

"I've got some sort of virus." He wrapped his scarf tighter. "I'm running a temperature." It was almost the first remark he had addressed to me all evening. He looked at me as though defying argument, wiped his nose, then smacked Ralph Pike gently on the back as a signal to go.

Almost before the airplane had stopped moving the pilot was out through the door waving a hand for Pike to hurry. "Is he all ready?" the pilot said to Harvey as if Pike couldn't be trusted to speak for himself.

"Set to go," Harvey confirmed. Ralph Pike threw his last unfinished cigar onto the ice. The pilot said, "He could practically walk across tonight. It's ice all the way."

"It's been done," said Harvey. "All you need is a rubber boat to cross the channels that boats have carved."

"I wouldn't trust no rubber boat," the pilot said. He tucked Pike into the front passenger seat and strapped him in.

"They're just thirty feet wide that's all," said Harvey.

"But about two wet miles deep," said the pilot. Then he smacked the motor cowling and said, "Wagons, roll; next stop Moscow."

We stood back and the motor started with a ripple of yellow fire. Harvey picked up the cigar butt with a tut-tut of annoyance. "Let's get out of here," he said. We got into the car but I was still watching the plane. It hadn't left the ice; an ugly skinny sort of structure that looked decidedly unsuitable for flying. It was heading away from me and I could see the twin yellow eyes of its exhaust which dilated as the plane changed its inclination and became airborne. A gust of wind caught it and it slid toward the ground, but only for a moment or so. Then it lifted a little higher, flattened out and set a course at sub-radar altitude.

Harvey was watching the plane too. "Next stop Moscow," Harvey repeated sarcastically.

"He could be right, Harvey," I said. "The Lubyanka Prison is in Moscow."

Harvey said, "Are you mad at me?"

"No, why?"

"When you have second thoughts about the kind of business you're in, you are inclined to bug the nearest person. Tonight I'm the nearest."

"I'm not trying to bug you," I said.

"Good," said Harvey. "Because even if you are leaving, we'll still be working together."

"Leaving?" I said.

"Don't snow me. You know that you're leaving."

"I don't know what you're talking about."

"Well, I'm sorry," Harvey said. "I thought you knew. The New York office wants you to do a short course."

"Really?" I said. "Well, I'm not sure about that."

"You're kidding."

"Harvey," I said, "I'm not even quite sure who the hell we are working for."

"We'll talk about it later," Harvey said. "And tomorrow perhaps you'll let me have a note of your expenses to date and I'll let you have some money. Will five hundred and fifty dollars for work to date be O.K.?"

"Fine," I said. I wondered if Dawlish would let me keep it.

"That's plus expenses of course."

"Of course."

As we got to Kämp Hotel on the Esplanade, Harvey stopped the car and got out. "You two take the car and go on home," he said through the window.

"Where are you going?" Signe asked from the rear seat.

"Never mind where I'm going. You just do as you're told."

"Yes, Harvey," said Signe. Then I moved into the driver's

seat and we drove on. I heard her fidgeting with her handbag.

"What are you doing?"

"I'm putting cream on my hands," she said. "That icy wind has made them rough, the hand cream will soften them. I bet you can't guess who I saw this afternoon. See how soft they are now."

"Don't put your hands over my eyes while I'm driving, there's a good girl."

"The one in the airplane. I let him pick me up at the Marski. I thought I would tell him how to spend his money."

"That cream," I said. "Have you been putting it on your head?"

Signe laughed. "Do you know he pays five marks each for his cigars and if they go out he throws them away?"

"Harvey?" I asked in surprise.

"No; that man. He says they taste bitter if they are relit."

"Does he?" I said.

"But the money wasn't for him. That money we left in the taxi. He had to pay it into a blocked bank account. You have to be a foreigner to do that; I couldn't do it."

"Really?" I said. I swerved to avoid a solitary drunk who dreamily crossed the road backwards.

Signe said, "That man who just flew off in the airplane taught me some words of Latin."

"He does that to everyone."

"Don't you want to hear them?"

"Very much."

"*Amo ut invenio*. That means 'I love as I find.' He said that all the important things in life are said in Latin. Is that true? Do all Englishmen say the most important things in Latin?"

"Only the ones who don't relight five-mark cigars," I said.

"*Amo ut invenio*. I'm going to start saying important things in Latin."

"If Harvey finds out, you'd better start saying 'Please don't blow your stack, Harvey' in Latin. You shouldn't have even given a sign you recognized that man. He hadn't even come to rest." *

"Harvey is a terrible old bear lately. I hate him." A taxicab stopped alongside us at the traffic lights. There was a small-screen TV that some Helsinki taxis fit onto the back of the driving seat. A couple were necking and smiling and glowing with blue reflected light from the TV. Signe eyed them enviously. I watched her face in the rearview mirror. "He's a terrible old bear. He's teaching me Russian and when I make a mistake with those awful adjectives he goes mad with rage. He's a bear."

"Harvey's all right," I said. "He's not a bear, he's not a saint; he has moods sometimes, that's all."

"Just tell me one other person who has moods like him. Just tell me."

"There's no one that has moods like him. That's what makes people more interesting than machines; they're all different."

"You men. You hang together."

The lights changed and I let in the clutch. There was no arguing with Signe in her present frame of mind. "Who does all the cleaning and cooking and looking after?" said Signe from the rear seat. "Who gets him out of trouble when the New York office is after his blood?"

"You do," I said obediently.

"Yes," she said, "I do." Her voice went up three tones on the last words, she sniffed loudly and I heard the click of her handbag.

* Come to rest—the period in which you make sure that a person is not under surveillance. A man who has come to rest can safely be contacted. There is no set time that this expression covers, it lasts until you are sure the man has no tail or until you are sure he has. A man tailed or suspected is said to be spitting blood.

"And all his money goes back to his wife." She sniffed.

"Does it?" I said with interest. She searched her handbag for the handkerchief, lipstick and eye pencil that are necessary parts of a woman's grief. "Yes," she said. "That thirteen thousand dollars—"

"Thirteen thousand dollars!" My surprise gave her renewed energy.

"Yes, that money that I took out to the taxi rank this morning. That was taken by that man and sent to Mrs. Newbegin's account in San Antonio, Texas. Harvey doesn't think I know that—it's a secret—but I have ways of finding out. The New York office would like to know that little item of information, I'll bet."

"Perhaps they would," I said. We had arrived outside the flats. I switched off the motor and turned around to her. She was leaning well forward in the rear seat. Her loose hair swung forward and enclosed her face like a pair of golden doors. She was wearing that coat with all the buttons and buckles that she had worn the first time I saw her outside Kaarna's flat.

"They would," she said. The sound came from inside the golden orb of hair. "And it's not the first money that Harvey has embezzled."

"Wait a moment," I said gently. "You can't throw accusations around without very firm proof of what you say." I waited, wondering if that would provoke her into further disclosures.

"I'll never throw accusations around," Signe sobbed. "I love Harvey," and out of the sphere of hair came little noises as if a canary inside was eating a hearty meal of seeds.

"Come along," I said. "There's no man in the world worth crying for."

She looked up and smiled dutifully through the tears. I gave her a large handkerchief. "Blow," I said.

"I love him. He's a fool but I would die for him."

"Yes," I said, and she blew her nose.

We all had breakfast together the next morning. Signe had gone to a lot of trouble to make Harvey feel he was back home in America. There was grapefruit, bacon, waffles, maple syrup, cinnamon toast and weak coffee. Harvey was in a good mood, balancing plates and saying, "This is something those Russkies do damn well" and "pip pip."

I said, "Just for your information, Harvey, no Englishman that I have met ever said pip pip."

"Is that right?" said Harvey. "Well, when I played Englishmen on the stage they said pip pip nearly all the time."

"On the stage?" I said. "I didn't know you had ever been on the stage."

"Well, I wasn't really an actor. I just barnstormed around after I left college. I was serious about acting in those days, but the hungrier I got the more my resolution sagged, until a guy I'd known at college talked me into a job with the Defense Department."

"I can't imagine you as an actor," I said.

"I can," Signe said.

Harvey smiled. "Boy, did we have great times. We were all so bad. The only guy who knew what he was doing was the manager, and we used to drive him out of his skull. Every morning the whole company would drag-arse onto the stage. He'd say, 'You're going to work your arses off today, the lot of you. Because I'm a tyrannous bastard. The critics are ignorant bastards, the audience mercurial bastards, and you are incompetent bastards. The only legitimate thing around here is the theatre.' Every morning he said that. Every morning. Boy, was I happy in those days. I didn't know it, that's all."

"Aren't you happy now?" Signe asked in alarm.

"Sure, hon, sure." Harvey put his arm around her and snuggled close.

"Wipe your face," said Signe. "You've got peanut butter on your chin."

"Romantic broad, ain't she?" Harvey said.

"Don't call me a broad," said Signe. She took a playful swipe at his face but Harvey caught it on the flat of his hand, then she struck at him with the palm of the other hand and they did a pat-a-cake routine. No matter how much Signe varied the speed, Harvey's hand was up there providing a wall against which her hand smacked, until he snatched his hand away and she toppled into his arms.

Harvey said, "We have to talk business, hon. Why don't you run downtown and buy those shoes you need?" He peeled a hundred-mark note from a big roll.

Signe took the money gleefully and ran out of the room shouting, "I can take a hint. I can take a hint," and laughing.

Harvey looked at his bankroll, and put it away slowly. When the door closed, Harvey poured more coffee for us both and said, "This has been a spectator sport for you so far, but now you are going to join the men."

"What does that entail?" I said. "Circumcision?"

Harvey said, "All our operations are programmed on electronic machines. Each stage is recorded on a tape machine and each operator reports the end of each stage to that machine and the machine will—providing all the agents on that scheme have also reported in—tell you the next stage."

"You mean you're working for a calculating machine?"

"We call it the Brain," said Harvey. "That's how we can be so sure that no slip-ups occur. The machine correlates the reports of all the agents and then relays the next set of instructions. Each agent has a telephone number. He phones that number and obeys the recorded instructions he receives. If the message contains the word 'Secure' that means the words following make up the introductory identification of someone who will contact him and give him orders. For instance: if you phone the number and the tape machine says 'Take a plane to Leningrad. Secure. The face of the city has changed,' that means you fly to Leningrad and stick around for orders from someone who will introduce himself with the words 'The face of the city has changed.' "

"I've got it," I said.

"Good, because those were exactly the orders for both of us this morning. We both go. When the next stage is complete you will be phoning and getting your own instructions. Don't tell me what they are. In fact, don't tell anyone."

"O.K."

Harvey passed me two New York numbers on the Hanover exchange. "Remember those numbers, then burn that paper. The second number is for emergencies and I do mean emergencies, not running low on Kleenex. And always call collect. The phone charges can't be drawn on your expenses."

Leningrad—Riga

> There was a little man, and he had a
>   little gun,
> And his bullets were made of lead, lead,
>   lead;
> He went to the brook, and shot a little
>   duck,
> Right through the middle of the head,
>   head, head.
>
> —NURSERY RHYME

CHAPTER 11

LENINGRAD is the halfway house between Asia and the Arctic. Normally it takes about six days to arrange a visit, even if you cable both ways. Harvey, however, had some way of speeding things, and we got the Aeroflot Ilyushin 18B evening flight from Helsinki just two days later. A Zim motorcar took us from the airport to the Europe Hotel which is just off the Nevsky Prospekt, the wide main street of Leningrad. Inside the hotel it looked as though the nine-hundred-day siege of World War Two was still going on. Pieces of broken plasterboard, old doors, tarpaulins and coils of rope had to be negotiated before we could get to the desk clerk. Harvey said he still had a temperature and must have something to eat before he went to bed. The desk clerk was a worried, gray-haired man with steel-rimmed glasses and a medal. He showed us into the buffet, and waitresses brought vodka and red caviar and stared at us in that curious but not impolite way that so many people do in Russia.

From the buffet we could see the restaurant where a ten-piece dance band was playing "Mambo Italiania" and about thirty couples danced various improvisations on the western dances according to whether they came from Leningrad, Peking, or East Berlin where the TV picks up the West Stations. Harvey insisted that he must have coffee as well as brandy, and although the big espresso machine had been cleaned and stopped, the plump waitress went off to fix some for us.

Harvey said that if he had the thermometer that was in his baggage he could show me whether he was ill or not, and that then I wouldn't think it was so funny.

I helped myself to some more red caviar and that wonderful dark sour bread, and watched the cashier noisily adding the takings on an abacus. Two waiters came into the buffet arguing, and then noticed that it wasn't empty and went out again. Then a very tall man in an overcoat and an astrakhan hat came in. He walked across to our table. "I notice," he said in good English, "that you have been so bold as to ask for food at this late hour. Are you discussing business, or may I join you?"

"Sit down," Harvey said, and he made a flick of the finger and said, "Mr. Dempsey from Eire, and my name's Newbegin. I'm American."

"Ah," said the man in that openmouthed way Italians express polite surprise, "my name is Fragolli. I am Italian. A little more of the same," he said to the waitress who had come to the table with Harvey's coffee and was watching Signor Fragolli with close interest. He made a circular motion with closed fingers. The girl nodded and smiled. "Stolichnaya," he called after her. "Is the only vodka I will drink," he explained to us.

"Hey Mambo. Mambo Italiana," he sang quietly to the music.

"You here on business?" Harvey asked.

"Business yes. I have been two hundred miles south of Moscow. You think here it is Russia in winter, but I have been in tiny frozen villages; you have no idea. I sell to the purchasing committees of the many regions. Four days of negotiations to make a deal, always the same amount of time. They make an offer, we argue then we discuss. I make a price, they say it is too much. I explain that a lower price will exploit my workers. They examine the figures again. I modify a part of the specification. On the fourth day we agree. They keep to their agreements exactly. They never default on a payment. It is a pleasure once agreement is reached."

The waitress arrived with a flask of vodka and more red caviar. Signor Fragolli was a large man with a deeply lined muscular face and a large hooked nose like a Roman emperor. He opened a white smile in his dark sun-bronzed face and tapped a knife against the silver champagne bucket in time to the music.

"What do you sell?" Harvey said.

He stopped tapping and groped into his black briefcase. "This," he said. He was holding a lady's girdle and he swiveled it like moving hips. The garters rattled.

"This I like," said Harvey.

We arranged lunch the next day. Signor Fragolli would meet us at 1:30 P.M. outside the Central Naval Museum which he insisted upon calling the Stock Exchange. The Museum is on the eastern spit of one of the hundred islands that make up the city of Leningrad, and the spit links two of its six hundred and twenty bridges. Here the river Neva is at its incredible widest, and the cold wind screams across the ice to the Peter and Paul Fortress. The Italian was a moment or so late, smiling and bowing apologies. He led the way down the slope to the river, now frozen solid from here to the north bank. Once upon the ice the distance to Kirovsky Bridge seemed even vaster. We followed the well-marked paths across the ice. A woman in a heavy coat, head scarf and fur-lined boots stood patiently holding a string which ran down through a circular hole in the ice. A small boy with her brandished a plastic gun and made banging sounds at us, but the woman admonished him and smiled at us. She had caught no fish, or perhaps she had thrown them back. When we were well past her, Signor Fragolli said, "The face of the city has certainly changed. Have you got it?"

"Yes," Harvey said. I noticed he kept his head bent downward, for even out here on the ice a parabolic reflector microphone could pick us up.

"I hope you haven't broken any of them?"

"No. I've been very careful," Harvey said.

That was all I needed to feel sure that Harvey had the half dozen eggs that were stolen from me at London Airport. I said nothing. They were going to be surprised when they looked more closely at those canteen eggs. Harvey and Fragolli both carried identical black briefcases.

"Change bags at lunch," said Fragolli. He gave a great peal of laughter with lots of teeth flashing. I suppose that was to fool anyone watching us from the riverbank. "One of you," he said, still smiling, "is going to Riga."

"Dempsey will go," said Harvey. "I must stay here."

Fragolli said, "I don't care which." He changed his position as we walked so that he could be closer to me. "You go to Latvia tomorrow. The 392 flight to Riga at 2:50 P.M. Stay at Hotel Riga. You will be contacted." He turned to Harvey. "You've put his photo on the brain index?"

"Yes," said Harvey.

"Good," said Fragolli. "The person meeting you will know what you look like."

"But I won't know what they look like?"

"Exactly," said Fragolli. "Is safer that way."

"Not for me it's not," I said. "I don't like the idea of my snapshots being found on one of your layabouts."

Harvey said, "There won't be any pictures floating about. The man who will contact you will probably be the airplane passenger."

"What do you want me to do?" I asked. "Apply splints and bandages?"

Harvey said, "The sooner you get it through your head that this organization doesn't make slip-ups the sooner you can relax and stop bugging me."

Perhaps he said that for the benefit of Signor Fragolli, so I just said, "O.K."

Fragolli said, "You are going to have to commit two thousand words to memory. Can you do that?"

"Not verbatim," I said, "not every word exactly."

"No," said Fragolli. "Only the formulas—quite short ones—need be verbatim."

"I can do that," I said.

I wondered how they would arrange my visa for Riga, but I didn't ask.

We reached the ice-locked boat. It was a great slab-sided craft with lots of wooden balconies and curtained windows. We picked our way through crates of beer and lemonade, and a man yelled "Tovarich" at us in a rather threatening way. "Tovarich," he yelled again.

Fragolli said, "It's because we haven't left our coats with him. It's not cultured to enter anywhere in an overcoat."

The floating restaurant had the same equipment that every other restaurant had. The cutlery was from the same state factory and had the same design and so did the plates, the menu, and the waiters.

We ate *piroshki* and bouillon and Fragolli told us what sort of morning he had had negotiating the sale of girdles. "You have no idea what remarkable minds the Russians have, cautious and devious perhaps, but clever yes. I sell my goods in many western countries, but these Russians . . ." He hissed at his fingertips to demonstrate his admiration, and his voice became low and conspiratorial. "We make a deal. Other customers just give me a number and a date. Eight thousand girdles model 6a in these sizes for this delivery date. The Russians, no. They want this garter clip to be one inch lower, they want this seam double sewn."

"Tricky," said Harvey.

"Yes," said Fragolli. "By changing the specification they insure that those garments are made specially for them. Elastic deterioration, you see. They don't want garments that have been months in the warehouse. Clever capitalist minds they have."

"Capitalist?"

"Certainly. Those old ladies selling bunches of flowers on the Nevsky Prospekt? Now no militiaman says anything to them, even though it is against the law. But to sell those flowers long ago, it could be a dangerous thing to do. If I could give one of those women a supply of girdles—" He stopped. "I have calculated that selling the girdles at normal price—and in Leningrad this day I could get double the normal price at least—but at normal price I could still retire at the end of one day's work. This country is hungry for consumer goods just as Europe about 1946."

"So why don't you do just that?" said Harvey.

Fragolli crossed the first two fingers of each hand in the universal Russian sign for prison and everything connected with it.

"Things will become easier," said Harvey. "You will soon be selling your girdles; all you can make."

Fragolli said, "There is a saying in Leningrad that a pessimist is a man who says that things were bad in the past, things are still bad, things will always be bad. An optimist says, things were bad in the past, are still bad, but nothing can be worse than this."

"So why do they put up with it?"

"When a baby is born in this country he is swaddled. Swaddled from neck to toe, like a log of wood. When you unwrap him to wash, he cries. He cries because the control and restraint has been removed. He is free. He is alarmed. So he is soon swaddled up again, and mentally he stays swaddled up until he dies."

"They don't do that swaddling so much nowadays," said Harvey.

Fragolli said, "Look at this waitress, for instance. She just cannot buy proper foundation garments. She has no proper brassiere or girdle."

"I like it like that," Harvey said. "I like my broads buttocked both sides."

"Non non no," said Fragolli. "I want to put foundation garments on every pretty woman in Leningrad."

Harvey said, "My ambition is exactly the reverse."

Fragolli laughed.

Harvey dropped his *piroshki* into the soup and broke it up with the spoon.

Fragolli said, "The Russian style. You eat your *piroshki* in Russian style."

"My father was a Russian," said Harvey.

"Newbegin is not Russian name."

Harvey laughed. "It is the word 'new' and the word 'begin.' My father used it when he came to America for a new start in life."

"I understand," said Fragolli. "I meet many Americans." He lowered his voice. "To tell you the truth, my company is forty-nine percent owned by an American company. The Russians do not like to do business with American companies so this is convenient arrangement for all concerned."

"Russians are realists," Harvey said.

"They are realists," pronounced Fragolli, and he too dropped a *piroshki* into his soup.

Harvey and I left Fragolli after lunch. Harvey said, "Relax. I didn't really send your photo to Riga. I've got my own system for identification but I'm not telling that Fragolli anything."

"What's your system?"

"They have television telephones in this crazy country. I have a call booked for Riga for three o'clock. We'll go now and take a look at this guy you are going to contact; it's a heap better than smudgy little photos."

Harvey and I took a cab to Pavlov Street. Number 12A is a small building that looks as if it might house an unskilled worker with a large family. It is really the public video trunk call office. We knocked at the door, and a woman let us in. She parked a pencil in her hair, looked at her wristwatch, compared that with the wall clock, asked us what time we thought it was, then we all went to a small room that housed a phone and an old-fashioned-looking twelve-inch TV set. We sat down and Harvey picked up the telephone. The woman turned a dial on the TV set and the screen flashed blue. Harvey said "Hello" four times, then suddenly he was talking to a bald-headed man who seemed to have four overcoats on at once.

Harvey said, "This is Mr. Dempsey, he's coming to see you tomorrow and he'll be staying at the Hotel Riga."

The man on the TV screen said, "It's cold here in Riga. Bring plenty of sweaters." Then he said would I move a little bit to the right so that he could see me, because the edges of the picture distort. Then the man in Riga asked if it was cold in Leningrad, and we said yes it was, and the man in Riga said you had to expect it now, and that the Riga Hotel was modern and well heated as long as it wasn't damp. Harvey said how much he had enjoyed his last visit to Riga, and how sorry he was that he wouldn't be going there, and the man at the other end said that Leningrad was one of the most wonderful towns in the world. Then Harvey said yes Leningrad was wonderful, and how it was called the Venice of the North on account of how wonderful it was. The man at the other end said yes, and how did Mr. Dempsey like it, and I said it was wonderful but I hadn't ever heard anyone call Venice the Leningrad of the South, and then there was a silence. I had spoilt the magic of the moment. That was when the little woman with the pencil in her hair came in and said that was the end of the time unless we wanted to extend it. Harvey said no we didn't, and then the man in Riga said good-bye, and we said good-bye, so the man in Riga said it again and was still saying it when he melted.

I was alone that last evening in Leningrad.

I went to the Maly Opera Theatre that night and saw Verdi's *Othello,* and with the voices still occupying my mind I decided to take a subway down the Nevsky and have a drink at the

Astoria. I went down the steps at the sign of the big neon M. I put a five-kopeck piece into the automatic entrance which won't prevent non-payers traveling but buzzes in order to embarrass them. A man in a fur hat, long black leather coat, white shirt and silver tie got into the carriage. I wondered if he had enjoyed the opera. I smiled at him and he nodded back without smiling. I reached for a packet of Gaulois, tore open the corner and offered them to him.

"No," he said. "No thank you."

"You are a cigar smoker, Comrade-Colonel?" I said.

"Yes," said the man, "but in our subway we . . ."

"Of course," I said. I put the packet away. I didn't want to break the law. "I don't want to break the law," I said. The man smiled but I was serious.

The train rattled along and we both hung on to the straps, looking at each other.

He was a heavy muscular man of about sixty. He had a round face that hadn't done much smiling until middle age, and an uptilted nose that perhaps had been busted and reset by a plumber. His eyes were small black sentries that marched up and down, and his hands were bunches of bananas unsold over the weekend.

I said, "I am getting off here and walking to the Astoria, where I will drink one hundred grams of port wine. I will listen to the band playing American dance music for perhaps twenty minutes, then I will walk back to the Hotel Europe."

He nodded and did not follow me as I got off the train.

I did exactly as I had promised. Less than half an hour later I left the front entrance of the Astoria and walked down the dark side street. When it's daylight in Leningrad and the buses and lorries are roaring along the wide Nevsky, and African delegates are being toasted at multicourse lunches at the Astoria, then it's easy to see Leningrad as the birthplace of

Communism. But when it's dark and the moon glints on the Peter and Paul Fortress, and two out of every three streetlights are extinguished for economy so that the puddles and newly fallen snow are discovered only by an errant foot, then it is once again St. Petersburg, and Dostoevsky is humpbacked in a slum behind Sennaya Square, and Pushkin is dying after his duel and saying "Good-bye my friends" to his rows of books.

Behind me I heard a slow-moving car. It was a large Zis —a car used only by government officials. The driver flashed the lights and the car drew alongside. The door opened, blocking my forward movement. From the back seat the voice of the colonel I had seen in the subway said, "Won't you get in, English?"

I got into the rear seat and the colonel closed the door. There was a lot of cigar smoke.

"So we meet again, Colonel Stok?" I said like they say it in films.

"Alexeyevitch."

"So we meet again, Alexeyevitch?"

"Yes." He gave an order to the driver, who switched off the car motor. "You are enjoying our Russian winter?" Stok stared at me. His head looked like that of a statue that someone had found and rolled home so that all the delicate parts had broken off.

"Yes," I said, "I'm enjoying the Russian winter. Are you?"

Stok tugged at his fleshy chin. "We have a saying in my country, 'For him who stands at the top of the tower there is no other season but winter.' "

"Yes," I said, although I still don't understand what that proverb means.

"You are involving yourself with a particularly foolish and headstrong group of troublemakers. I think they are exploiting you. When I move against them do not expect me to treat you differently from the way I treat them. It may be that you are investigating these evil people on behalf of your government, or it may be that you are ordered to cooperate with them. They are troublemakers, English; but they will find that I am more expert at making trouble than they are."

"I believe you," I said. "But in my experience there aren't many evil people around. Just ill-informed, misguided and ignorant ones."

Colonel Stok said, "In Russia our people are not misinformed."

"There are many people who think that water has no taste," I said, "because we were born with it in our mouths and it's been there ever since."

Stok didn't reply. "Hotel Yevropeiskaya," he shouted to the driver. The car moved. "We will take you to your hotel," he said to me. "It is not a good night for walking."

I didn't argue. If it wasn't a good night for walking, Stok would know.

CHAPTER 12

THERE are fifteen republics in the Soviet Union. Each one constitutes a separate ethnic unit, has a self-sufficient economy, a flag, a supreme soviet, a council of ministers and, most important, is placed between the area we call Russia and the world outside. The three Baltic republics are Estonia, Lithuania and Latvia. They huddle close and drink at the trough of the Baltic along with Sweden and Finland.

I caught the Aeroflot 392 flight from Leningrad to Riga. It left at 2:50 P.M. and was crowded with people in heavy coats and fur hats who changed their minds constantly about leaving their outer clothing in the small wardrobe at the front of the cabin. There was some confusion about the seat numbering: two women with arms full of overcoats and a crying baby had the same seat ticket that I had. This was sorted out by a ravishingly beautiful air hostess who distributed boiled sweets to all concerned and reprimanded a tovarich for smoking.

The plane climbed across the smoky suburbs of Leningrad and over the Elektrosila plant. Brick suburbs gave way to big wooden houses, then single-story houses which became more and more isolated until there was nothing but grizzled, frozen marsh. Winter had closed the eyelids of the land and the snow that covered it was ill-fitting and dingy like a secondhand shroud. Lake Peipus moved slowly under the starboard wing, scene of Alexander Nevsky's great battle when the Knights of the Teutonic Order probed too far eastward and went, complete with horses and heavy armor, through the ice-crust and into the deep black water.

The trimly uniformed stewardess—definitely wearing western foundation garments—brought a cellophane envelope for leaky fountain pens and a plastic cup of fizzy lemonade. I smiled at her, and she jammed a copy of *Pravda* into my hand, her smile still ticking over. Below us the landscape shone in great brown and white patterns like the coat of a well-groomed piebald horse. We began the descent above the Gulf of Riga and dropped toward the military airport. In the seat in front two passengers recognized the farm where they lived and wanted me to see it too. We nodded, smiled and pointed down, while a dual-seat jet-fighter screamed off the runway in a climb that indicated that the instructor was pushing the buttons.

The stewardess said, "You come from London?" She offered me a tray of boiled sweets.

I took one, and thanked her.

"I know a poem about London," she said.

"I know a limerick about Riga," I said.

She nodded and passed on. The plane came down for a smooth landing amid the radar gear.

The Hotel Riga is built on the site of the old Hotel Rome just across the street from the opera house. The pavements were crowded with women sweeping snow, and fur-hatted soldiers in padded fatigue coats and dirty boots. All the while long lines of lorries trundled along the streets as if it was 1945 and the retreating Wehrmacht only a couple of miles away. The dual-language signs—in Latvian and Russian—heightened the illusion. As fast as the street cleaners worked, more snow swept down upon the street, shining like tracer bullets on the dark winter air. I turned away from the window and sank down upon the bed.

I went to sleep that afternoon fully dressed, and I didn't wake up until 7:45 P.M. I washed and changed my clothes, and walked through the old part of the city with its strange crouch-backed medieval buildings like a Hollywood set built for Garbo. I walked as far as the castle, where the tram tracks jut out toward the far bank of the Daugava River to show where the bridge was torn away from under them. I picked my way through the narrow streets where the old bent buildings leaned together for warmth. I wasn't followed. I suppose my shadow calculated that I would soon come in off the streets, or perhaps he was using the opportunity to go through my baggage. By comparison with the cold cobbled alleys, the hotel restaurant was a scene of throbbing gaiety. A small orchestra was playing "Lights of Moscow" and the waiters were clattering metal dishes and semaphoring with table napkins, and there was that air of subdued hysteria that you get in a big theatre when the orchestra is tuning up.

The restaurant was like many of its kind throughout the

Soviet Union, although perhaps better cared for than most. The parquet was shined, the tablecloths starched and the waiters had clean shirts. At a table near the window sat a delegation of Africans, and another table nearer to the dance floor had South-East Asian faces that nodded every time their Russian host spoke. Here and there sat groups of army officers in baggy trousers and boots, with enamel medals on their chests. Each time the music began, half a dozen unsteady men wandered through the restaurant asking the women to dance. More often than not the women declined but this did not discourage the tipsy men. I ordered red caviar and black bread and butter and two hundred grams of vodka. I ate slowly and watched the dance floor. I tried to guess which of the women were the Russian wives of men stationed here and which were Latvian girls.

An unkempt man with a torn shirt collar and a large bundle sat down opposite me. He asked me for a light and I offered him one of my Gaulois. He inspected it carefully, thanked me and lit it. He asked me if I was English, and I told him Irish. He told me that this was not a good time of the year to see Riga. June, he said, was the time to come here. He ordered another two hundred grams of vodka.

One of the army officers at the next table called across to my companion, "Businessman?"

He leaned over to me. "They want pineapples," he said.

"Is that so?" I said.

"Yes," he said, "and I have the best ones in town."

We watched one of the army officers get to his feet. He was a short fair-haired man with gold epaulets and the black flashes of the tank units. The other officers were teasing him, but he did not smile. He walked across the restaurant to the long table near the dance floor, where the delegation sat. He clicked his heels and bowed briefly toward a beautiful Eurasian girl. She got up and they completed a rather formal fox-trot amid the strange gyrations of the more experimental couples. After the dance he escorted her back to the rest of the delegation, and returned across the floor to us. He whispered something into the ear of my disheveled companion, who produced a bundle wrapped in old copies of *Pravda*. It was a large pineapple. Rubles changed hands.

My companion winked at me. "Are pineapples difficult to get in your country?" I watched the officer present the pineapple to the girl.

"Not as far as I know," I said. "Why can you get them when no one else can?"

He put an index finger alongside his nose. "I fly them up from Djakarta," he said. "I'm an Aeroflot pilot."

The band played "When the Saints Go Marching In." "This is my favorite song," said the man from Aeroflot. "I shall find a girl to dance with." He indicated dancing by making a stirring motion with his index finger and nearly knocking the vodka flask over, and then he lurched off toward the music. "Guard my pineapples," he called.

"Yes," I said.

Latvia—or at least Riga—is more sophisticated than Leningrad or Moscow. If you ask for breakfast in your room they have difficulty in understanding the idea, but they will do it. A suggestion like that in Leningrad is subversive. In Riga the waitresses wear clean uniforms with white starched caps in the Mrs. Beeton tradition; in Leningrad they wear greasy black suits. So when, late that night as I was just about to go to bed, I heard a discreet knock at the door I was not amazed to find a waiter in a claw-hammer coat pulling a heavily laden food trolley into my room.

"I didn't order anything," I said.

His broad back just kept coming through the door as if he was laying a cable. Once inside he turned and smiled.

"I didn't know you could get KGB * men from room service," I said.

Colonel Stok said, "I would be obliged if you would speak more quietly." He went across to the washbasin, picked up a drinking glass and putting the top of it against the wall, applied his ear to the base. I held up a bottle of Long John that I had brought from Helsinki. Stok looked at me blankly—still listening through the wall—and nodded. By the time I walked across to him, Stok had the glass in the drinking position. The evening suit was not a good fit and he looked as though he were part of a Marx Brothers film.

He said, "Within the next hour you will receive a phone call."

Stok sipped his drink and waited as though he expected a round of applause.

"Is that what you call revolutionary consciousness?"

Stok looked at me calmly, trying to read the small print in my eyes. "Yes," he said finally, "revolutionary consciousness." He tugged one end of his bow tie and the knot came undone. The tie tumbled down his shirtfront like a little cascade of ink. Stok proceeded with his prediction: "Within an hour you will receive a phone call. It will arrange a meeting somewhere along the Komsomol Boulevard, probably near the October Bridge. If you attend that meeting I shall be forced to treat you as I shall treat the others. However, I advise you strongly not to go because you will be in danger."

"Danger from whom?"

Colonel Stok was as big as an old oak wardrobe. Maybe some of the carving had got damaged in transit, but he was as

---

* See Appendix 2. Soviet Intelligence.

firm and heavy as ever. He walked across the floor, and although he caused little sound, the whole room vibrated with his weight. "Not from me or any of my men," Stok said. "I promise you that." Stok drank the whisky in one gulp.

"You think these other people you mentioned will do me harm?"

Stok took off his evening dress jacket and put it over a hanger that was lying on my open suitcase. "I think they will," said Stok, "I think they will do you harm." He arranged the coat on the hanger, wrenched at his wing collar and unclipped the shirt stud. The starched front of his shirt parted with a clatter, he dropped the handful of studs into an ashtray and kicked off his black patent-leather shoes. He flexed his toes on the carpet. "My feet," he said. "I suppose a young man like you wouldn't understand what pleasure it gives me to remove tight shoes." He arched one foot like a cat's back, and said, "Aahh."

"And that's momentary interest," * I said.

Stok said nothing for a moment, then he looked through me and said, "I touched Lenin. I stood beside him in Vosstaniye Square in July 1920—the Second Congress—I touched him. So don't use Lenin's words to me. Momentary interest." Stok crossed his arms across his face and began to pull his shirt off, and his words were lost beneath the white cotton. Beneath his shirt was a khaki singlet. Stok's face emerged flushed and smiling. "Do you know the words of the poet Burns?" He hung his trousers on a hanger. He wore long underwear and elastic garters held his socks.

"I know 'To a Haggis,' " I said.

Stok nodded. "I read a lot of Burns," he said. "You should

---

* Momentary interests (Communist jargon)—a complex idea that defined those demands by the proletariat that were shortsighted, therefore ill-advised. It means giving in for the sake of comfort.

read him more. You would learn a lot. 'We labor soon, we labor late, to feed the titled knave man.' Burns understood. The man who taught me English could recite Burns by the hour." Stok went across to the window and looked through the side of the curtain like they do in gangster films. "Aren't you going to offer me another drink?" he asked.

I poured a slug of whisky into the glass. Stok drained it without even a pause to say thanks. "That's better," was all he said. He walked across to the food trolley and removed the starched cloth with a flourish. Instead of metal serving dishes there was an officer's uniform laid out there, complete with peaked cap and well-shined high boots. Stok reached for his riding breeches, buttoned himself into them, tucked his shirt in, then walked across to where I was sitting. He flexed his toes again.

"You wonder why I am warning you, instead of rounding you all up? Well, I'll tell you. If I round up all these criminals and troublemakers, no one will say 'What a clever man is Colonel Stok to grab those people before they could cause our country trouble.' They will say 'Look how many subversives have been working under the very nose of Colonel Stok.' You understand this, English. We have known each other before. My desire is that these criminals leave my district and abandon their fantastic dreams."

Stok tied his tie, using all the muscles of his fingers as though it was made of metal instead of cloth. He slipped into his coat and shook his arms to make his shirt cuffs appear.

"What fantastic dreams do they have?" I asked.

Stok pinched the big knot with his fingers. Then he poured himself another drink. "Don't try to make a fool of me, English."

"I just want to know."

"They think that the Soviet Union is on the verge of overthrowing its tyrannical overlords. They think that people walking on the street out there are dreaming of the moment when they can become capitalist serfs again. They think that we all lie awake dreaming of going to America. They think they can distribute pamphlets and gold, and a vast army of monarchists will materialize overnight. That's what I call fantastic dreams. You understand?"

"Yes," I said.

Stok put on his uniform cap and a thigh-length padded jacket of the sort that Russian troops wear as fatigue dress when it's very cold. There were now no badges of rank to be seen. He walked across to the window, and producing a knife, ran it around the paper sealing strip, then opened it. He opened the outer window as well, and stepped out onto the fire escape. "Thank you for the use of your room," said Stok.

"One good turn deserves another," I said. He picked up his whisky.

"You speak the truth," said Stok. "Well, do as you wish. It's a free country." He downed the drink.

"You mustn't believe all you read in *Pravda*," I said.

Stok walked down into the darkness.

I poured myself a drink and sipped it. I wondered what to do. There was no question of contacting Dawlish. I wasn't so concerned with Midwinter's security but it would take ages to phone New York. Perhaps Midwinter had already outthought Stok. I didn't think so. Stok was something no computer could deal with; perhaps that's what I liked about him.

CHAPTER 13

ONE hour and ten minutes after Stok left, the phone rang. "The hell with you" I said to the phone but after the third or fourth ring I answered it. The phone said, "Western clothes. Secure; two extra shirts. Komsomol Boulevard near October Bridge."

"I'm staying right here," I said. "I'm sick."

"That's all," said the phone.

"Don't wait for me," I said. I replaced the receiver and said it again. I walked across to the bedside table and poured myself a large, large shot of whisky. The hell with them all. An operation like this must be a write-off, the odds against it were too great to make it worth pursuing. But I didn't drink the whisky. I sniffed it and whispered an obscene word to it, then I put on my coat and overshoes and walked out of the hotel.

I walked through 17th June Square, and the Domsky Cathedral was shiny with moonlight and snow. Parked outside the Polytechnic there were two small taxi-vans that are hired at ten kopecks per kilometer. Nearby were two men talking. Each was taking an unnatural interest in the view beyond his companion's shoulder. One of the men called to me in German as I passed them. "Do you want to sell any Western clothes?" It was the bald man I had spoken with on the video trunk call screen.

"I have a couple of extra shirts," I said. "Woolen ones. I could sell those if it's permitted."

"Good," said the man. He opened the door of one of the taxi-vans. I got in. The driver revved up enthusiastically and turned onto the October Bridge. On the far bank the sky was red, for the heavy industry of the Lenin region doesn't close down at midnight. On the river bank a huge sign said, THE BALTIC SEA IS A SEA OF PEACE.

The van was crowded with men in damp overcoats and their weight made it difficult to control over the hard bumpy ice. The wipers began to wheeze as the snowflakes built up into hard wedges of ice, and some of the men in the back were stamping their feet on the floor of the van trying to improve their circulation. No one spoke. The headlights of the taxi-van behind us flashed as it hit bumps in the road and the interior lit up the faces of the men in the van with me. The bald man popped a clove of garlic into his mouth.

"You like garlic?" he asked, breathing at me.

"Not second hand," I said.

"I have a cold," said the bald man. All Russians believe that garlic cures the common cold. I picked at a crust of ice that condensation had formed upon the window. The whole world was white; a great canvas backdrop untouched by paint. Here and there a faint pencil line indicated where a line of trees or a valley would one day appear. And all the time the snow fell; not once but many times, scooped up by the wind and hurled back in huge opaque whirlpools that obliterated even the pencil lines. We drove for an hour. In the tiny villages just one or two lights still burned. Twice we nearly drove into a horse and cart and we passed three lorries. When we finally stopped, the van behind slid on the hard ice and narrowly missed colliding with us. We were in open country.

"Get out," said the bald man. I opened the door and wind flicked against my exposed flesh like steel-tipped whips. The two vans parked under the trees. The bald man offered me a cigarette.

"You're an American?" he said.

"Yes," I agreed. There was no point in providing him with facts.

"I'm a Pole," he said. "So is my son there." He pointed toward the driver. In Latvia, Roman Catholics refer to themselves as Poles. "The others are Russians," he said, "I don't like Russians." I nodded.

The bald man leaned closer and breathed garlic at me. "You, me and my son are the only ones working for Midwinter. The others are . . ." He made that sign of two fingers laid across two fingers.

"Criminals?" I asked. I shivered from the cold.

He sucked at his cigarette and then wet his lips distastefully. "Businessmen," he said. "That's the arrangement."

"What is?"

"An army lorry is due along this road in a few minutes. We'll wreck it. They take the contents, we take the documents."

"What are the contents?"

"Rations. Food and drink. No one here ever steals anything but food or drink. They're the only things that you can dispose of without a permit." He laughed garlic at me.

"What documents?" I asked. "The ration strengths?"

"That's right," said the bald man. "Best way to check the manpower of the units along the coast here." He threw the stub of his cigarette into the snow and walked into the center of the roadway. I followed him. Two men were staring at the road. The bald man extended a toe and slid it experimentally across the glassy surface of ice. They had melted snow with a little water from the car radiators and now it was freezing into a mirror of ice. "The lorry will be helpless on it," said the bald man. Some of his confidence rubbed off on me. Just for one moment it all seemed possible. I'd like to see those ration strengths, perhaps it would go well. I pulled my scarf tighter and shivered; who was I kidding? From the top of the rise a torch flashed twice.

"Now," said the bald man. "It will have to do." He tapped the ice with his toe. "The lorry is coming." We all crouched behind the trees. I could hear a heavy lorry in low gear.

"You don't think we can do it," whispered the bald man.

"You're damn right I don't," I said.

"We'll show you. Clean, cheap, fast and not a firearm in the vicinity."

I nodded. The bald man looked around to make sure that none of the "businessmen" were within earshot. "You tell Midwinter," he said, "not to send them any guns. It's the *promise* of guns that makes them cooperate with Midwinter. If they ever *got* guns . . ." He smiled. The reflected light from the snow underlit his face. His nose was red but his grin was tired, like a clown without greasepaint. Behind his head the lights of the lorry were flashing as it bumped over the hard ridges of ice.

There was something nightmarish about the slow approach of the lorry. I could help these lunatics or I could fight them on behalf of Stok; neither of those ideas appealed to me. I thought of all the warm beds that I could have been in and I kneaded my fingers that were going numb with cold. The lorry changed into a lower gear as it reached the final slope. The driver must have seen the prepared patch of ice reflected in the moonlight for I saw his white face lean close to the windshield. The front wheels began to slip and then the rear wheels hit the ice patch and they too began to spin. The lorry stopped. The driver revved the motor but that only made things worse. The lorry slid sideways across the road. Eight of the men came running out of the trees and heaved at the sides of the lorry. It moved slowly toward the drainage ditch. The driver gunned the motor but that only threw off sprays of fine snow and the motor howled until I thought it would burst. The lorry tipped gently into the ditch and wedged there, its offside front wheel clear of the ground. With appalling crudity they had disabled the lorry. The engine stopped and for a moment there was the silence that can only exist in a forest. Then there was a clang as the driver opened the door and climbed down. He showed no surprise.

His arms were raised above his head but not raised so far that he showed any fear, either. Someone brushed a hand across him for a gun but finding none pushed him to one side. They began to untie the canvas at the rear of the lorry. There was a sudden sound of compacted ice falling from the under-side of the lorry and some of the men looked startled. The soldier grinned and reached for a half-smoked cigarette behind an earflap of his fur hat. His movements were slow but his eyes were quick. I threw him my matches. He lit the cigarette keep-ing both his hands high and visible.

When the canvas was open one of the men climbed inside. "That's Ivan," said the bald man, "he's a dangerous bastard." There was a glow from a flashlight and Ivan's voice read off the markings on the boxes. The bald man translated his words to me. There was a babble of Russian. "Dried milk," said the bald man. More Russian; "tea," said the man "and a sack of fresh lemons." More Russian. "Excrement," said the man, "he has found a machine gun." He leaped over the tailboard of the lorry like greased lightning. It didn't need a Russian scholar to understand that the bald man was claiming that the docu-ments and the guns were for him, only food and drink for the "businessmen." They both jumped down from the lorry, they were still arguing loudly. Ivan was carrying the machine gun. He began to prod the bald man with the barrel of it. They stood swearing at each other, both aware that everyone was watching. The bald man said, "The American sees what you do." He pointed at me. "There will be no more money from the Americans." Ivan grinned and stroked the gun. The bald man repeated his threat. I wished he would shut up. It seemed like a good argument for eliminating me. The other men were standing well to one side expecting violence and the soldier finished his cigarette and put his hands into his pockets instead of holding them high. The bald man screamed loudly at Ivan. They were both standing very still and the snow built a lacelike pattern over them. For one moment it seemed that the bald man would carry the situation through by sheer force of character. But he didn't. He aimed a swift blow at the gun. It wasn't swift enough. A burst of fire cut the bald man into two at point-blank range and propelled him headlong into the ditch, like a blow from a sledgehammer. Ivan fired again, short experimental bursts as if he'd got a new powerdrill from under the Christmas tree. The magazine ended and there was only a faint click from the trigger mechanism. The smoke drifted on the air and the sound echoed like a football rattle across the silent snow. Only the bald man's foot was visible over the ditch. Ivan lifted the sling of the gun and slipped it over his head. He wore it like a sommelier's key, an order of merit or a symbol of kingship. From his pocket he produced a new magazine. He fitted it with care.

No one spoke; they began to unload the cases from the lorry. They made the driver help them but I stood to one side stamping my feet to keep warm and watching the horizon with keen interest.

Two heavy bombers moved across the sky at about ten thousand feet. Ivan brought me a battered metal box from the driver's cab. He opened the lid to show me a batch of dirty dog-eared cards inside. He gave me a flamboyant salute. I smiled. He smiled too, and stabbed me in the gut with the gun barrel hard enough to make me suck in my breath. He still

smiled. His friends called to him, they had finished transferring the boxes from the lorry to the two taxi-vans. I could
see no reason for keeping me alive. So I smiled nervously and
slammed him in the mouth with the metal box, trying to kick
him in the groin as he sagged but his heavy overcoat protected
him well. I held the metal box and chopped at him with the
side of my hand but it struck the sharp metal of the gun and
I felt the flesh tear as one round fired. The men scattered and
the bullet whined away into the snowflakes. Ivan backed away
from me. I kicked at his leg but almost overbalanced. Ivan
smiled. There was blood on his mouth but he kept smiling
because he had the machine gun. Boy-wonder karate expert,
I thought, and I hoped that my sister would get the hi-fi and
the record collection; some of the Goodman discs were valuable.

That was when the soldier hit Ivan with the tire lever. Ivan
toppled toward me creaking like a rusty hinge. I ran. I didn't
look behind. I blundered through the dark forest bumping into
tree trunks and stumbling over roots. The Russian soldier was
just ahead of me. From the road came the sounds of men
shouting and then a long burst of machine-gun fire. The soldier
dropped. I went flat. There was more firing and I could hear
chips of wood being torn from the trees. I crawled over to the
soldier. His eyes were closed. The gun fired again. It seemed
closer. The forest was dark and low upon me, and only the
gunfire gave me any sense of direction. I remained still. There
was more shouting and about twenty yards to my left a man
ran noisily. More shooting, then there was no movement. I
guessed it was the bald man's son. I had cut my hand on the
gun; it wasn't bleeding much but the little finger was bent sideways and I couldn't move it. I wrapped a clean handkerchief
around it. It was black under the trees and a white mist of dis-
lodged snow hung close to the ground. It was quiet. I prodded

the inert soldier but he seemed pretty dead so I got to my feet and moved slowly and quietly away from the noise and excitement.

I walked almost to the edge of the forest, then I heard the noise. Something was moving through the trees. Something larger than a man. Something much larger than a man. I stared into the gloom. The noise of breaking twigs stopped but the breathing continued. It wasn't human breathing. I hugged a tree trunk, and became as thin as a Blue Gillette. The large breathing thing out there began to speak. The voice was metallic and resonant. It spoke Russian. It came nearer, still speaking and almost invisible—a white-cloaked cavalry officer on a horse.

"Approach carefully," said a metallic voice, "they have guns."

"Yes sir," said the rider. He was speaking into a walkie-talkie.

Through the trees I could see the valley. A large cavalry patrol moved across it stage by stage like bedbugs across a clean sheet. I put the metal box containing the army ration strengths down on the ground.

The horseman was watching me; he switched off the radio and nudged his horse closer. The leather creaked but the hooves were silent in the snow. Built into the saddle was a small Doppler radar set. Above his head the aerial sang gently in the cold wind and the screen shone blue in the rider's face. It was not a pleasant face. He moved his heels slightly and the horse edged toward me like a police horse controlling a crowd. I pushed against its hard muscles; the nerves twitched under the smooth coat. The icy metal of the stirrup stuck to my fingers and the sour breath of the horse was hot upon my face. The rider swung his map case away from his thigh and opened his revolver holster. I knew a few useful words of Russian.

"Don't shoot," I called. The horse, reluctant to hurt me, fidgeted and kicked up clods of snow but the rider urged him nearer until the pistol was inches from my face. He raised the gun and without hurry brought it down upon my skull. The horse shied a little and the butt cleaved into the side of my head almost taking my ear off. My vision went red and I groped toward the stirrup and stuck to the icy metal. Frostbite, I thought, then the gun butt came down more accurately and everything split into two like a badly adjusted range-finder and I slid into the black snow.

CHAPTER 14

I MOVED very slowly out of unconsciousness. I moved not into consciousness but into delirium. My hand was as large as a football and throbbed with a pain that extended to the shoulder blade. All was dark except for a tiny glimmer of red light. Was it a tiny light close-to or a gigantic light far away? I tried to move but the pain from my hand was overwhelming. I lapsed into unconsciousness. Many times I moved from one state to the other until I mustered the strength to cling to the twilight zone without slipping back into darkness.

Upon me rested heavy cold weights and under me was a smooth, curved surface like the bottom of a gargantuan test tube. I ran my good hand across the surface. The weights moved, tumbling over me like a cold sack of potatoes, and I eased my head around them in order to breathe. Near to my face a human hand was moving. The hand was attached to an arm and the arm belonged to one of the weights. The hand moved slowly nearer to the edge of a blanket that was over us. It moved slowly and almost imperceptibly; its finger and thumb poised greedily, ready to grip the frayed edge. It was a bath I was in. The hand continued to move. A large stained bathtub. The hand moved faster, passed the blanket edge and stopped, bobbing gently in space like a mascot hanging from a car mirror. It was a dead hand, waving a tiny, posthumous good-bye. Two dead bodies were heaped upon me. I wondered if this was a pipeline to hell. I moved slowly, letting the dead men slide under me. One was the bald-headed man and the other was his son.

I climbed over the dead bodies and looked around the washroom. My eyes had grown used to the dim red emergency lights by now. Cisterns were belching and gurgling nearby and a tap on the wall dripped into a bucket with a deep musical note. There were three washbasins fixed to the far wall; over the center one was a pocked mirror one corner of which had broken and swung away on the screw to live a life of its own. Suddenly there was noise of a toilet flushing. The door of a W.C. opened and a soldier emerged buckling his belt. He stared and came slowly toward me. He had trouble fixing his belt buckle but his eyes did not leave mine. As he neared me his steps became more deliberate until he was in slow motion. I was stretched full-length upon the bodies, my battered hand resting on the rim of the tub. The soldier looked at my swollen hand and then back to my face. His skin was dark and his eyes bright and moist. An Armenian perhaps. He held his trouser front with one hand and with the other he reached forward to prod me.

Had he prodded any other part of my anatomy I would not have yelled. My hand was lacerated, deformed, and bulbous with pus. I screamed. The soldier leaped away, crossing himself and gibbering; some ancient prayer perhaps or a magic sign. His back thudded against the wall and he scraped along it toward the door, still giddy with fear. As he got to the door he snatched his eyes away and blundered through the doorway. His unbuckled trousers slid and tripped him headlong into the corridor outside. I heard him scramble to his feet and his metal-tipped boots took him down the stone corridor at better than the track record.

Very slowly I took my weight on the good hand and slid my feet over the rim of the tub. I had aches in muscles I never knew I owned. From a standing position the bathroom was even colder and smellier than it had looked before. I went across to the dripping tap and held my swollen hand under the cold running water. I splashed more over my face. It looks therapeutic in movies but it made me feel worse than ever. My hand hurt just as much and now I was shivering with cold. I tried to turn the tap off but it still dripped. I staggered across to the washbasins. I looked in the mirror. I don't know what I expected to see, but as always when you have a tooth out or get kicked half to death the change in appearance is nowhere like commensurate with the pain. I touched my swollen lips and my ears and had a roll call of my limbs, but apart from my hand, an incipient black eye and a few abrasions, there wasn't much evidence of my encounter with Russian free enterprise and Soviet cavalry.

I was ill. I was in pain. I was frightened. Upon all, there was the overwhelming pall of failure. I stared at myself and wondered what I was doing there. I didn't identify with the tired, frightened failure that stared back at me from the mirror. I wondered if Harvey had arranged the whole thing, betrayed me to Stok. Perhaps Signe had told him that we had made love. That was the sort of thing she would delight in saying, but would Harvey believe her? Yes, he would. Or perhaps London had betrayed me. It had been done before, it would be done again. Who was responsible? I wanted to know. If this was how it was going to end I wanted to know. The responsibility for failure rests upon the one who fails. I failed. I shivered and reached for the hot tap but changed my mind. The basin was spattered with bright, fresh blood. A dirty hand towel had blood on it. Splashes of it had hit the wall behind the basin and there were three oval blots of it on the floor. It was bright and shiny, very fresh, and not at all like tomato ketchup.

I tried to be sick in the toilet but even that I failed to do. I sat down. I shivered. Psycho-shock, I told myself, a way to soften you up for interrogation. Psycho-shock, having you regain consciousness piled under corpses, don't succumb, but I continued to shiver. In the corridor there were orders given and monosyllabic assents. Colonel Stok swung the door open with a crash. He was shirtless, a great hairy muscular figure with bad scarring on his upper arms. He was dabbing at his face with a large wad of cotton wool. "I always do it," he said. "I cut myself when I am shaving. Sometimes I think I will go back to using my father's razor." Stok leaned toward the mirror and bared his teeth at his reflection. "I still have some of my own teeth," he said. He prodded his teeth. "I have a good man—a good dentist—these state dentists are no good. It's better to have a private dentist." Blobs of blood had reappeared on his chin. "They take an interest in you, private dentists."

Stok seemed to be speaking only to his own scrubby reflection in the pockmarked mirror, so I said nothing. He tore small pieces of cotton wool off the wad and stuck them to his face with blood, while singing "The Motherland Hears, the Motherland Knows" in a scratchy basso. When he was satisfied with the blood staunching, Stok turned around to me.

"So you did not heed my advice."

I said nothing, and Stok walked across and looked down upon me.

> *"Wee, sleekit, cow'rin', tim'rous beastie,*
> *O what a panic's in thy breastie!*
> *Thou need na start awa sae hasty,*
> *Wi' bickering brattle."*

Stok quoted it with an excellent Highland accent. "Robert Burns," pronounced Stok, " 'To a Mouse.' "

I still didn't say anything, but I had my eyes open and I looked at Stok calmly.

"Are you not going to speak?" said Stok mockingly.

I said:

> *"Fair fa' your honest sonsie face,*
> *Great chieftain o' the puddin'-race."*

"Robert Burns. 'To a Haggis.' "

Stok joined in the last three words as I said them, and then he laughed so loud that I thought he would shake some of the cracked tiles off the wall. "To a Haggis," he said again, the tears of delight welling in his eye. He was still laughing and saying *To a Haggis* when the guard came to take me downstairs and lock me up.

Stok's temporary office was at the end of a long corridor lined with dusty panes of glass that almost permitted you to see beyond them into the honeycomb of bureaucracy. One door had HEALTH BUREAU stuck on to its glass panel in raised letters. Parts of some letters had been chipped away, but a careful paint job had cured them. Inside the office there were midget desks and a huge plans chest and a poster about putting fires out and another that showed two wooden-faced men and artificial respiration. Beyond this opened a small glass-sided cubicle from which a senior clerk could watch for frivolity among the underlings. Stok was sitting there speaking into a telephone that looked like a prop from *The Young Mister Edison*.

My clothes had been dried and rough-ironed. They had that smell of coarse soap that is as endemic to Russia as the smell of Gaulois and garlic to Paris. I sat in a small easy chair, the stiff clothes seeking out the bruises and abrasions of the night, my hand throbbing with pain.

Stok replaced his phone. His uniform was clean and pressed and his buttons were shiny. Behind him through the thin curtains the sky was beginning to grow dark. I must have been unconscious a long time. The guards saluted. Stok pulled a small chair close and rested his big shiny jackbooted feet upon it, then he lit a cigar and threw a cigar and matches to me. The two guards watched this with surprise.

Stok said *"Spasibo"* to the guards, and they said *"Tovarich Polkovnik Stok"* to him and withdrew.

"Smoke it," said Stok, "don't smell it."

"If it's just the same to you," I said, "I'll do both."

"Cuban. Excellent," said Stok.

Then we spent five minutes blowing cigar smoke at each other, until Stok said, "Lenin didn't smoke, hated flowers, never had a soft chair in his office, had only the simplest food, liked reading Turgenev and always had his watch fifteen minutes slow. I am not like that. I like all things that grow from the soil. The first thing I demand when I move into a new office is one soft chair for myself and another for my visitors. I like rich bourgeois food on the rare occasions that I have it. I don't much like Turgenev—I think the death of Bazarov in *Fathers and Sons* is unconvincing and unfair to the reader— and I always have my watch fifteen minutes fast. As for smoking, there are nights when it's been friend, fire and food to me. Many such nights."

I smoked and nodded and watched him. The small pimples of cotton wool were still stuck to his bright new chin but his eyes were dark and old and tired.

"Exciting friends you have," said Stok. "Gay, temperamental and devoted to private enterprise." He smiled.

I shrugged.

Suddenly Stok said, "They tried to kill you. Fifteen of them. We arrested ten, including two that died. Why did they try to kill you? Have you been meddling with someone's girl friend?"

"I thought you had spent all night asking them."

"I have. I know why they tried to kill you. I just wondered if you did."

"I'll always welcome a second opinion."

"Your old friend Newbegin wants you dead and out of the way."

"Why?"

"You were sent to spy on Newbegin and he doesn't like it."

"You don't believe that?"

"No interrogation I conduct ends until I get a story that I believe." Stok opened a brown dossier and looked at it in silence, then closed it again. "Trash," said Stok. "The people I arrested last night are trash."

"What does that mean?"

"It means they are antisocial elements. Delinquents. They are not even people with political errors. Trash."

There was a tap at the door and a young officer came in. He addressed Stok by his rank alone—usually a sign of friendship in the Soviet Army—put another limp file of papers on the desk, and then whispered into Stok's ear. Stok's expression was unchanging, but I had an idea he was working hard to keep it so. Finally Stok nodded and the guards major stood to one side of the desk.

Stok opened the file and signed the corners of eight sheets of paper. Then from the back of the file he took six more sheets of paper, perused them hurriedly and then signed those too. He spoke slowly to the papers which were still receiving his attention. "Ten men were taken into custody and we require"—he turned the pages without haste—"thirty-five sheets of paper covered with reasons and thirty signatures from four different police authorities. I am buried under the paper work. And do you know"—he leaned across the table, staring at me and tapping the open file softly with his huge fingers—"if tomorrow I decide to release one of them, there will be over three times as much paper work." Stok laughed a hoarse laugh as though the prisoners had pulled that trick on him and he wanted to show that he didn't mind.

"Things are tough all over," I said.

"Yes," said Stok. He drew on his cigar carefully, then waved it at the major. "Guards Major Nogin. GRU," Stok explained. The major looked surprised at being introduced to a prisoner, but he played along with it. "The major has just become the father of an eight-pound boy," Stok said, and then there was a lot of soft rapid Russian, which was probably Stok wising the major up on me and my department. Then Stok gave Major Nogin a cigar, and the major smiled at both of us and left the room. "He is a nice fellow for a GRU * officer," Stok said.

I smiled.

Stok said, "Baltic Military District GRU is handling the whole thing. The District Military Council sent me over to the Area Military Commissariat as an adviser, but these young

* GRU. See Appendix 2.

men don't want an old man's advice. They have handled the people that NTS * sent here, and they can quite well handle these new people." Stok gave an angry flick of his gigantic fist. "We don't send men into other countries to interfere with their internal affairs, why should you send your criminals here?"

I said, "What about the suppression of the Budapest rebellion?"

Stok shouted, "What about the Bay of Pigs? What about Suez? Tell the truth, English, the thing that sticks in your throat is that we were successful and you were not."

"Yes," I agreed wearily, "you are successful and we are not."

"Modern victories are not won by movements of armies but by imperceptible change of molecules. Victories must be won inside the hearts of men."

"I prefer my victories inside their heads," I said.

"Come along, English. We soldiers must not talk politics. Our job is to take the stupid and impossible fantasies of our politicians and try to make them work in terms of flesh and blood." Stok stood up and put his hands on the small of his back and threw his head back like a man in pain. "I am tired," he said.

"I'm half dead," I told him.

He took my arm. "Come along then, we'll support each other."

"I'm hungry," I said.

"Of course you are, and so am I. Let's go somewhere civilized and have a meal." He looked at his wristwatch. "But I must be back by nine-thirty. Tonight Moscow will take its revenge."

* NTS. See Appendix 3.

"What are you talking about?"

"Football," said Stok. "Tonight on television."

The Luna Café on Soviet Boulevard faces the gardens and the old Liberation monument that had been built there several regimes back and—so it is said—was something of a milestone in municipal graft. Already there was a small queue of young people at the café door, for this was Saturday night and the boys had put on their one-hundred-and-thirty-ruble English wool suits and the girls had fifty-ruble pointed shoes wrapped in a parcel, for they were far too valuable to wear out on the icy streets. Everyone stood aside for the barrel-like KGB colonel in full uniform and his scruffy civilian companion. We got a small table near the orchestra, which was faking jazz music from their memories and shortwave radio.

Stok took the menu. "What about port wine?" he asked.

"I prefer vodka." A lot of vodka might numb the pain in my hand.

"They don't sell vodka," said Stok. "This is a nice, cultural place." He had chosen a seat that faced toward the door, and he watched the young couples entering. The dance floor was crowded.

"When I was a young man," said Stok, "we had a song called 'When Tears Fall a Rose Will Grow.' Do you know that song?"

"No."

Stok ordered two glasses of port wine. The waitress looked at the marks on my face and at Stok's uniform. Her face was kind but rigid.

"If it were true, then this would be a land of roses. You have a word meaning unlucky people?"

"Losers."

"Ah, that's a good word. Well, this is a land of losers. It's a land where doom hangs upon the air like poison gas. You have no idea of what awful things have happened here. The Latvians had Fascists who were more vicious than even the Germans. In Bikernieki Forest they killed 46,500 civilians. In Dreilini Forest five kilometers east of here, they killed 13,000. In the Zolotaya Gorka, 38,000 were murdered."

While Stok was talking I had seen a familiar figure enter the door. He had left his outer clothes downstairs and he wore his cheap Latvian suit with its wide trouser bottoms as though it was Savile Row. He sat down on the far side of the room and I caught only a brief view of him through the dancers, but it was undoubtedly Ralph Pike still at large.

". . . the old, the pregnant, the lame," Stok said. "They killed them all, sometimes with the most terrifying and prolonged torture. The Germans were so pleased to find such enthusiastic murderers that they used Riga as a clearinghouse for people they wanted killed. They sent them here in trainloads from Germany, Holland, Czechoslovakia, Austria, France, from all over Europe, because the Latvian-recruited SS units were the most efficient killers."

Ralph Pike suddenly saw me. He didn't make any sort of sign of recognition, but he gulped at his drink with urgency.

". . . We have dossiers on hundreds of such Latvians. War criminals now living in Canada, America, New Zealand and all over the world. You would imagine that people guilty of such terror would remain quiet and be thankful that they have escaped justice, but no. These scum are the foremost troublemakers. Your friend there is such a person as I describe; a war criminal with more murders of children upon his conscience than I would care to name. He thinks his crimes are forgotten, but our memories are not so short."

Ralph Pike had taken on a strange rigidity. I glimpsed him only through dancing couples. He leaned back in his seat, casually turning his head to take in the whole room. Two tables to his left I recognized the handsome young guards major who had just become a father.

"You wouldn't think he was like that," Stok said. "He looks so respectable, so bourgeois."

Pike was staring at me and at Stok's uniformed back. "He's wondering whether to kill himself," Stok said.

"Is he?" I said.

"Don't worry, he won't. People like him are not losers. They're survivors, professional survivors. Even on the gallows such men would not bite a poison pellet."

The dancers opened and my eyes met Pike's. He was holding his glass of port wine and swallowing hard. The music was a vintage piece of Victor Herbert, "Sweet summer breeze, whispering trees."

"Warn him," Stok said. "Warn your comrade he's in danger. You must have a prearranged signal and I'd like to see it in action."

"Who is it you are talking about?"

"Very good," said Stok. Pike had noticed Guards Major Nogin now. Stok waved to the waitress and said, "Two more port wines."

I said, "If you are going to arrest him, do it. Don't play cat-and-mouse like a sadist."

Stok said, "He killed over two hundred people. Six of my men taken prisoner in 1945 were tortured by this man personally." Stok's face had gone rigid and he didn't look like himself, just as those mathematically accurate waxworks never look like the people they portray. "Do you think he should go free?" Stok said.

I said, "I happen to be in custody, remember?"

Stok shook his head in disagreement. "You are a casualty, not a prisoner. Now answer my question." Stok's mouth was tense with hatred, he could hardly force the words through it.

"Take a hold on yourself," I said.

"I could walk across there and kill him very slowly," Stok said. "Very slowly, just as he killed them."

Major Nogin was looking expectantly toward our table and Ralph Pike couldn't take his eyes off the major. He knew that he was just awaiting Stok's signal.

"You'd better get a grip on yourself," I said. "Major Nogin is awaiting orders."

The music played,

> *Stars shining softly above;*
> *Roses in bloom, wafted perfume,*
> *Sleepy birds dreaming of love.*

Pike was talking to a waitress and gripping her wrist very tightly. It was impossible to witness Pike's terror without identifying with it. The waitress stepped back from him and wrenched her arm free. Ralph Pike was positively radiating doom by now, and in Latvia such radiations are quickly picked up. I wondered if Pike had a Latin tag for this moment; perhaps *"bis peccare in bello non licet"*—in war two blunders aren't permitted.

Stok said, "Do you seriously and honestly tell me that such a man should go free? Truth now."

"What's truth," I said, "except a universal error?"

Stok's huge hand leaned across the table and tapped my chest. "Shooting is too good for him," Stok said. The music played *"Safe in your arms, far from alarms."*

I said, "You've done your piece and said it nicely." I brushed his hand away. "You've made sure that I am seen talking to you at the time of this man's arrest in a public place. You will now release me. The resulting implication being that I bought my freedom at the expense of his. My organization will write me off as unreliable." I nursed my hand. It was swollen now like a blue boxing glove.

"Are you frightened?" asked Stok, without delighting in it. Perhaps he was being sympathetic.

I said, "I'm so afraid that the motor areas are taking over, but at least reflex actions are true to oneself, which is more than I can say for blind hatred." And that's when I waved at Guards Major Nogin and set in motion the arrest of Ralph Pike.

Daylight shall come but in vain,
Tenderly pressed close to your breast,
Kiss me, kiss me again.

CHAPTER 15

THERE are three styles in cities. There are river cities—London, and Paris—and waterfront cities like Chicago and Havana, and there are island cities. Stockholm and Venice are island cities. So are Helsinki and Leningrad and so is Manhattan, that sparkled in the dusk like a wet finger dipped into the caster sugar of electricity. The plane dropped a wing toward Brooklyn and the dark water of Jamaica Bay and nosed down the traffic pattern of Kennedy Airport.

Kennedy Airport is the keyhole of America. You peer into it and glimpse the shiny well-oiled pieces, the bright machine-finished gleaming metal; it's clean and safe and operates smoothly. It's a great keyhole.

I got off the Air-India jet spitting betel nut and nursing a swollen hand. The airport was crowded with hurrying people, men in Stetsons or tartan jackets, men carrying suits in bright polyethylene bags. I found myself hurrying too, until I realized that I had no destination: I wondered how many people around me had fallen into the same trap. A woman with all her baggage and a raucous infant in a wire buggy wheeled it over my foot, and a woman in a yellow smock rushed out of a shop yelling, "Did you just buy a Scrabble game?"

"No."

"You forgot your instructions," she said. "They didn't enclose the instructions."

The loudspeaker was calling, "Skycap to the information center."

The woman in the yellow smock said, "It's not like you didn't pay for it. A Scrabble game is complicated."

"I didn't buy it," I said. A lady with a lot of packages marked *Shannon duty-free shop* said, "I'd just love chickenburger and French fries. I haven't had real good French fries since I left San Francisco."

The woman with the Scrabble game rules waved them in the air. "Unless you know how to use it," she sighed, "a Scrabble game is just a boxful of junk."

"Yes," I said. I turned away from her.

"It's not like you didn't pay for it," she said again.

The lady with the duty-free packages said, "Not even in Paris. Not real good French fries."

A man in an Air-India uniform said, "Are you Mr. Dempsey? Air-India passenger?" A transistor radio was playing so loud that he had to shout. I nodded. He looked at my passport, then handed over a large envelope. Inside there was three hundred dollars in bills, two dollars in small change sealed into a plastic bag labeled SMALL MONEY, and a thick bundle of political literature. One pamphlet said that eighty percent of all U.S. psychiatrists were Russians, educated in Russia and paid by the Communists to indoctrinate Americans. As a first step they tend to make sexual attacks on their female patients. Another booklet said that the mental health program was a

Communist-Jewish conspiracy to brainwash the U.S.A. Two booklets said that the President of the U.S.A. was a Communist and suggested that I should ". . . buy a gun now and form a secret minuteman team." The last thing was a bright blue bumper sticker: *Are you a Commie without knowing it?* I stuffed the whole wad back into the envelope and phoned the Brain. The metallic voice said, "No instructions. Call tomorrow at this same time. Have you read the literature? Record your reply, then ring off."

"I read it," I said. It was all very well for Dawlish to tell me to take orders from the Brain, he didn't have to obey them.

I threw my baggage into a battered cab. "Washington Square," I said.

"Tunnel or bridge?" said the driver. "I always ask 'em. Tunnel or bridge?"

"Bridge," I said. "Let's keep the East River where we can see it."

"You bet," said the driver. "Six bucks."

"Could we find a doctor somewhere on the way in?" I asked him. "I think I've got a broken finger."

"You're British, aintcha, fella? Well, I'll tell ya sumpin. Just one thing dough don't buy ya in this town, fella—total silence. Know what I mean? Total silence."

"I know what you mean," I said. "Total silence."

I joined the cast of the relentless 3D movie that calls itself Manhattan, where it's always night and they keep the lights on to prove it. I prefer to arrive in New York at night, to lower myself into the city gradually like getting into a bathful of very hot water. The rusty taxicab clattered down the spine of the city and the driver told me what was wrong with Cuba and we went past the silent skyscrapers, kosher pizzerias, glass-fronted banks, bagel factories, Polish gymnasiums with belt-vibrators for rent, pharmacies selling love potions and roach killers, and all-night supermarkets where frail young men were buying canned rattlesnake. New York, New York—where the enterprise is free if nothing else is.

From my hotel at the foot of Fifth Avenue I made short forays into the neon between soaking my cuts, counting my abrasions and nursing anxiety to sleep. On the third night in New York I settled down to watch one of those TV programs where relaxed, informal chatter had been perfected by hours of intensive rehearsal. Outside I could hear rain falling upon the fire escape and bouncing back against the window. I closed the window tight and turned up the heat.

I seemed to have spent most of my life in hotel rooms where room service wanted money in advance and the roller towels were fixed with a padlock. Now I had graduated to the Birmingham Rug and Dufy print circuit, but I wondered what I had sacrificed to do it. I had few friends. I stayed well clear of the sort of people who thought I had a dead-end job in the Civil Service, and those who knew what the job was stayed clear of me. I poured myself a drink.

On the TV, a man in an open convertible was saying, "It's sunny and hot here in Florida. Why not fly down tonight? You can take twenty-four months to pay." My broken finger hurt like hell. I soaked it in hot water and antiseptic and I drank a little more whisky. By the time the phone rang I was well beneath the label.

"Stage Delicatessen," the voice on the phone said. "Eight three four, Seventh. Immediate. Secure. Are you waiting to go in?" I wondered what would happen if I ignored the call or pretended it wasn't me, but I had a strong feeling they knew it was me. I had a feeling that if I had been somewhere in the midst of the mob at Madison Square Garden they would have still got that metallic voice to talk to me. So I put my head under a cold shower and climbed into my raincoat and the doorman whistled up a cab for the Stage Delicatessen. The schlock-shops were afire with sale signs and smiling suckers, and the cops were buttoned tight and growling. A man in a blue poplin raincoat was standing outside the delicatessen waving a bundle of show-biz newspapers. He ignored the code introduction.

"O.K., Slim," he said as I arrived. "Let's go."

I said, "I'm going nowhere till I've had a hot pastrami sandwich." We crowded into a melee like the Eton Wall Game. We both had a sandwich, the man in the blue raincoat saying, "We'd better make it snappy" between every bite. Waiting for us was a black Ford Falcon with a DPL (diplomat's) license plate. We got in and the Negro driver gunned it away without a word. We passed Columbus Circle. Blue raincoat buried himself in an article headlined BLIZ BOFFS BORSCHT BIZ and chewed on a toothpick. The car radio was saying, ". . . New Jersey Turnpike traffic moderate, Lincoln Tunnel, heavy. Route 22 moderate, Holland Tunnel moderate. Folks, this is the time of year to think about buying a new car . . ." The driver tuned to another station.

"Where are we heading?" I asked.

The blue raincoat said, "You follow your orders, feller, I'll follow mine, right?" The driver said nothing but we were at Broadway and the Seventies and still heading north. Suddenly the driver turned left and pulled up before one of those little medieval castles on the West Side that are owned by people who like to stare tall buildings in the toenails. The car stopped. The chauffeur reached for the car-phone.

"Let's go, bud," said blue raincoat. He stuffed the bundle of papers into his pocket and pulled a face as if the toothpick was causing him some sort of pain. "The old man's as touchy as sweating gelignite tonight," he said. The bottom half of the building was towers, balconies and metal grills, and the top half was very Flemish merchant. He didn't ring the bell so we just stood there looking at the massive door.

"What are we waiting for?" I asked. "Won't they lower the drawbridge?"

The blue raincoat looked at me, quietly mapping the course of my jugular vein. There was a lot of chain-rattling, then the door opened with a faint buzz. Blue raincoat pointed at the open door, then went back to the car. The driver and blue raincoat waited until I entered and then they drove away south. Maybe they were going for another pastrami sandwich.

The fittings and furnishings inside the house were old. In America that either means you made it, or you just got off the boat. Just in case there should be any mistake about it, these old items were spotlighted by Swedish lamps.

The door had been opened by some sort of electric release, but two Negro footmen in gray silk—complete with stockings —stood inside the door and said "good evening, sir" in unison. A tall man walked into the hall to greet me. He was dressed in a red coat, cut away from chest to knee with long yellow lapels that became a cape collar. His breeches were made of shiny white silk and so was his waistcoat. His hair was white and powdered and long enough to be tied in a small black silk bow. It was the uniform of an eighteenth-century soldier. I followed him along the marble hall. Through a doorway to the right I saw two more soldiers opening a crate of champagne with their bayonets. I was ushered into a high-ceilinged room dark with oak paneling. There was a long refectory table around which sat seven young men all in the same red-coated uniforms. They were drinking from pewter tankards. Their hair was uniformly white and long. A young girl in a long, low-cut dress with a sash and apron sat on a settee beyond the table. The whole scene looked like something soaked off a box of chocolates. The man who had shown me in reached a pewter tankard down from the Welsh dresser and filled it with champagne. He handed me the tankard and said, "I won't be a minute."

"Take your time," I said.

The door at the far end opened and a girl in a similar serving-wench dress, but of silk and with a richly embroidered apron, came in carrying a small cardboard box. Mozart wafted through the door. The girl with the box said, "Has he broken his hand?"

The first wench said, "Not yet," and the second wench tittered.

One of the soldiers said, "A new boy." He waved a thumb at me over his shoulder.

"He's come to talk with the General." He said it like I had aisle seats for the day of judgment.

The wench with the box said, "Welcome to the Revolutionary War." A couple of the soldiers grinned. I swilled down the half pint of champagne as if it was bitter lemon.

She said, "Where you from?"

"I'm from Sci-Fi Anonymous," I said. "I'm selling subscriptions to the Twentieth century."

"Sounds awful," she said.

The first soldier returned and said, "The General will see you now," with awesome regard for the word "general." He reached a cocked hat down from the Welch dresser and put it on carefully.

I said, "Do you think I should pipe-clay my alligator shoes?" but he just led the way into the hall and up the stairs. The music was louder here. It was the second movement of the Mozart A Major Concerto. The soldier walked ahead of me, holding his sword in his left hand so that it didn't clatter against the stairs. At the top, a long red-carpeted corridor was lit by antique oil lamps. We walked past three doors, then he opened the next and showed me into the study. There was an inlaid desk upon which silver ornaments had been placed with that carefully posed look photos in *House and Garden* have. On one wall there were ancient documents—some merely signatures—framed in modest elegance, but apart from that the walls were plain. If that's what you call walls lined in silk. There was a communicating door in one corner of the room and from behind it came the third movement of the Mozart, which was working itself up to that frantic minor-key Turkish routine which I've never thought a good enough ending for such a great beginning; but then that complaint went for just about everything in my life.

The music ended, there was applause and then the door opened. Another one of these antique soldier boys came into the room and said, "General Midwinter" and both the Redcoats went into a state of paralyzed rigidity. The applause continued.

Midwinter came into the frame of the door and turned back to the room beyond to clap gently with his white-gloved hands. He was speaking to someone and beyond them I could see a brightly lit room with vast chandeliers and women in white dresses. From the dark study it was like glimpsing daylight through a manhole.

"This way," the General said. He was a tiny man, dapper and neat like most small men, and he wore a gold-encrusted eighteenth-century English general's uniform with its complex aiguillette and the thigh-length boots. He pointed with his general's baton and said, "This way, men" again. His voice was soft but with a hard mechanical edge like a speak-your-weight machine and he said "men" like his friends said "General."

The General tucked the baton under his armpit and clapped his hands softly as the small orchestra walked through his study. When the last violin and cello had disappeared, the

General switched on the desk light and settled down behind his tidy desk. He rearranged a couple of silver paperweights and brushed his long white hair with his hand. A large emerald ring flashed a spot of light into a dark corner of the room. He motioned me to a chair and said, "Tell me about yourself, boy."

I said, "Can we cut the crowd scene?" and he said, "Sure; beat it, you two." The two sentries saluted and left the room. General Midwinter said, "What's your phone number?"

I said, "I'm at One Fifth Avenue, that's Spring 7-7000."

"Five million, nine hundred and twenty-nine thousand," said Midwinter. "That's the square of it. The square root of it is 277.49. I can do that with any number you name," he said.

"So could my father; it's a knack, I guess."

"Is that why they made you a general?" I asked.

"They made me a general 'cause I'm old. Old age is an incurable disease, see. People think they ought to do something for you. Me they made a general. O.K.?" He winked at me and then scowled as though he had thought better of it.

"It's O.K. with me."

"Good." The word carried a certain amount of menace. Midwinter leaned forward and the harsh crosslighting emphasized his age. His flesh was soft—a badly fitting rubber mask that around the eyes showed a moist pink edge. The yellow skin, freckled brown, shone like the well-fingered ivories of a barroom piano.

His white gloved hands played possum on the desk top until one of them walked across to the baton, picked it up and hit the desk top a sharp blow.

"They told me you were belligerent," said Midwinter. "I said I didn't mind 'cause I'm a little belligerent myself."

"Looks like neither of us is going to grow out of it."

"In your case, I'm not so sure." He tapped the baton on the desk and dropped it with a loud clatter. "When you see

the setup we have—not only here but throughout the world—
you will join us all right."

"You are a probationer. This is a symbol of the faith we
have in you." He picked up one of those brown shiny golf balls
that I had seen at Pike's and rolled it across the desk to me.
I picked it up and looked at it. "Inside that sphere is a sample
of American soil—the soil of freedom. I hope you will treasure
that piece of soil, remain true to it; a symbol of the simple
faith of a free people rooted in a free soil." He tapped the desk
as though it were all there in a diagram that I should have
already looked at.

"When you come back from training, we will have tested
you; then we will be trusting you."

"Suppose you decide that you won't be trusting me?"

"Then you won't be coming back," Midwinter wheezed.

"Then perhaps it's me that should be mistrusting you," I
said.

"No, no, no," said Midwinter in a fatherly voice. "I like you.
Come to me, confide in me. I am the one person you can trust
around here. Always trust a financier because he is investing
the stuff that counts. If you pay money to an artist, how can
you tell if he's going to be famous a couple of years from now?
You submit yourself to a doctor; well, who knows how many
guys he's slaughtered? It's strictly between him and the A.M.A.
An architect; maybe he had a smart assistant last year; you
may end up with the dumbest heap of concrete you ever saw.
But a financier—when he lays it on the line it's going to be
portraits of Presidents cashable in solid U. S. anyplace on the
globe. So don't ever say a financier doesn't measure up; he's
the only one who does." One of the soft white animals had
gone to sleep and the other went across the desk to sniff at it.
"Get me?" said Midwinter.

"Got you," I said. Midwinter nodded and wheezed a wheezy laugh.

"Let me tell you something, son," he said. "Making a lot of money is no fun. When you get rich you find that the rich are soft and stupid and want to talk about parties for their daughters. Your old friends—your real friends—don't want to see you anymore. Poor people don't want a millionaire among them reminding them of some way in which they failed to make it. So it's lonely being a rich old man. Lonely." The animal with an emerald on its leg tugged at Midwinter's sleeve-lace.

I said, "Poor old rich men are something of a cliché, aren't they?"

Midwinter said, "I got nothing against clichés, son. It's the quickest method of communication yet invented, but I get you. You think I'm a lonely old man looking for a tomb in a history book. I love. It's as easy as that. I love. I love my country. Get me?" The animal with the baton smacked the sleeping animal in time to Midwinter's staccato pronouncements. From the next room I heard a riff of a clarinet and toot of a trombone. "Get me?" Midwinter said again.

"Yes," I said quietly.

"No," said Midwinter. His voice was loud but without animosity. He leaned across the desk and looked at his hands and the baton and at me, and then he winked. When he spoke again it was in a low persuasive tone. "You don't understand the kind of love I have for this great country we live in. Love's not built that way—my way—anymore. These days love is marriage and its compensation is alimony or success. Love these days is bravery under fire and the compensation is medals and fame. Love is public duty or a political donation and the compensation is a pension or maybe an embassy. Love is some dame you left back in St. Louis or a fast haul in the back seat of an automobile." One of the white animals tapped his waistcoat. "My love is nothing like that. My love is this great company of brave young men who are proud to make their country strong. I love my country and my token is to make the thing I love, strong. Get me, boy? Get me?" He was agitated.

"Yes sir," I said very loud. The baton waved in the air.

"Strong," said Midwinter, and the animal with the baton smashed the sleeping animal in the belly and there was a terrible noise of splintering wood. One leg kicked convulsively and the sleeping animal died with its feet in the air. "I knew you'd get me," Midwinter said. "I knew." And he picked up his poor dead broken hand and removed the white glove. The wooden fingers of his false left hand were bent and damaged and he turned it slowly under the light. My own swollen hand seemed to hurt even more as I watched him.

The door opened after a brief tap and the wench with the cardboard box came in. The dance band began to play "Smoke Gets in Your Eyes." Midwinter was still looking at the revolving hand. She bent over and kissed Midwinter on the cheek. "You promised," she said reproachfully. From somewhere across the city came the lonely scream of a police car. "They don't make them strong enough," said Midwinter. He had lost the intensity that his love had generated and was in a postcoital triste. She kissed him again and said, "You mustn't get overexcited." She turned to me. "He gets overexcited," she explained. She rolled back the sleeve to reveal the place where the false hand fitted to the arm. Midwinter waved his baton at me. "I like you," he said. "Go and have a swell time at our fancy-dress party. We'll talk some more tomorrow. We can fix you a costume if you feel conspicuous in your street clothes." He winked again as if it was his way of dismissing visitors.

"No thanks," I said. "Uniforms bring me out in a rash."

That house was one of the few places where I preferred to be different from the others.

I moved out among the Nell Gwynnes with cast-iron facials and the Redcoats who rode a Jaguar unafraid. The chips were down, the levels were split and the Scotch trickled over the rocks. Harvey was there in a Redcoat uniform, smiling and doing his neat little dances and pretending to drop plates and saving them at the last minute, and the girls were saying "Ooo" and slyly studying each other's hairdos and shoes. I stood watching Harvey, trying to get beyond his moods to the man underneath. His timing was exact; even when he moved in a clumsy way, he never knocked anything over. He was the sort of fielder who never runs but is always there when the ball lands. His eyes were clear but his white wig was askew. I felt sure that he was more than a little drunk, but his voice never slurred or changed from that flat resonance that makes so many Americans sound as though they are speaking over a bullhorn.

Harvey spotted me on the rim of his audience. "You old sonufabitch," he said in a relaxed idle way and he leaned forward and grabbed my arm to be sure I wasn't a hallucination. "'Bout time you smiled, you miserable old swine. You look drunk," he said. He flagged a waiter down and grabbed two drinks from the silver tray. The waiter began to move away. "Stay right there," Harvey said. "Stand there stood, like a real waiter should." Harvey insisted that I drink three gigantic martinis before he released the waiter. Harvey watched me down the drinks and he downed three just to keep me company. "Now let's go," he said, dragging me toward the door. "The only thing worth having at these crazy pantomimes is the booze."

Harvey grabbed two more drinks for good measure, then did a little dance. The band saw him and picked up the rhythm.

It was all—or more—than Harvey needed and the dancers cleared a path as he did a Gene Kelly, relaxed and skillful right there in the middle of the dance floor. As he drank from the two glasses so he was able to strut wider and leap higher until, with the glasses empty, he was spinning and soft-shoe shuffling and the dancers had stopped dancing and were finger clicking and hand-clapping and the atmosphere built like a house of cards—thin and precarious but high and beautiful. The enthusiasm spread to the band, the drummer steadied him and the trumpet urged him to attempt and complete stances beyond his normal skills. The E.S.P. boys would say that it was the telepathic radiations of the audience that enabled Harvey to do that dance. Certainly they were all rooting for him and just as certainly Harvey responded, and he did things that night that would have attracted a talent scout from the Bolshoi. When the band sensed that Harvey was growing tired they moved him toward a finale and spread a musical carpet and drew a musical curtain and the trumpet milked the applause. Harvey stood there grinning and flushed and the waiter stepped forward with another great silver tray with just two drinks on it and some wag took down a piece of greenery and formed it into a crown and the soldiers drew their swords and provided an arch under which Harvey walked. He went out onto the balcony and the applause was still echoing around the ballroom.

Harvey said, "Hey, they like us. You're not bad," which was nonsense because all I had done was follow Harvey's steps and fake pauses when they became too difficult to follow.

Harvey grinned and said, "I knew three of those big martinis would do it. I know you only too well."

The rain had stopped. The balcony was cool and the night was dark as far as Broadway, where a slab of writhing electricity changed the color of all the windowpanes on the other side of the street. Harvey produced a couple of cigars and we looked at the glow above the dark city and smoked, and Harvey said, "It's a millionaire's toy," and I said, "Yes, with eight million working parts."

"Working parts," said Harvey. "Yes." The street below was empty except for a girl walking along sobbing quietly and a boy behind her trying to explain. "They wouldn't have killed you," Harvey said. "Rough you up a little, yes; but they would never have killed you. It was Stok that made it dangerous by sending that cavalry patrol to pick them up."

"Better a devil you know than a devil you don't know," I said.

Below on the street the sobbing girl let the boy comfort her, then behind us there was a click from the balcony door. The serving wench who had been carrying the General's spare hand in a cardboard box stepped out onto the balcony to join us. "Harvey darling," she said in that same reproachful tone she had used on General Midwinter.

"What's wrong, honey?" Harvey said. "Won't the General lend you his plane?"

"You know," said the girl. "I came out of the study with the General and there you are cutting up, Harvey. Don't you understand how terrible it makes me feel?"

"No," said Harvey.

"It makes me feel terrible. Embarrassed, Harvey; that's how it makes me feel."

Harvey screwed up his eyes and stared at her. "You know something, honey?" he said. "Drinking makes you very beautiful."

"I haven't been drinking, Harvey," she said patiently as if this was a dialogue they had been through many times before.

"No," said Harvey triumphantly. "But I have."

"If your marriage means nothing to you, Harvey," she said, "then your self-respect should. I'll be ready to go home in fifteen minutes." Then she swept away skillfully, rustling her long dress for maximum effect.

"My wife," said Harvey in explanation.

"Yes," I said.

"One of these days I'll wire up her electric toothbrush—" He stopped. It was a joke, I suppose, but he didn't grin.

"She spies on me. Do you know that? My own wife spies on me. To hear her talk you'd think I was the hired help. To hear her talk you'd think that guy Midwinter was the right hand of God."

"That's what you'd think if you heard anyone around here talk about Midwinter."

"Right. These punks think he's MacArthur, George Washington, Davy Crockett and Jim Bowie all rolled into one."

"But you don't?"

"I didn't say that. I think he's a great man. Seriously. A really great man and a powerful man. Midwinter will never be the President of the United States but he will be close to the President. When the forces of conservatism take control of this country then Midwinter will be the power behind the throne . . . and maybe I do mean the throne." Harvey smiled. "But he doesn't trust anyone. He doesn't trust anyone."

"That's a common failing among people in our business."

"Aw, but this guy taps phones, intercepts mail, checks up on friends and relatives. He even puts agents in to spy on his own staff. That's pretty crummy, wouldn't you say?"

"All I'd say is, why are you so sure this balcony isn't bugged?"

"I'm *not* sure, but I'm too drunk to give a good Goddamn is all." Harvey suddenly thought of something else. "Tell me something, you bastard," he said. "Why did you change over the eggs in that package?"

"I told you, Harvey, the package of eggs was stolen from my baggage on the way to London Airport."

"Tell me about that again."

"I already told you. It was the same man who followed me from the doctor's surgery. Full-face. Black horn-rimmed spectacles. Medium height."

Harvey said, "You said, projecting ears, bad teeth, long hair, sounded like an Englishman who wanted to be taken for a Yank, bad breath. You gave me a long description."

"That's right, the horn-rimmed spectacles were adapted to make his ears project. He was an American who put flat cockney vowel sounds into his American accent to sound like an Englishman assuming an American accent. He used a hairpiece to cover a bald patch on top of his head. (It didn't come near the hairline so if he hadn't kept tapping it no one would have noticed it.) He blacked out a couple of his front teeth with stage cosmetic and made his breath smell with chemical—oldest trick in the business to prevent people looking you in the face close-to. He stole the baggage after it had been through customs." I paused.

Harvey was grinning. "Yes," he said. "It was me."

I went on. "I'd say he was a transit airline passenger on a refueling stop who got off his airplane, changed into a pair of overalls in the toilet, drove off with a vanload of baggage, took what he wanted and was back on his plane well within the time his flight was called, to continue his journey without even going through customs. Not bad for someone who had just barnstormed around after leaving college."

Harvey laughed and said, "Elevator shoes, contact lenses to change the eye color, dirtied fingernails and a trace of coloring on the lips to make the face seem pale. You forgot all those."

Harvey stared down at his toes and watched them while they did a little dance.

"You think you are a pretty smart bastard, don't you?" Harvey said. He was still looking down and still doing a little dance. I didn't answer. "A pretty smart bastard." Harvey split the words into syllables and made each syllable a step in his dance, then he changed the accents around and danced the same remark again. He zinged an end to his dance with one foot high in the air. He turned his face to me. "You made sure your prediction about Pike came out O.K., didn't you? You're like these dames who see two knives crossed on the table, then start a row to prove it's a bad sign. Pike gets burned. You have a nice chat with Stok."

I think Harvey wanted me to hit him. Whether he wanted to be hurt and suffer, or an excuse to hit me back, I don't know, but I'm sure he wanted me to hit him.

Harvey said, "You were having a nice chat about Turgenev. You knew Stok wouldn't harm you. As far as he's concerned you are a representative of the UK Government. If he cracks down on you, London would crack down on all the fringe people who go in and out of the Soviet network there. No, providing you are reasonably discreet you are safe anywhere in Russia. That's what makes me sick. You laughing and chatting with Stok while our boy was sitting there petrified."

I said, "Stok's O.K. compared with some of the people I work with, let alone compared with the people I work against. Stok knows which side he's on. So do I. That's why we can talk."

"Stok is a bloodythirsty ruthless bastard."

"So are we all," I said. "Half-ruthless, half-doomed."

"Maybe you should have walked over to Pike and told him that. Half of us are ruthless and the other half are doomed. You should have told Pike which half he belonged to."

"We are all half-ruthless and all half-doomed. That's what I mean."

"You're drunk," said Harvey, "or you wouldn't be so corny."

The balcony door was open. I looked through it to see why the music had stopped. General Midwinter was in front of the band smiling benignly at the closely packed guests and holding his gloved hand high as if he was auctioning it. The guests were silenced.

"We interrupt your pleasure for a brief prayer," said Midwinter. He bowed his head and so did everyone. "Dear Heavenly Father," Midwinter intoned, "help us to awaken our beloved country to its great danger. Help us to cleanse it and hold it safe from the godless forces of Communism that surround it and threaten it from within. In Jesus's name we ask it. Amen." The guests said "Amen."

I looked at Harvey but he was staring at his feet, which twitched for another little dance. I eased my way through the crowds that were watching Midwinter climb down from the platform. Mercy Newbegin pushed past me.

"How does Harvey know what I said to General Midwinter?" she asked me as she passed.

I shrugged. How the hell did he know what I'd said to Colonel Stok?

CHAPTER 16

NEXT morning my phone rang at 9:45. I had a headache. A voice that called me "old boy" suggested that I "toddle over the road and meet me in Greenwich Village at the corner of Bleecker Street and MacDougal. I'll be wearing a green tweed overcoat and a brown felt hat."

I'll bet, I thought, with a small Union Jack flying from the crown of it. So I walked across Washington Square and along MacDougal where there are coffee houses for rich vagrants. The black chairs and marble tables were silent and empty and men in white aprons were sweeping the floors, carrying ice and emptying the garbage. Two kids were playing draughts with Coca-Cola caps on the steps of an art-jewelry studio. A dozen stray cats were asleep under a Con-Edison awning and so were two winos. I stopped at the corner of Bleecker Street. It was a bright cold day with a freezing wind blowing on the crosstown streets. There was no sign of anyone resembling the tweedy man that phoned. Outside Perazzo's Funeral Church there was an old-style funeral. There were six black Fleetwoods with Negro chauffeurs, and flower arrangements as big as lots. Three men in black overcoats and dark glasses were fussing around the long cars, and a small crowd had gathered to weep and wonder. I watched the first of the Fleetwoods roar away with headlights shining and felt a nudge in the kidneys and heard a soft voice.

"Don't turn around, old fruit. No point in both of us knowing what I look like. Billet doux from the old firm. Lots of luck and all that, don't you know." He paused. "Fascinating people, eh? Carries great status, a fine funeral, you know."

"Does it?" I said. "I'll bear that in mind."

"That's the spirit. You'll love the Village. Fascinating. I live here. Wouldn't live anywhere else. Love the Village. Fascinating people, eh?" He prodded my ribs with something that turned out to be a manila envelope.

"Yes," I said.

I gripped the envelope. He moved away and I heard a murmur of protest as he trod on feet and pushed ribs to move back through the sightseers. I gave him two or three minutes to disappear, then drifted away as the last hearse disappeared.

A sign on the wall said, LIVE AND TRADE IN THE VILLAGE. I walked past it and headed north to have breakfast.

In Washington Square a camera crew was measuring the width of the arch and being important. It was one of those days when police academy cadets were controlling the traffic and miles of brightly colored taxicabs slithered very slowly up the avenue of graceful skyscrapers like banded snakes between jungle trees. On Eighth Street the wind was lifting discarded newspapers like wounded pigeons. The sky was low and pregnant with rain which would fall as soon as the wind dropped. Even now the air was damp with the threat of it.

I went into the Cookery Coffee Shop. I got a seat near the window and ordered Canadian bacon and a pot of coffee. At the next table a group of kids in white cricket pullovers and sneakers were arguing about who ordered two helpings of French toast. A middle-aged woman passed along the street on roller skates, and across the road a fat man was fixing a notice: *Only a few days to go. Accountant will do your tax forms—$5.* He felt the first dabs of rain and held out his palm to inspect the circles of water as though they might be gold or a map of the city.

I opened the manila envelope the Englishman had given me. There were four letters addressed to me at my London flat. Jean had opened them. One was the Military Historical Society Bulletin, two were receipted bills for gas and phone—Jean had paid them. The fourth was a letter from the landlord about making too much noise late at night. Me, that is, not my landlord. There was also a note from Jean.

The note from Jean said:

> Dawlish passed the January expenses O.K. so you were right after all, you clever thing. Your washing-up lady left a message that she was three weeks in arrears and she was going to see her brother in Brighton—whatever that means

—anyway I took it out of the petty cash and paid her. You forgot to stop the milk. Mr. Dawlish says I should tell you that the Pike brothers are both Latvians but hold British passports. They have been members of some very dodgy Latvian old-pals clubs but nothing else is known. No form, etc., of course.

They are a very clever family the Pikes, they all hold medical qualifications, but Ralph Pike (the younger one, who took a trip you know where) has biochemical qualifications too. He was probably sent there to take a look at some local biochemical machines because even a quick glance would be very revealing to an expert, and Ralph Pike is an expert. We are sure at this end that the Pikes wouldn't be a party to exporting the virus to (or in even the slightest way aiding) the place you've just been. On the contrary, politically they are as far right as it's possible to go without falling off the edge.

I can't do much to answer your queries about Kaarna. He knew that there was a group of people interested in selling a stolen virus. He decided that they were British (for no reason that we yet know). He had a rudimentary training in science and probably offered to look at the virus and give an opinion as to its value in order to gain information. That's why he was in a white jacket (I remember that you said he looked like a phony dentist in a toothpaste ad). The postmortem now states quite categorically that he was not killed by any sort of missile (the open window must have been a red herring). He was killed by a needlelike instrument (punctured wound, the report says, but it was four and a quarter inches deep) going into his kidney, renal artery, peritoneum and loop of jejunem. This seems to suggest an assailant unknown to him coming up behind him with a weapon in the right hand, holding him around the neck with the left arm (fabric traces in the teeth) to prevent his shouting. "A skillful piece of placing," the Helsinki path. lab said. We haven't mentioned eggs to the Central Criminal Police in Helsinki but the Security Police are getting interested and we may have to give them at least some explanation of the raw egg on Kaarna's body. Did you get your clean laundry? I told them it was urgent, but I don't think their van does you on Tuesdays. I divided some of those files into sub files and we have got rid of quite a bit of it now so you needn't be frightened of coming back to weekend working. Mr. Dawlish told me to give you a summary of the virus. (It's enclosed) It's a bit fourth-form biology, but then you were a little fourth-form biology yourself the last time I saw you.

All my love darling.

JEAN

A blue flimsy attached to the letter said:

This is to tell you about those raw eggs on Kaarna and in the box from Pike. Viruses have a regular geometric shape. They are bigger than protein molecules but smaller than bacteria. They cause polio, smallpox, foot-and-mouth, flu, cattle diseases, plant diseases, sore throats and cancer. New ones are discovered every week. They attack man, plants, bacteria and animals. Some viruses attack bacteria, others attack body cells. They live in a host cell which they invade. It is a medical problem to attack the virus without attacking the normal cells. When the virus takes over a cell it takes over the master plan or system of instruction of that cell and the cell is thereafter directed to reproduce itself with the virus already in command.

Transport of the virus.

The virus lives at body heat—37° C—and can be reared in a fertile hen's egg. Candle the egg to see which way it is sitting, trepan the egg, inject virus into the yolk via the hyaline membrane (tough white skin), replace shell section.

The particular virus in which we are interested is an antivirus virus. It enters the body by droplet infection—e.g., nasal passage—stimulates the reticulo-endothelial system to produce an amino-acid complex like interferon. This attacks the growth of other viruses by attacking the foreign nucleic acid before it gets into the cell.

I hope this is of some use to you. It took me four hours at a boffin-house and lasted through two sherries, three bottles of wine, a little brandy and a proposal (of marriage). Bring some records. How about Coltrane, Kirk & Rollins?

JEAN

I sipped my coffee. I wondered whether they were using my secretary Jean to do the work of other departments. I wondered if they passed that Trade Union (Positive Vetting) File over to someone else or whether they were keeping it for my return. None of those public school boys would be able to do that job with the instinct that I would be able to bring to it. Yet some of the people concerned would be people I was at school with; and in any case, it would call upon questions and allegiances that I had continuously pushed into the rear recesses of my mind. I dreaded that file landing on my desk, and yet to make clear how much I wished to avoid it would . . . I was deep into a descending spiral when I heard a tap at the window against which I was sitting. It was pouring now, but standing right there on the shiny 8th Street pavement was Signe. She was standing there crammed full of enthusiasm and energy like a bomb on a short fuse. Her skin was tanned and freckled like a brown farm egg. When she smiled that big smile with her slightly too big mouth and too many very white teeth it was as if the explosion was starting to blow the top of her head off. Rain was bouncing off the street like corn stubble and Signe's hair was plastered against her head like a pot of mustard that someone had poured over her. She wore a man's yellow oilskin coat that was many sizes too big for her and the rain made it even shinier, flashing there like a neon sign advertising gold.

She tapped on the glass again. Several customers looked at Signe and made soft noises of approval. I beckoned her to come in and have coffee but she shook her head and tapped on the glass again and mouthed the words "I want you," like a trapped goldfish.

I left two dollars and a half-eaten bacon sandwich on the table and walked out into the street. Signe wrapped her yellow oilskin arms around my neck and planted a kiss on me. Her sharp nose was icy cold and her face wet with rain. She was bubbling over with words and explanations and kept pumping my arm and staring at my face as though she couldn't believe it was really me.

She said, "Did you go to General Midwinter's fancy dress party last night? Was it wonderful? Don't tell me if it was, I couldn't bear it. I wanted to go. Did you see General Midwinter? Isn't he marvelous? Did you see Harvey? We're finished, Harvey and me. Harvey and I. His wife was there, wasn't she? Did they have champagne? I love champagne. Will you buy champagne if I cook dinner tonight? Just the two of us. Don't you adore that house? Did you dance? Was the band good? What was Mercy Newbegin wearing? Was everyone in costume? What time did it finish? Did they have oysters? I adore oysters. I'll get oysters for us tonight. Oysters and champagne. Isn't Mercy Newbegin awful? Did you get to talk with her? Isn't she awful? What was she wearing? What sort of shoes? Did they dance the Paul Jones? I hate all women. Except two that you don't know. I didn't go because Harvey and I are through. And also I didn't want to see that Mercy Newbegin. Also I didn't have any proper shoes." She stopped. She looked up at me and said, "I didn't think I'd ever see you again. You don't hate me, do you?"

"Why should I?"

"Well, I'm always weeping on your shoulder. Men don't like that. Especially hearing about other men. It's natural. I wouldn't want you to tell me about your love affairs."

"Wouldn't you?" I said. "I was just going to tell you about my love affairs."

"Were you truly?" she said with a flattering amount of alarm in her voice.

"I'm just teasing," I said.

"Good," she said. "I don't want you to have any women in your life except me."

I was surprised. "I'm surprised," I said.

"I'm zipreezed," Signe mocked.

"You're getting very wet. Shall I try to get a cab?"

"No, no, no," she said. "I live on Eighth Street and I like walking in the rain."

"So do I."

"Do you really?"

"On account of my father who was a Saudi-Arabian rain-maker." Signe's hand squeezed mine. "He broke his heart when his village got connected to the mains."

Signe looked up into my eyes. "How terrible. Tell me about it."

I told her.

Signe's apartment was in a small block built over a row of shops. The hallway was bleak and one window was broken. Signe lived on the first floor. Her hall was papered with straw paper and there was a strange set of horns upon which Signe hung her yellow oilskin coat. She tapped it. "Hang up your coat. Plastic elk horns."

"I didn't know you hunted the great plastic elk."

"It was there when I moved in. Horrible, isn't it?" She swished her fingertips through her hair and sent a spray of water over me.

"Take it easy," I said. "I once gave away a dog that did that."

"I'm sorry," she said. "I forgot you English hate water." She disappeared into the bathroom and reappeared with her head under an enormous towel which she kneaded sensuously. "This way," the towel said. She led me into the kind of large room that Americans call a studio. It was papered in white and gold. On the walls were small pieces of wood that I later learned were the sculptures of one of Signe's ex-boy friends. Highly polished floorboards peeped around the white carpets, the curtains were ruffled and there were white shades with bobbles. On the floor there were three whodunit paperbacks and a copy of *The Village Voice* with face powder spilled on it. It was easy to spot the big-city items that Signe had added to the furnished apartment. There were a couple of fairground signs from Third Avenue antique shops, a polar bear rug and two huge basketwork chairs that looked like witch doctors in full gear and creaked when sat upon. Signe leaped across the room like a rubber kangaroo and landed flat upon the sofa. She bounced and cuddled herself into half a dozen bright scatter cushions.

"My apartment!" she yelled. "Mine, mine, mine!"

"Yes," I said.

"Sit down. I'll make you some coffee."

"I abandoned a perfectly good bacon sandwich," I said.

"Pooh on your bacon sandwich. I shall make you something delicious."

"What?" I said suspiciously.

"I'll see what's in the icebox. Sit down and stop looking so English."

"How do the English look?" I asked. I had ceased protesting that I was Irish.

"Embarrassed." She giggled. "Too many elbows and too many feet."

I moved a pair of cotton slacks, a brassiere, a housecoat, a page of a letter in Finnish, a jar of Pond's cold cream, some roll-on deodorant and a half full cup of cold coffee in order to sit on the basketwork chair.

"Ah, there it is," Signe said, coming back into the room and taking the cold coffee from me. "Do you take sugar and cream?"

"Cream, no sugar." I dried my trouser legs in front of the fire until Signe returned with a toasted ham sandwich and coffee.

"I'm through with Harvey," she said. "You're steaming."

"I always steam when I'm alone with girls. What happened?"

"I couldn't put up with him. Those moods. One moment he's all smiles, the next moment he snaps my head off."

"That's right. That's what he does all right. He does it to me."

"He even does it to Midwinter. They are getting fed up with him too."

"Who?"

"The organization. Our organization. Even they are fed up with his moods."

"It doesn't make him less efficient," I said.

"It does if everyone hates him, doesn't it?"

"Yes it does, I suppose."

"He told me he would kill you. That's why I was so frightened for you."

"It's nice to know someone was," I said. "But why would Harvey kill me?"

"You know why."

"No, I don't know why."

"You don't have to shout at me."

"No, I don't know why."

"Why couldn't you say it quietly the first time? It's because you are checking up on him."

"You don't believe that?"

"I do believe it. You overplay your part. You're always pretending you don't know who General Midwinter is and you don't know what the organization is. No one could be as ignorant as you pretend to be." She waited for me to reply.

"That gives me a chance to be a villain or a fool," I said. Signe agreed.

I said, "Harvey thinks I am employed by Midwinter to check up on him?"

Signe pursed her lips at me. "Kiss, kiss," she said. I went across to her and kissed her.

"Do you call that a kiss?" she said.

"Make it do for now," I said.

"General Midwinter says you are to move in here with me."

"You are lying again, Signe."

"No, truly. He doesn't like using hotel switchboards to transmit orders. The Midwinter organization pays the rent for both my apartments—New York and Helsinki—so I can't argue when they send me guests. I've prepared for you. Come and see."

I went into the bedroom. There was a double bed with flowered sheets, and on the pillows a pair of pajamas and a negligee.

"Our boudoir," said Signe. She opened a wardrobe and swept back the hangers to make room for my nonexistent dozen suits. I opened a cupboard and about fifty pairs of Signe's shoes fell over me. Signe clapped her hands and laughed. "I love shoes," she said. "I *love* shoes." She picked up the shoes in armfuls and stacked them away with obsessional care, keeping the toes carefully in line. When she spoke it was to the shoes. "You will stay?" she said anxiously. "I get awfully frightened at night. The cats knock the garbage cans over and last week someone got into the front hall and smashed the mirror and the door. That's why it looks so awful down there. The police caught him but his mother came round next day in a Jaguar and paid the landlord three hundred dollars not to prosecute. You will stay, won't you?" She wrapped her arms around me and sought my spine with her fingertips.

"I wouldn't want you to be frightened at night," I said.

I went back to the hotel to collect my baggage, a quarter-full bottle of whisky, two paperback books (*The Thirty Years' War* by Wedgwood and *The Complete Guide to New York City*), one worsted suit, four cotton oxfords, socks and underwear in one small fiberboard case.

The phone rang. The same metallic voice spoke. "You will move into Miss Laine's apartment today," the voice said. "You will be going south for training within a few days. If you require money record an affirmative now."

"I need money," I said. "Only machines don't need it." This time I rang off before the machine did.

It was an idyllic weekend. Midwinter didn't call. Harvey didn't try to kill me—as far as I know—and Signe and I wandered around Greenwich Village gawking and scoffing, eating and shopping and arguing without malice. On a Saturday the Village is crowded: girls with dirty hair and men with pink pants and poodles. Shops full of rude paintings, rustic sandals, cut-price records, any tie in the window 80¢, primitive jewelry and cold storage in our own vaults $2 up. Frantic electric signs were ticking like wire brushes and the trumpet call of police sirens played a countermelody to the bass gearboxes of ancient buses. On the corner a girl selling the *Catholic Worker* gave a cigarette to Socialism What It Means. The sun, incandescent orange, dropped slowly onto Pier 56 and made the buttes of Midtown Manhattan shine like fool's gold.

We had dinner in the Village, a French restaurant where the Provençal dressing is warm ketchup, and it's all candle-light and striped aprons and waiters with waxed moustaches who talk like Maurice Chevalier.

"Ow izz zat for madame et monsieur?" the waiter said and left without waiting for a reply.

I said, "Evryzink izz what we call in my countree zipreez-ingly ockay."

Signe seemed very happy and my pleasure was watching her. She wore a white dress that made her shoulders look even more tanned than they were. Her hair gleamed like a hastily polished brass pot, its tiny dents reddish-brown. Her eyes were dark and carefully made darker, but her lips were without lipstick and her face had only the merest dusting of powder.

"I'm glad you talked me out of Poetry and Jazz."

"So am I," I said.

"A nice restaurant or a settee is the best place to spend an evening."

"That's it," I said.

"I met Harvey in a restaurant," she mused. "I was with a nice boy. I wanted the sugar and rather than wait for the waiter to return or ask this boy to get it, I asked Harvey for the sugar. Harvey was all alone. I said, 'Can I have the sugar?' and he picked up a knife from the table top and pretended to carve his heart out, put it in the sugar bowl and presented it to me. I thought he was fun but I didn't take much notice, especially since this boy I was with was angry. The next moment the waiter came back to Harvey carrying a little cake with twenty-six candles, all alight. He put it down in front of Harvey and Harvey sang—quite loudly all by himself—Harvey sang 'Happy Birthday to Me' all through. Then everyone there clapped and people sent him drinks and we all got talking."

"What then?"

"We had a love affair. Frantic. For those first few weeks we couldn't keep our eyes off each other. Couldn't keep our hands off each other. And talk. Obsessively. Staring at each other while having dinner or being at a party, then go home, go to bed and talk. Talk, make love a little. Talk, talk as though you can tell each other everything you've ever done or seen or said or thought. I can't tell you how I love when I love. I'd just look into Harvey's eyes and there was a silent scream that drained me, like I had a baby inside me that never stopped sobbing. It was great but it ends. It always ends."

"Does it?"

She smiled. "It does when you are in love with a moody crackpot like Harvey. Let's forget him. Let's talk about you. They'll send you for training to San Antonio, Texas. Can I visit you there?"

"You know more about it than I do," I said. "Sure, come and see me."

"Three weeks from tonight. Nine-thirty. There's a club on Houston Street. They have to call it a club or they're not allowed to serve hard liquor. If I write it down, will you be sure to be there?"

"I'll be there," I said.

"That will be wonderful. Now let's order champagne. Pol Roger '55. I will pay for it."

"You don't have to pay," I said and ordered it.

"I love champagne."

"So you keep saying. How about moving on to something else, shoes for instance?"

"You are fishing. I'll tell you what else I like." She thought deeply. "Champagne, hot scented baths, Sibelius, tiny kittens, very, very, very expensive underwear that you hardly know you're wearing, and skiing at night and going into the big stores on Fifth Avenue and trying on all the three-hundred-dollar dresses and shoes and then saying that I don't like any of them—I do that quite often—and . . ." She wet her lips with her tongue to indicate deep thought ". . . and always having a man madly in love with me—because that gives you confidence when you're mixing with people—and I like outsmarting men who try to outsmart me."

"Quite a list."

The waiter brought the champagne and thumped it around in a bucket of ice to persuade us that it hadn't come out of the refrigerator. It went *pop* and Signe leaned forward into the candlelight so that all the customers could see her, and sipped at the champagne and narrowed her eyes at me in a gesture of passion that she had seen in some bad film. I cranked the handle of an old-time movie camera and Signe sipped her champagne and the waiter said, "izzz evryzink all right, madame?" and Signe started coughing.

| *San Antonio*

He loves me, he don't,
He'll have me, he won't,
He would if he could,
But he can't, so he don't.

— NURSERY RHYME

CHAPTER 17

I WAS the sole passenger. I left New York in Midwinter's Jetstar. The Weather Bureau was predicting light rain and snow flurries and the cirrus was thickening, but over San Antonio, Texas, three and a half hours later, the night was crystal clear. The landscape was green. The trees were dense with leaves. The air clung like a warm facecloth. Men moved in the leisurely evening warmth like alligators across a mud flat. I loosened my shirt collar and watched a couple of generals being saluted by their chauffeurs. On the seats there was a tall man in Stetson and jeans and a Mexican girl listening to a Spanish station on her transistor radio and flipping the gatefold of *Playboy*.

"You looking for Colonel Newbegin?" called the man in the Stetson. He hadn't moved a muscle.

"Yes," I said. He stretched himself lazily and picked up my

case. On his shoulder a silk patch read MIDWINTER. FACTS FOR FREEDOM.

"Let's go," he said. He rolled a cigarette across the width of his mouth without using his hands. I followed him. I'd follow anyone who can do that.

Harvey was sitting in an olive-drab station wagon. Across the front of it was painted *Keep your distance* in mirror writing. We drove through the humid night and things flew into the beam of the headlights. We headed north—away from the city—on U.S. 281 as far as State Highway 46, which forms a great arc around the town. At the tiny village of Bergheim—three houses and a gas station—we turned onto one of those narrow tracks that don't even get a farm road numeral. The driver took the road carefully as it dipped and turned, and forded rivers that shone like a newly tarred road and roared and pounded against the floor. Large animals drinking bounded back into the undergrowth blinded by our lights. At one curve in the road the driver stopped and flashed his main beams. A torch flashed. We drove slowly to where a sentry stood. He shone his hand lamp into the car and then, without speaking, opened the gate across a side road. In the flow of the headlights I read the note: *Department of Agriculture Experimental Station. Animal traps dangerous to you are set in this area. Proceed no further*. Then there was a skull and crossbones and the word DANGER very large. The signs were repeated every ten yards. We drove two hundred yards and then the driver switched a dashboard control marked *garage doors* which sent a radio recognition signal to the second compound. The sentry there came out and flashed his lamp around and then we entered a high steel-mesh fence that said *Department of Agriculture. YOU are in danger. Do not move. Shout for assistance, there is a game warden near to you. Danger 600 volts*. The signs were illuminated by spotlights which marked the fence-lines for miles in each direction.

"Welcome to Texas," said Harvey.

The Brain was three buildings that looked single-story from here outside but they went deep into the rocky hillside. Tinted glass filtered the bright morning sunlight, and powered swivel shutters excluded it at will. Harvey was dressed in a khaki uniform with colonel's insignia on the collar. On his sleeve there was a Facts for Freedom patch.

We walked past the Brain along the chalky-white cart track. Here and there on the hillside I could see sheep and the goats grazing among the wildflowers and stunted trees. High above, a trio of hawks faltered on the rising air and the only sound was the scraping of insects.

Harvey said, "All Midwinter personnel comes here for training in intelligence work. Some are management development students, they are between twenty-eight and thirty-six years old and they stay here for fifteen weeks. Some are Advanced Management students between thirty-seven and fifty. Their course lasts thirteen weeks. At least eighty percent of them have previous intelligence experience although we do recruit directly from other commercial organizations (especially ones that Midwinter has an interest in), and sometimes even from college. They learn straightforward administration applied to intelligence work. We show them some of the dirty tricks, but it's pretty elementary because none of those boys are likely to be used in any sort of field work. They don't get much more out of it than they would from reading a James Bond paperback but it makes them understand a few of the problems the field men face. So that one day when they are sitting on their fat butt in Frankfurt or Langley and some poor guy's written seven point nine two centimeter automatic rifle instead of seven point nine two millimeter, they won't want to fire him for bad writing. Jesus, it's hot. Well, that's the gut * course, so they are called gut men. The Operations Students—the fieldmen—are called spitballs around here. Watch for the cactus. We'll join the main path in a moment. There's a spitball course going through now, you'll join it for a couple of days." Harvey scrambled up some roughly cut footholds, held on to a gnarled gray tree and offered me his other hand. At first sight this was like English countryside, but close to, where you could see the baked cracked topsoil, the dead convoluted trees, bleached stones like animal skulls and huge pear cactus in bright yellow flower—close to, the land was hard, dry and pitiless.

Harvey helped me up and pointed to a concrete runway just below us. "That's the strip. We call that Longhorn Valley, so that's Longhorn Strip. We can't get a large plane in there of course but it's useful having our own field sometimes." He looked at his watch. "This hill we are on is called Loving Alto. Alto is Mex for a bald-top hill and Loving was an old trail boss who first named it." Harvey sank down into the parched grass. On the hillside facing us I could see four turkey vultures scavenging in the carcass of a raccoon. "Gee, it's good to feel that hot sun," said Harvey. I watched a line of furry caterpillars playing follow-the-leader across the path. Harvey looked at his watch. "Above where the river shines," Harvey said. Out of the drone of insect life around us I could distinguish the sound of an airplane engine. I followed Harvey's pointed finger and saw the plane not very high above the horizon.

"He'll hang out the laundry right across the valley," Harvey said. Almost as Harvey said it a parachute inflated under the plane. "First the conduction officer," said Harvey. "That gives

* Gut course—easy course (U.S. college slang).

the other students confidence. Now they go." Six parachutes puffed like Indian smoke signals across the sky. "They're going nicely," Harvey said. "They'll be right on target. We do three daylight drops, two at night. The instructors are U.S. Army Special Warfare Center people from Fort Bragg. Really tough."

"That's nice," I said.

We watched the men bundle up their parachutes and move off through the dense undergrowth, chopping at it with jungle machetes. Now and again there was a tiny puff of smoke and the smack of a hand grenade or a burst of machine-gun fire. It didn't seem my sort of thing at all and I gave Harvey a glance to indicate it.

"You'll enjoy it," Harvey said. He walked on. "Down in the valley they say they found dinosaur tracks—"

"Freeze! Freeze!" a shrill voice sang out. I froze and so did Harvey. It took me a full minute to recognize the soldier in the bush. He had a tough tanned face and clear eyes. He wore a mottled camouflage jacket and a lightweight Stetson and carried an automatic rifle. He moved slowly and cautiously through the dead roots and broken timber.

"Newbegin and student Dempsey of the new intake," Harvey said.

The man with the rifle said, "Remove your index tag real slow. Put it on the ground and back up."

We removed the tags from our shirt fronts, put them on the ground and stepped backward. The sentry picked up the tags, stared at the photos and at our faces. "Colonel Newbegin, sing out your number backwards."

Harvey said, "308334003 AS/90."

I said, "I don't have the slightest idea."

"He's today's intake," Harvey said. "Didn't I tell you?"

"I suppose that's O.K. then," said the guard grudgingly. "I've seen you around before, Colonel Newbegin, sir."

The sentry brought the cards to us. I said, "What kind of gun do you call that?"

"The A.R. 10," said Harvey. "Fairchild Aviation, Armalite Division, developed it using— aluminium and foamed plastics. Seven hundred rounds per, at two and three-quarter thousand f.p.s. Quite a baby, weighs nothing." He turned to the sentry. "Let him feel the weight of it." The sentry passed it to Harvey. "Eight pounds. Fantastic?"

"Fantastic."

"Twenty-round magazines using seven point six two Nato cartridge. See the new type flash suppressor. It's quite a baby, the A.R. 10." Harvey took it and swung it round experimentally. His face tightened, his teeth bit into his lower lip, "Raise 'em!" he yelled. We didn't move fast enough. "Raise 'em I said. Get your Goddamn pinkies grabbing cloud." He turned upon the sentry. "Hit dirt," he said. "Twenty push-ups. Twenty. Count 'em. Not you, stupid," he said to me. "You didn't turn over your gun." The sentry looked mournful. He was a Mexican boy about eighteen years old. They were employed around the compound as permanent sentries. "Twenty push-ups," Harvey said again.

"Harvey," I said, "let it go. It's too hot for playing at Belsen."

Harvey looked doubtful but he let me take the gun from him. "Here, kid," I said and threw it to him. The sentry took advantage of the pause to slip away into the undergrowth.

"You shouldn't have done that," Harvey said resentfully.

"Come on, Harvey. You're the pleasure-loving, all-laughing boy who is successful by accident. This pursuit of efficiency isn't your speed at all."

"Perhaps you are right," said Harvey. Then he raised his voice. "Now from here, you can see the buildings more clearly.

See how the three largest buildings surround the little flat windowless one. Kind of arrogant, that little building looks, doesn't it? That's where we're going now. We call that the Brain. The other buildings are schoolrooms and a gymnasium for the spitballs and gut men. Those walkways join the three buildings together because we sometimes have cosmics here. That is to say, students whose faces we don't want the other students to see."

"Man in the iron mask," I said.

"Right," said Harvey. "Next stop the Bastille."

The only part of the Brain building above ground level was a reception hall. The outer doors were as heavy as a bank vault and inside, the air here was clean, dry and quite cold. To the left there was a long line of cubicles with colored doors and a large numeral on each. Two uniformed men sat inside an armor-glass fishbowl in the center of the floor. Inside the turret there were twelve small TV screens by means of which the guards monitored the approaches to the building and knew when to open the electric door. I could see the tiny figures of Harvey and myself moving on two of the screens as we walked across the floor. It was white, and so gave optimum visibility on the screen.

"Go ahead," the second guard said. Harvey took off his identity tag and inserted it into a machine like a railway station weighing machine upon which he stepped.

Harvey explained. "The identity tags are changed every week. The metal strip at the side of the card holds an electrical charge—like a piece of recording tape; this machine reads that, to make sure it's of the current pattern while at the same time photographing me and my tag and weighing me. If one of those things doesn't tally with the record of me on the machine then the doors will lock—including the doors to

the elevators—and alarms will sound in about twenty places
on the compound as well as in New York."

I put my card into the machine. The guard said, "Cubicles
twenty-one and twenty."

"What now, Harvey?" I said.

"You go in the cubicle—it's quite large—undress and step
into the shower. The shower will stop automatically and warm-
air blowers will dry you off. You will then change into a set
of white coveralls which are made of paper. Leave all your
belongings in the clothes you take off, the door will automatically lock behind you. Don't keep your wristwatch on,
because the last doorway you step through will be a counter.
The smallest item will trip it and start an uproar, so don't
forget anything. Your glasses and keys you put through a small
slot. You'll see the notice about it."

"In three languages?" I asked.

"Eight," said Harvey.

Harvey and I came out the other side looking like a couple
of spooks. "The whole building," Harvey explained, "is sealed
and dust free." We entered an elevator and went down. *Stand
still* said a sign on the wall opposite the elevator exit.

Harvey said, "That's a TV monitor. The guard at the entrance can watch who is moving from floor to floor." We stood
still. Harvey picked up a green phone and said, "Visit 382 on
pink level." The sign flashed the word CLEARED.

We went down a long corridor to a door bearing a sign
Latvia pilot operation. Inside there were long banks of computers making a low musical noise like a child's spinning top.
"These are operational," Harvey said. "Riga is the pilot operation, that's why we are watching it so closely. These machines
are programming our operation there. Each and every act of
every agent comes out of this machine.

Harvey told me how each part of the computer was named

after a section of the human brain: the *Medulla, Pons* and *Midbrain*. He showed me how the items of information called *neurons* were filtered by the *synapses*. I said yes to everything but to me machines tend to look alike. Harvey led me to a room which he unlocked with a key. It was a large room with a dozen or more men pushing switches and loading reels of tape into gray machines. Some of the men wore earphones with dangling plugs which they occasionally plugged into a machine, nodding professionally like doctors sound a chest.

"Nu think," said Harvey. He pointed to a row of eight doors along the far wall. "Its an indoctrination laboratory."

"Go into number four," said one of the attendants. "We're going to stream him in a couple of minutes."

Inside door number four was a light lock and beyond it a dark cubicle like the flight deck of a large airliner. There was a curious smell of spice in the room. A man sat in a low leather bucket seat and watched a TV screen. Some pictures were in color and some in black and white. Some of the pictures were stills, some were movie. There was a picture of a village street, the houses were battered clapboard and there were a lot of horses around. On another TV screen at the side there was an endless stream of associative words in Russian script and Latvian—*horse, house, people, street*. They were stream-of-consciousness words, Harvey explained later, a constant enrichment of the students' vocabulary. Over a loudspeaker came a voice speaking Latvian, but Harvey handed me earphones that carried an English translation. ". . . until you were sixteen," the commentary was saying." Then your Uncle Manfred arrived. He was a soldier." A photo of Manfred came on the screen. "That's how Uncle Manfred looked in 1939 when you were sixteen. You saw him again in 1946. He looked like this. You saw him for the last time in 1959. He looked like this. Now I'm going to stream Uncle Manfred's life for you but before

I do, here are some questions." The associative screen stopped its flow of words. "These two bottles on the screen, what do they contain?"

"Green top is yoghurt, silver top is milk," said the student.

"Good." The bottles disappeared and a street scene appeared. "What is the name of this cinema and what was showing there at Easter weekend?"

"I never go to the cinema," said the student.

"Very well," said the commentator, "but you must have noticed the posters. Isn't this where you line up for the tram coming home from work?"

There was a long pause. "I'm sorry," said the student.

"We'll have to do local geography again," said the commentator. "We'll leave it for now and stream Uncle Manfred a few times."

Pictures of a man were flashed upon the screen in rapid succession. They were in chronological order and you saw him grow older before your eyes. The lines on his face and the slope of his eyes varied as the pictures changed. It was an uncanny thing to watch. I shivered. Harvey noticed me. "That's right," he said. "That's how it makes me feel. Mind you, that's just a short sequence they are streaming. Later they will stream longer and longer episodes until a whole life whistles past in about three minutes. It goes right into the subconscious, of course; no memorizing involved."

"Again," said the voice, and the screen showed the whole set of pictures through again.

"In five days," said Harvey when we were outside the cubicle, "we can indoctrinate a man so that he really believes his cover story better than he believes his own memory. By the time that man gets to Riga he will know his way around the town and every detail of his life from the day his father gave him a light brown teddy bear to the TV program he watched last night. He doesn't need to remember facts and figures, he actually sees the things and people of his cover-story life. We photograph special setups—his motorcycle, his dog, we use actors to make a movie of his relatives sitting in the rooms where he grew up. We show him photos and movies of his hometown when he was a kid. By the time he leaves here no one could crack him, he believes his own cover story, he is schizophrenic. . . . Did you notice that smell in there? It's always the same temperature and humidity and has that scent so that the mind is conditioned by environment."

Harvey stepped up to a door marked RECREATION. "What about a little recreation?" he asked. "This is where we keep the curvy blonde."

I said, "I knew this was science fiction."

"By the time those indoctrination students have done their training they deserve a break," said Harvey. "They just stay here twenty-four hours per day talking nothing but the language of their region from the minute they wake up till the time they go to bed in those tiny cubicles over there. Even then they don't get a break, because they are awakened suddenly at night and asked questions in some language they are not supposed to speak. If they even look like they are going to answer they get an automatic extra twelve hours. They learn fast, believe me. They learn fast."

Inside the recreation room there was a bar-counter with coffee, doughnuts, iced milk, hot soup, Alka-Seltzer, bread and a toaster. Harvey poured two glasses of milk and put two doughnuts on paper plates. We sat in fiber-glass easy chairs. There were a dozen magazines, a TV set, four telephones— one red one marked EMERGENCY—and a small illuminated panel which gave a current weather report. *Low today 70° Downtown San Antonio 79° Humidity 92% Pressure 29.6 Partly cloudy, Wind from southeast at 12 m.p.h.* There was no blonde except for a lady on the TV who was showing us Saniflush in the new unbreakable plastic bottle.

"It's complicated, eh?" Harvey asked between bites on the doughnut.

"That's the understatement of the year," I said.

"Cost over a billion dollars," Harvey said. "Over a billion. The old man—General Midwinter—has a private suite at seven floors below ground level. I'm not allowed to show you in there but that's quite a terrific place too. He even has a swimming pool there. The pumps that change the water in that pool cost three thousand dollars each. It's fantastic; the lighting is arranged so that you'd think it was daylight down there. He can see the surrounding country on color TV if he wants to. Really fantastic; sixteen guest bedrooms, each with a bathroom as large as my sitting room."

"It's nice to know that when he survives World War Three he'll have guests."

"I'd sooner be a crisp than survive. I had four months on permanent duty here. I went out of my mind."

"Yes," I said.

"I don't want to bore you," Harvey said, "but you should understand that these heaps of wire can practically think— linear programming—which means that instead of going through all the alternatives they have a hunch which is the right one. What's more, almost none of them work by binary notation—the normal method for computers—because that's just yes/no stuff. (If you can only store yeses and noes it takes seven punch holes to record the number ninety-nine.) These machines use tiny chips of ceramic which store electricity. They store any amount from one to nine. That's why—for what it does—this whole setup is so small."

"Yes," I said.

We finished our milk. "Back to the salt mines," said Harvey, standing up. "And if you want to do me a real favor, stop saying yes, for Christ's sake."

Harvey went through two doors and down a moving staircase. "This is what we call the Corpus Callosum; it's the most complex computer in existence today. The machines in this building cost over a hundred million dollars to develop and the machine equipment and construction set Midwinter back nearly as much again. These operators are all college graduates with postgraduate qualifications in either math or a similar subject."

We walked through a small data room. Operators were using punch machines and then transferring the results onto tape. Two men were standing under a no-smoking notice trying to hide a burning cigarette, and one college graduate with a postgraduate qualification was sitting under a sign that said THINK TALL reading an illustrated journal called *Voodoo Monsters Invade Earth*.

"You saw the operational machines," said Harvey. "They are working on the Latvia project. If the Latvia project is successful then the total resources of the Brain will come into use." He paused before a locked door marked MAIN PROJECT. Two guards stood outside, khaki-clad and motionless as shopwindow dummies. They exchanged code words with Harvey, then each of them opened his shirt and fished out a small key on a neck-chain. There were three keyholes marked *Alpha, Beta* and *Kappa*. Harvey produced a key for the third, and a red light came on over each lock. Harvey opened the door. This room was gigantic, like the hangar deck of an aircraft carrier. The banks of computer machines stretched away into the distance and there were only a few dim lights glowing. Our footsteps echoed as though there were other people walking to meet us from the far end. The machines were only ticking over. *Non-operational* the plastic ticket said. Over the banks of machines

were signs: DISTRICT 21 INCLUDING ODESSA, DISTRICT 34 AS
FAR AS ENVIRONS OF KURSK, MOSCOW CENTRAL AND DIS-
PERSED CENTERS OF GOVERNMENT WHATEVER THEIR LOCA-
TION, COASTAL ZONE 40.

The machines hummed and snick-snicked as if they had
been warned to keep their voices down. The thin oil that coated
each vital component, the enamel and metal tapes, were warm
enough to aromatize the air as fast as the air conditioning
changed it. The smell was sobering and efficient like ether and
antiseptic, as though this were the casualty ward of a vast
hospital run by machines for machines.

"This operation in Latvia." I found myself speaking in a
whisper, "What is it doing that these machines will do for the
rest of Russia?"

"Usual thing," said Harvey. "Sabotage of communications,
cache of arms, instruction in guerrilla warfare, preparation of
landing fields and drop zones, clandestine radio, beach reconnaissance, underwater demolition, contact with ships and aircraft, then G-2 work for the military. Usual stuff."

"Usual stuff?" I said. "If that's usual stuff for God's sake,
don't ever try to surprise me. This is total war looking for a
place to wage!"

"Stop worrying," said Harvey. "It's solely for Midwinter.
Three-dimensional chess, that's how to look at it. Three-dimensional chess for a millionaire."

"Fool's mate," I said.

CHAPTER 18

HARVEY lived with his wife and two children a few miles outside town on the road to Laredo and the Mexican border. I drove through the city instead of around the loop. It's not a typical American town, not one of those low modern places with chrome and neon and glass; the Alamo City is beat-up, chewed at the edges and in need of paint. I passed the second-hand clothes shops and the sign that said *Used books and guns* on Commerce Street. The Texans share the town with Mexicans, and they share it with soldiers. It was seven P.M. and already military police were sniffing around the clubs and bars of what Texans call "occupied Mexico." Out on the far side of town signs were jammed down the highway: Liquors, Drugs, Breakfast All Day, Speed radar control, Watch for deer roaming at night, Exit, fasten seat belt, Mexiteria; all you eat $.10, Hot Pizza to go, Gas, Regular 25.9, Tomatoes 35¢. I watched for the gas station on Harvey's map and turned off onto an unmade road that kicked up stones against the underside of the Rambler and laid a film of dust across the tinted windshield. There were whole fields of dead tree stumps here, like a World War One battlefield. In places the topsoil had broken, revealing bleached stones that were luminous in the fading light. A long way ahead of me, on a narrow farm road, were half a dozen cows. A man in a pickup truck slammed his hand against the door and shouted "Wow-wow." The sound was louder than the buzz of cars along the highway I had left. My tires rumbled across a cattle grating; I watched for a marker board of the Screw Worm Quarantine Line. I turned there and followed the twin scars that marked the track to the house.

The slope was covered with white and yellow wildflowers, and near to the house was a cluster of small trees. The house was narrow, transparent and bright with yellow light. One end was supported on steel legs and the other end bit into the rock. Under the high side there was a gray Buick that I had seen Harvey driving and a long black Lincoln Continental that looked like the President of the United States had come over for pizza and beer.

Harvey waved from the balcony and dropped ice cubes into a large glass. There was a scent of wildflowers and grass cooling after a hot day. Harvey's two kids were chasing around the trees in their pajamas. Mercy Newbegin called to the kids. "C'mon now; time for bed." And there were more Indian war whoops and whistles and cries of "Another five minutes, mom, huh?"

Mercy Newbegin said, "O.K., but exactly five now."

She came through into the sitting room where I was nursing a martini. The house had a simple luxury. It was little more than a glass-sided army hut but there was plenty of mahogany, ebony and zebra skin, and a tall cone of polished copper in the center of the floor became a fireplace at the touch of a switch. Harvey was lounging full-length across the sheepskin seats that followed the wall around the corner. Mercy sat down next to him.

"Did you see the Brain?" Mercy asked me. She was wearing lacy raw-silk pajamas like people wear in drink advertisements.

"Did he see it!" Harvey said. "He had the full transfers-between-airports-taxes-tips-and-porters-included-plan-A-tour. And he took it like a hero."

Mercy said, "I don't know why you have to speak like that, Harvey. Surely you're interested in the way the Brain works. It's your job, after all."

Harvey grunted.

Mercy called, "Are you children in bed yet?"

There was a jumble of children's voices, then the smaller child looked around the door. "Is Simon in here, Daddy?"

Harvey said, "No, I don't believe so. Simon's the cat," he explained to me. "He was a war profiteer."

The child said, "He wasn't, Daddy."

Harvey said, "He was, Hank—your mother and I weren't going to tell you." Harvey turned to me. "During the Korean war, see, this cat—"

Hank said, "No he was not," very loudly, he was angry and pleased both at once.

Harvey said very reasonably, "Then why does he go around wearing that ankle-length overcoat with the astrakhan collar? And smoking cigars? Explain that if you can."

Hank said, "He wasn't a war profiteer, Daddy. Simon doesn't smoke cigars."

Harvey said, "Not when you are around maybe, but when he goes across to see the Wilsons' cat . . ."

Mercy said, "Cut it out, Harvey. You'll give my children a complex before you're through."

Harvey said, "Your mother doesn't want you to know about Simon's cigars."

Mercy said, "Come along, Hank. Bath time." She marched him out. I could hear the child saying, "Candy cigars, Mommy, or real ones?"

Harvey said, "Mercy's got a kind of thing about the old man—Midwinter. She feels she has to support him. You know what I mean?"

"He seems to rely on her," I said.

"You mean his hand. He's a showman, Midwinter. Never lose sight of that. He's a pitchman from way back."

Mercy Newbegin came back into the room and closed the sliding door. "There are times when you make me scream, Harvey," she said.

"So scream, honey," Harvey said.

"You know more ways to foul up my marriage than any other man living."

"Well, that's only right, honey, I'm your husband. What is it you need, a little more romance?"

"I need a good deal less."

Harvey said to me, "Women are never romantic. Only men are romantic."

Mercy said, "It's a little difficult for a woman to be romantic about her husband's amours." She smiled and poured Harvey another drink. The tension was gone.

Mercy smoothed Harvey's hair. "I went to a sale today, honey."

"Buy anything?"

"Well, they had this sale of nylons for 28 cents below what I usually pay. Two women tore the nylons I was wearing—really good ones. Another dragged a baby carriage across my ninety-dollar shoes. Net gain: one dollar sixty-eight. Net loss: one pair of two-dollar nylons and one pair of ninety-dollar shoes." The screen slid back. Hank said, "I'm washed, Mommy." Mercy said, "Say good night quickly then."

Hank said, "Simon wasn't really a war profiteer, was he, Daddy?"

"No, son, of course he wasn't," Harvey said in a kindly tone. "He was just doing his bit toward victory." Harvey turned to me suddenly. "We have another cat named Boswell; a labor leader. He's organized every cat in the neighborhood except

Simon. Boy, is he ever a crook. He takes more kickbacks than. . . ."

Hank got very excited. He yelled, "He's not, Daddy! He's not, Daddy. He's not, he's not, he's not . . ."

Mercy picked Hank up and put him over her shoulder. "Off to bed," she said.

Hank yelled, "You'll give me a complex, Daddy, before you're through!"

Dinner was set on the patio. From this end of the house—the end on legs—there was a magnificent view. Through the cleavage of two low hills the lights of San Antonio rippled in the warm rising air. Harvey said, "I'm a city boy but this cow country has a lot of magic. Imagine great herds of longhorns —perhaps 3,000 head—walking across that landscape north, to where there was plenty of money and an appetite for beef. This was the starting point for those cattle drives. Tough guys like Charles Goodnight, John Chisholm and Oliver Loving pioneered routes to the railheads at Cheyenne, Dodge City, Ellsworth and Abilene. You know what sort of journey that would be?"

"I've no idea," I said.

"I did a trip along the Goodnight train to Fort Sumner, then took the Loving Train to Cheyenne. That was in 1946. I bought a war-surplus jeep and followed the Pecos River just like Loving did. From here to Cheyenne is 900 miles as the crow flies, the trail is nearer 1,400. I took it real slow, I did it in ten days but in 1867, Loving took three months to do it. Rustlers, outlaws, storms that had rivers breaking their banks, Indians, droughts. These trail bosses. . . ."

"Is Harvey playing cowboys and Indians again?" Mercy said. "Help me with the trolley, Harvey."

"It's interesting," I said.

"Don't let him hear you say that," she said, "or he'll get his guns out and demonstrate the 'border spin' and the 'road agent's shift.' "

"The border shift and the road agent's spin," Harvey corrected wearily. "Get it right."

We sat down and Harvey speared fried chicken onto the three plates. "Yes, sir," he said. "The end of the trail was little old Dodge where Earp would challenge any man wearing his plow handles north of the railroad tracks."

"Look what you're doing, Harvey. Serve the food properly or let me do it."

Harvey said, "Yes, ma'am. The kinda hombres who'd raise hell and put a plank under it. . . ."

"You haven't opened the wine, Harvey. The chicken will be cold if you don't stop it."

"Let me open the wine," I said.

"I wish you would, Mr. Dempsey. Harvey gets so excited sometimes. He's just like a big child. But I love him."

I opened the wine carefully; it was a very fine Chambertin.

"Quite a wine," I said.

"We made sure it was a good one. Harvey said you knew about Burgundies."

"I said he liked them," Harvey corrected.

"What's the difference?" said Mercy without wishing an answer.

Mercy Newbegin was a good-looking woman who looked even better in the light of the flickering candles. Her frame was small. Her arms looked frail and very white against the raw silk. Women would say she had "good bones." Her skin was tight across her ivory face and although one suspected that the tautness was maintained by a beauty parlor, it didn't lessen the harmony of the face, in which brown eyes seemed bigger than they really were, like a sun at sunset. She was a silk and satin girl; it was hard to imagine her in denim and cotton.

"Doesn't that General Midwinter have style?" she said. "He has his own train. He has houses in Paris, London, Frankfurt and Hawaii. They say the servants prepare food and set his table every day in each of these houses just in case he arrives. Isn't that something? And that plane—you came down in it— did you ever know anyone with two four-motor jet planes for private use?"

"No," I said.

"It makes me discontented, the life he lives. Here I am stuck in Texas for weeks on end. The droughts make the chiggers unbearable and the floods bring out the rattlesnakes and copperheads—"

"Grab some chicken," Harvey said, "while it's still hot."

Mercy handled the porcelain and silver with her elegant hands and measured out the wild rice and Caesar salad. Mercy gave me a chance to stare deep into her limpid brown eyes. "I'll bet even your Queen doesn't have two four-motor jet planes for her private use. One of them with interior décor of a nineteenth-century sailing clipper. Even your Queen—"

"You'd better not get into a hassle with this guy," Harvey interrupted. "Maybe he doesn't know a squeeze play from a loud foul, but once he senses he's being got at he can be a vicious S.O.B."

Mercy gave me a smile like homogenized gossamer. "I'm sure it's not true."

"That's just the two of us then," I said, and Harvey laughed.

"You British are such clever losers," Mercy said.

"It comes with practice," I said.

"Let me tell you about this guy," said Harvey, pointing a fork at me. "The first time I ever saw him was in Frankfurt. He was sitting in a new white Jensen sports car that was covered in mud with a sensational blonde, sensational. He was wearing very old clothes, smoking a Gaulois cigarette and listening to a Beethoven quartet on the car radio and I thought, Oh boy, just how many ways can you be a snob simultaneously? Well, this guy—" he paused for a moment to remember the name I was using—"well, this guy Dempsey knew."

"I can never remember names," Mercy said. "I remember when I was at college, men would phone me and I wouldn't have any idea who they were. So I would say, 'What kind of car do you have now?' and that would help me to remember. It would also help me to decide whether I should go out with them." Mercy laughed delicately.

"Husbands are a byproduct of marriage," said Harvey.

"A waste product," corrected Mercy Newbegin. She laughed and touched Harvey's arm to show that she didn't mean it. "I keep telling Harvey to sell that Buick. Can you imagine what people think, with him in a Buick? Especially with General Midwinter thinking so highly of him. A Buick just isn't us, Harvey."

"It isn't you, you mean," said Harvey.

"You could go to work in my Lincoln," said Mercy. "That has style."

"I like the Buick," said Harvey.

"Harvey is so anxious that we live only on his income. Why, it's so foolish. It's sinful pride. I've told him, sinful pride, and it's me and my children who suffer."

"You don't suffer," Harvey said. "You still buy your Mainbocher dresses, you still have your horses . . ."

"On Long Island," said Mercy. "I don't have them here."

"So you go home to Long Island once a month," said Harvey. "You go to St. Moritz every February, Paris for the Spring collections, you are in Venice in June, Ascot in July. . . ."

"With my money, darling. I don't take it out of your housekeeping." She laughed. She had perfectly proportioned features and perfectly proportioned hands and feet, and small even teeth that flashed as she smiled. When the conversation deserved to be punctuated she threw back her head and gave a perfectly proportioned peal of carefully modulated laughter. She turned to me. "I don't take it out of his housekeeping," she said and laughed again.

CHAPTER 19

AT 6:45 the following morning my visit to the Brain began in earnest. In the mess hall I had orange juice, cereal, ham and eggs and coffee. There was scarcely time for a cigarette before we were hustled over to the equipment store. We got six khaki shirts and pants, one belt, one knife with knuckle-duster handle, socks and sets of underwear and a lightweight Stetson. We changed into these outfits and assembled in Classroom 1-B at 7:45 A.M. Each uniform shirt had a large red shoulder patch with a white grid like three capital F's jammed together. On my shirt Harvey had arranged that I wore the word OBSERVER, which meant I was able to remember a prior appointment when the going got rough. The badge meant Facts for Freedom, the instructor explained. He was a crew-cut Harvard man with sleeves rolled up and collar buttoned down. Around the room there were signs that said THINK TALL. Every classroom had at least one of those signs in it. The foreign students spent a lot of time having the meaning of that slogan explained to them. I don't know if they ever fully understood it. I didn't. In other parts of the building there were signs saying *50% of the U.S.A. is Communist dominated, Pornography and titillation are the weapons of*

Communism and *Without you the U.S.A. will become a province of a world-wide Soviet system.*

Neither the instructors nor the other students knew anyone's real name, or even what they were giving as their name. We were given numbers. The first nine days of instruction —there were no days off ("Communism doesn't stand down on Sundays")—were devoted to desk learning. Geography, with special attention to the disposition of the Communist bloc and the Free World. History of the Communist Party. Marxism, Leninism, Stalinism, Materialism inside the USSR. Class Structure of foreign countries. Strength of Communist Party in various foreign countries.

On the tenth day eight of the men on my course went to spend three days studying photography, four did locks and keys, and seven went to study Roman Catholicism. (They were agents who would find their work easier if they posed as Catholics.) The rest of us had a series of lectures on Russian and Latvian etiquette, literature, architecture, religion, and recognition of uniforms and fighting vehicles of the Soviet Army. We were then given a simple exam which mostly consisted of crossing out the most stupid answers in order to leave the least stupid one. On the fourteenth day we moved to a different section of the training building. This was to be Active Training.

I nursed my damaged finger, and showed it to anyone who wanted me to join in the rough stuff. Each course had a "conduction officer" who stayed with it all through the training. The training included knife work, cliff climbing, gun firing, plastic explosives, railway destruction, night exercises, map reading and five parachute drops—three by daylight and two at night. Apart from the Negro student and one of the Bavarians, all the students were on the best side of thirty and they could run rings round us older men who saw only dubious advantages in agents who could run, jump and do forward rolls.

I had three days of Active Training. I had strained a muscle in my back, one of my toes looked septic, my finger was worse, and I was fairly certain that one of my jacket crowns was loose. Mind you, I'm always fairly certain that one of my jacket crowns is loose. I was probing around with my tongue and trying to decide about this when the phone by my bed rang. It was Signe calling from downtown San Antonio.

"You won't forget our dinner date tonight?"

"Of course not," I said, suddenly remembering.

"The Burnt Potato Club at nine-thirty. We'll have a drink and decide where to go. Right?"

"Right."

The Burnt Potato is a bar on Houston Street, downtown San Antonio. Outside there is a scrollwork of pink neon that says STRIPTEASE. SHOW NOW ON. TWELVE GIRLS. In the doorway there is a royal flush of girlie-pictures. I opened the door. The long room was dark but a tiny light behind the bar showed the bartender which shot glass held a full measure. I took a seat at the bar and a girl with sequin nipples nearly trod on my hand. The music ended and the girl took a bow and disappeared behind some plastic curtains. The barman said "S'it gonbee?" and I ordered a Jack Daniels. There were two girls near the jukebox but neither was Signe. My drink came and a girl's head came through the plastic curtains and shouted "Nineteen jay" to one of the girls at the jukebox. The jukebox moved convulsively and loud beat music began. The stripper gyrated slowly upon the tiny square of painted hardboard at the end of the bar. She unzipped her dress and hung it decorously on a coat hanger. Then she removed her underwear without overbalancing—a feat for which she was applauded

—and did a mammary swiveling walk along the bar top. I moved my hand away. The rhythm and movement became more orgastic until both ended in a sudden breathless silence. Another girl stepped out.

The bartender said, "What you think of the show?" He gave me my drink and a membership card. I said, "It's like eating chocolate with the wrapper still on."

"That's the trouble," said the bartender. He nodded.

I said, "Did you have a blond girl in here about nine-thirty?"

"Hey, is your name Dempsey?"

"Yes," I said. He passed me a note that was propped behind a bottle of Long John. The note said, *Urgent Sachmeyer's*. Then there was an address over in the Mexican sector near the Expressway. It was written in lipstick. As I put the note in my pocket the door swung open and two military policemen came into the bar. Their white caps and batons shone in the soft light reflected from the stripper's flesh. They watched the girl for a moment, then walked softly behind the row of men at the bar. The whole bar held its breath—then the two cops slid gently and silently into the street.

"Your doll?" asked the bartender. He didn't wait for a reply. "Great doll."

"Yes," I said.

"See, my name is Callaghan from the old country," he said.

"Yes," I said. "Well, I'm going to move along now."

"She's a joker, that girl of yours. Her friend came in and said 'reach for the sky' and pretended he had a gun and she played along with him right up to the time they left together. He was making all kinds of gags, too. She wrote that note while pretending to look in her handbag. They're real crazy friends, your friends. I like a sense of humor. You can't get along without it. Especially in my job. Why, take just the other day— Hey, you didn't finish your Jack Daniels."

The address Signe had written was south of Milam Square. Behind the Banana and Produce Company a derelict building was aflutter with torn posters. *First choice for District Judge Papa Schwartz, Reelect Sanders to legislature, Free parking for Funeral Home.* The streets were jammed tight with narrow shop fronts and grimy cafés. Religious statuettes and rat-traps shared a shopwindow with dog-eared movie magazines and loaded dice. I found the shop I wanted: an open Bible and a quote from it in Spanish written across the glass in whitewash. A large plastic sign in the doorway said SACHMEYER. DENTIST. *First Floor. Go Up.* I went up. There was a plain-fronted wooden door with a sign that said COME IN. It was locked. I felt along the ledge at the top of the door and sure enough the key was there. I let myself in. The first room was a waiting room, a ramshackle place where gray stuffing oozed from knife slashes across the plastic seats. I went into the surgery. It was a large room, with two windows, which flashed with neon from the sign outside. The neon sign made little clicks as it changed color. In the alternate pink-and-blue light I saw trays full of forceps and scalers, mouth lamps, mirrors and drills, and two trolleys with more of them. There was an X-ray machine, rolls of cotton wool balanced upon the water heater, matrix holders and impression trays, and small glass shelves smiling with false teeth. There was a huge adjustable chair with one of those disk lamps above it. In the dentist chair there was a man. His body slumped lifelessly like a torn rag doll. His head had slipped out of the supports and his hands almost touched the floor. He was a large man with a hooked nose and a deep-lined worried-looking face. From his mouth crawled a long, dead centipede of dried blood. He was pink and then blue and then pink and then blue. A motorcycle cop with his siren on went roaring along the elevated Expressway that was level with the surgery window. The siren died away into the hot distant night. I went close to the body. In the lapel there was an enamel badge with the FFF symbol. I don't know how long I remained staring at him but I was disturbed by the noise of voices in the waiting room. I picked up a dental chisel and resolved to sell my life dearly.

"Liam. Is that you, darling?" It was Signe's voice.

"Yes," I said.

"What are you doing in the dark, dearest?" she said, swinging into the room and switching all the lights on. Harvey was right behind her.

"We were waiting for you downstairs," he said. "Didn't expect you would prefer it up here with the molars." He laughed as though that was a particularly witty thing to say. There was another man behind Harvey who took off his jacket and slipped into a white coat. "I don't think I'd better join you," he said in a heavy German accent. "This fellow will be coming around any moment now."

Signe said, "Look at Liam's face."

"Thought you'd discovered a vile plot?" Harvey asked flippantly.

"Dr. Sachmeyer does the teeth of the American students at the Brain," Signe said. "You can spot a man's nationality from looking at his dental work. Dr. Sachmeyer has to give them European mouths."

"I'm starved," said Harvey. "Shall we have Chinese food or Mexican? Git along." He pointed his fingers like pistols and Signe raised her hands. "Dinner on me," said Harvey. "Maverick limey has negotiated the Hellfire of the Brain and the almighty trail-boss Midwinter has summoned him for a special assignment."

"What sort of assignment?" I asked.

"Assignment Danger. Da-da-da-di-da-da," said Harvey, imitating the opening chords of a TV serial.

"What kind of danger?" I asked, although I had already decided that Harvey was a little drunk.

"Being with the duchess," said Harvey, indicating Signe who struck him playfully. I had the idea they had been quarreling and hadn't quite made it up.

"That's the kind of danger I can handle," I said.

Harvey's hunger got the better of him only fifty yards down the street and even though Signe was keen to go downtown, Harvey had his way. It was a wide-open Mexican restaurant where the menu was painted across the window. The TV high in the corner was tuned to KWEX and the Spanish commentator was getting as frantic as the fighters. Below the screen, oblivious of the carnage, sat a group of downtowners radiating Guerlain and Old Spice and mixing with real people. Harvey ordered the complex Mexican food and it arrived promptly.

Harvey was clowning around pretending to be a gunman, which was his way of being sarcastic to me. Signe was being reserved and held my arm tightly all the time as though she was frightened of Harvey.

"What are you fidgeting around for?" Harvey asked her.

"It's so hot in here. Do you think I could go to the powder room and take off my girdle?" she said.

"Go ahead," said Harvey, "have a good time." But Signe didn't move. She was staring at me.

The word "girdle" solved a problem. The man in the dentist chair was the hook-nosed girdle salesman, Fragolli, who had been our contact in Leningrad. He didn't know anything about America. How could he possibly have American dental work? Harvey and Signe had hustled me out of there too quickly.

"That's right," I said midway through a mouthful of frijoles. "You two have been snowing me." I got up from the table.

Signe grabbed my arm tightly. "Don't leave," she said.

"You both lied," I said.

Signe looked at me with a wide-eyed look of sadness. "Stay here," she said and touched my fingers and stroked them.

"No," I said.

She lifted my hand and put the fingertips into her soft half-open mouth. I pulled my hand away from her.

One of the men at the corner table was saying ". . . where the most potent forces of nature were first revealed to man; that's why they call the swimsuit a bikini," and the downtowners all laughed.

Lighted shops painted yellow patches on the pavement and huddles of men stood here and there talking, arguing and gambling. The shop lights illuminated them as though they were valuable items on display in a museum. There was a curious all-enveloping blueness that nights in the tropics have, and on the air was the sweet smell of cumin and hot chili. I hurried back the way we had come, splashing through the puddles of yellow light and past a shop full of blue boxers fighting a vicious silent war. I brushed through a group of Mexicans and broke into a run. Past the Bible in the window I swung into the doorway of Sachmeyer's and up the stairs. At the door of the waiting room there was a man in shirt sleeves fanning himself with a straw hat. Under his arm was a heavy shoulder holster. Behind him in the doorway there was a policeman in blue shirt, bow tie, white crash helmet and riding breeches.

"What's the hurry?" said the tall cop.

"What's going on?" I said. To a policeman an immediate answer is a sure sign of guilt.

The man with the straw hat put it on his head and produced a lighted cigar from nowhere. He inhaled. "Dead punk in the dentist's chair. Now suppose you answer one of mine. Who in the name of Christ are you?" A siren grew very loud. There was a scream of tires outside.

"I'm an English reporter," I said. "I'm gathering local color."

Two more cops were clattering up the stairs with drawn guns. The switched-off siren was taking a long time to die. One of the cops behind me on the stairs put an armlock on me. The detective with the cigar spoke in the same unhurried voice. "Take this guy down to the station house. Show him a little local color. Maybe he'll tell you how he gets to know about murders in the city before you do."

"It's just local color I'm after," I said. "Not contusions."

The blades of the siren were still making a very low groan. The detective said, "Take it easy with the limey, we don't want Scotland Yard horning in on the case." All the policemen laughed. That detective must have been at least a captain.

The prowl-car boys handed me downstairs and gave me the hands-flat-against-the-roof-of-the-car routine while they frisked me. I stared into the blinding glare of the revolving light. Behind me I heard Harvey's voice say, "Hello, Bernie," and the voice of the detective said, "Hi, Harv." They were both being very relaxed. A bumper sticker on the police car said, *Your safety; our business.*

Harvey said, "This is one of our boys, Bernie. The General wants me to send him to New York tonight."

The cop finished frisking me and said, "Get in the car."

The detective said, "If the General's gonna be responsible for him . . . see, I might wanna see him again."

"Sure sure sure," said Harvey. "Listen, I've been with him for nearly three hours, Bern."

"O.K.," said the detective. "But you are kinda running up a backlog in my favor account."

"Yeah, I know, Bernie. I'll talk to the General about that."

"Do that," said the detective. I was glad it was so near election time. He shouted to the two cops to turn me over to Harvey.

"Come back and finish your frijoles," said Harvey. "That's how people get indigestion, jumping around like that in the middle of the meal."

"It isn't indigestion I'm frightened of," I said.

| *New York*

Hey diddle dinkety, poppety pet,
The merchants of London they wear
scarlet,
Silk in the collar and gold in the hem,
So merrily march the merchant men.

—NURSERY RHYME

CHAPTER 20

FIVE o'clock in the morning. Manhattan was blue with cold. In the hot lushness of southern Texas it had been easy to imagine that summer had arrived, but thirty seconds in New York City corrected that illusion. I was moving through midtown Manhattan in General Midwinter's chauffeur-driven Cadillac—the one with leopard skin seats. Five o'clock is the top-dead-center of the Manhattan night. Just for one hour the city is inert. The hearses have been brought up to the doors of the city hospitals but they haven't yet begun to load. The last cinema on 42nd Street has closed and even the billiard rooms have racked the cues and shut down. The cabs have vanished but the office cleaners haven't appeared. The fancy restaurants are closed but the coffee counters aren't open. The last wino has curled into newspaper and stretched out on the last bench in Battery Park. Down in Washington Produce Market they are huddled around the oil-drum fires. The news desks have released their radio cars as it's so cold even muggers have stayed at home, to the regret of patrolmen longing to thaw their ears in the precinct house. The city's seventy thousand wild cats have pounced upon pigeons in Riverside Park or Norwegian wharf rats in Washington Market, and now they too are asleep under the long lines of still cars. Even the Spanish-speaking radio stations are subdued. The only movement is compressed steam roaring along at three hundred miles an hour under the roadway, escaping now and again with a spectral puff, and the shuffle of wet newspapers as far as the eye can see down the long, long streets to the bloodshot dawn.

The car followed Broadway all the way to Wall Street, stopping outside a glass cliff that reflected the smaller buildings as though they were trapped inside it. A thin, shirtless man with a pistol and squeaky shoes unlocked the glass door, relocked it and led the way to a bank of lifts that were labeled *Express 41 to 50 only*. The man with the pistol chewed gum meditatively and spoke quietly as people do at night. "It's wonderful, ain't it?" he said. "Modern science." He pushed the elevator button for the third time.

"Yes," I said. "It's just a matter of time before the machines are pressing buttons to call people."

He repeated that to himself as the doors closed him out of sight. The elevator moved fast enough to make my ears pop and the numbers flickered like bingo results. It arrived with a ding. A man stood there in white trousers and a sweat shirt that said MIDWINTER MINING ATHLETIC TEAM across the front of it. "S'way feller," he said, and walked down the corridor making cracking noises by flicking a white towel against the air. At the end of the corridor there was a gymnasium. In the exact center of it, cycling methodically, was General Midwinter. "Come here, boy," he called. He was wearing a large pair of white shorts, a white singlet and white cotton gloves. "You made good time." He said it as if speaking to a packing case, pleased by the efficiency of his organization and transport. "I hear you felt the strain a little on my Active Course." He looked at me and winked. "I'm cycling from New York to Houston," he said.

"Five and three-quarters," said the man from the Midwinter Mining Athletic Team. Midwinter pedaled in silence for a moment or two, then he said, "Keep yourself fit, boy. Healthy mind in a healthy body. Get rid of that surplus weight."

"I'm happy the way I am," I said. Midwinter stared at his handlebars. "Self-indulgence goes hand in hand with titillation and pornography. Makes a country soft. These are weapons of Communism." His forehead was moist with his exertions. "The Russians hate pornography," I said.

"For themselves," said Midwinter. He was puffing a little now. "For themselves," he said again and waggled a finger at me. It was about this time that I realized Midwinter's winks were nervous twitches. He said, "They used to build ships of wood and men of iron. Now they build ships of iron and men of wood."

"The Russians?"

"No, not the Russians," said Midwinter.

The man in the athletic team shirt said, "Six miles exactly, General Midwinter." Midwinter climbed off the exercise machine, careful not to give away an extra inch. He reached behind him for a towel without looking to see if it was there. The man in the athletic team shirt made sure it was there, then he put a rubber glove over Midwinter's cotton-clad false hand. Midwinter walked across to the locker room and disappeared into the showers. There was the noise of water and Midwinter's loud voice said, "There are only two sorts of minds left today. Either you are going to have everything done for you by the Government, like you are some sort of invalid. Either you are going to have everything from diapers to derbys made in some State factory and your body'll wind up on some dump where they make fertilizer."

I said, "Spending my afterlife as fertilizer is the least of my problems."

Either Midwinter didn't hear or didn't choose to. His voice went on, ". . . or you believe that everyone is free to fight for what he believes is right." The sound of the water stopped but Midwinter didn't lower his voice. "That's what I believe. Luckily there's an awakening in this country of ours and a lot of other people are declaring that's what they believe too." There was a silence and when Midwinter appeared again he was in a white bathrobe. He stripped the rubber glove from his cotton-clad hand with a sucking sound, and threw it to the floor.

"I'm interested in facts," Midwinter said.

"Are you? Not many people are nowadays."

Midwinter spoke in a soft voice as though he was cutting me in on a very special deal. "A Gallop Poll found that eighty-one percent of Americans preferred nuclear war to Communism. In Britain, only twenty-one percent felt that way. Red-blooded Americans are rallying to anti-Communist leaders; no time now for internal arguments. The U.S.A. must double its spending on armaments. We must get an effective military satellite into orbit and the Russkies had better know we'll use it—we mustn't fritter away the lead as we did with the Atomic bomb—*we must double our expenditure right away*." He looked at me and did that nervous twitch with his eyes. "Got me?"

"I get you," I said. "It's that same America that broke away from George the Third because sixty thousand pounds was too much to pay toward the cost of the military. But even if what you suggest is a good idea, won't the USSR just go ahead and double her arms budget too?"

Midwinter patted me on the arm. "Maybe. But we spend ten percent of our gross national product at present. We could double that without suffering; but the USSR already spends twenty percent of her gross national product. If she doubles that, boy she will crack. Get me—she'll crack. Europe's got to stop hiding behind Uncle Sam's nuclear power. Get some of those Teddy Boys into uniform, get tough. Close ranks, hit them hard. Get me?"

"From where I'm sitting it sounds dangerous," I said.

"It is dangerous," said Midwinter. "Between 1945 and 1950 the Reds expanded at the rate of sixty square miles per hour. Retreat brings the threat of war closer because finally we're going to hit them, and I say the sooner the better."

I said, "I'm as keen on facts as you are, but facts are no substitute for intelligence. You think that the best way to contribute to a dangerous situation is to raise a private army out of your profits on cans of oil and beans, frozen orange juice and advertising, and to operate your own undeclared war against the Russians." He waved his good hand in the air; the large emerald ring flashed in the cold morning light.

"That's right, son. Khrushchev once said that he would support all interior wars against colonialism because he said, quote, they are in the nature of popular uprisings, unquote. Well, that's what I'm going to do in the territory the Reds occupy. Get me?"

I said, "That's the sort of decision I think only governments should make."

"I believe that a man is free to fight for what he believes is right." Midwinter's eye twitched again.

"Perhaps he is," I said. "But it's not you that does the fighting. It's poor little sods like Harvey Newbegin."

"Ease down, son," said Midwinter. "You are on rich mixture."

I looked at Midwinter and regretted trying to argue with him. I was weary of war and sick of hate. I was tired, and frightened of Midwinter because he wasn't tired. He was brave and powerful and determined. Politics was simple black-and-white toughness—like a TV western—and diplomacy was just a matter of demonstrating that toughness. Midwinter was formidable, he moved like a flyweight levitated by his confidence, he had all the brains that money could buy and he didn't have to look over his shoulder to know that plenty of Americans were marching behind him with side drum, fife and nuclear big stick. But a good agent should have a fast brain and a slow mouth, so I took it slowly. I said, "Is this your way of protecting America, employing second-rate hoodlums in Riga? Subsidizing violence and crime in the USSR? All that does is strengthen police and governmental power there."

"I'm talking about—" Midwinter said in a loud voice but this time my voice carried through.

"O.K. Inside America you are doing even more to assist the Russians. You spread false accusations and false fears through the land. You smear your Congress. You smear your Supreme Court. You even smear the Presidency. What you don't like about Communism is that you're not giving the orders. Well, I prefer America with ballot boxes and I prefer my orders to come out of a face instead of a telephone. You can't look a telephone in the eyes to see if it's lying."

I walked across the gymnasium and the sole survivor of the Midwinter Mining Athletic Team stared at me.

Midwinter moved fast. His good hand clenched my arm, "You'll stay," he said in a low voice. "You'll hear me out." I pulled away from him but the big man in the sweat shirt put himself between me and the door. "Tell him, Caroni," said Midwinter. "Tell him he's going nowhere till he hears me out." We stared at each other.

"O.K.," I said. "Now let go of my arm, you're creasing my only good suit."

"You're tired," said Midwinter. "You're on edge." His face moved from phase one—threat—to phase two—conciliation. "Caroni!" he shouted, "Get this feller a winter-weight suit, shoes, shirt and stuff. Take him along to my shower. And Caroni, give him a workout. He's been on a plane all night. Get him spruce. We'll have breakfast an hour from now."

"O.K., General," said Caroni without expression.

Midwinter said, "I'll stay here, Caroni. I'll do another three miles on the machine. That'll bring me to the Tennessee state line.

I had a shower and Caroni put me on a slab and punched hell out of my surplus fats while explaining some of the finer points of coronary heart disease. A suit—Dacron and worsted herringbone—came along as if by magic in one of those blue Brooks Brothers' boxes. By the time I was ushered up into Midwinter's private apartment at the top of his office block, I looked like I'd come to sell him insurance.

There was a table set with Scandinavian silverware and bright yellow linen. Unlike his uptown mansion this apartment was full of stainless steel, modern abstract paintings and the sort of chairs that have to be designed by architects. Midwinter was sitting under a Mathieu in a strange wiry throne that made him look like an actor in a bad film about spaceships. He had a pair of 10 x 50's glued to his face and was staring out of the window.

"Know what I'm watching?" he said.

From here the view was magnificent. There was the Statue of Liberty and Ellis Island and, scarcely visible in the mist, the tip of Staten Island. The waves of the bay were cold and gray, and each one was flecked with dirty spume. Half a dozen tugs lurched toward the Hudson River, and the Staten Island ferry was beginning to pack the commuters tight.

"One of the big boats coming in?" I asked.

"I'm watching hawks, three foot across, peregrine falcons, they eat small birds." He put the binoculars down. "They live in those ornamented buildings. Gothic church towers they like especially. I watch them hunting most mornings. Real speed. Real style." He turned to look at me "Say," he said suddenly very loud, "that suit looks great! Did Caroni get that for you?"

"Yes," I said.

"Well, I'll have him get me one just like it."

"Look, Mr. Midwinter," I said, "I appreciate compliments from rich busy men especially insincere ones because they don't have to butter up anyone if they don't want to. But sometimes it makes me uneasy, so if it's all the same to you I'd rather hear what you want right now."

"You are a direct young man," said Midwinter. "I like that. Americans like a little preamble before business—a little how's-your-lovely-wife-and-beautiful-children—before soliciting the order. You British don't do that, huh?"

"I wouldn't want to mislead you, Midwinter," I said. "A lot of them do."

Midwinter put the binoculars on the table and poured coffee for both of us. He was well into the scrambled eggs on toast before he spoke again and then it was only to inquire if I was enjoying it. The last morsel disappeared and Midwinter fidgeted with his lips and patted them with a napkin while staring at me. He said, "Your friend Harvey Newbegin has deserted."

"Deserted?"

"Deserted."

"In my vocabulary you only desert from armies. Do you mean he has left your employ?"

"I mean he has left the country." He watched me carefully. "Surprised, eh? I had his sweet little wife on the phone during the night. He went across the border—the Mexican border—right after he left you last night. We figure he's going over to the Russians."

"What makes you think so?"

"You disagree?"

"I didn't say that."

"Ah!" shouted Midwinter. "You agree, eh? Sure, son. He set you up for that beating you took. If those Russian cops hadn't moved in you'd be dead. To tell you the truth, I'd sooner have you dead and my boys still free but that doesn't change the fact that Harvey had them give you the treatment. Then after the Communist cops had you in captivity they suddenly took you to witness an arrest. Why do you think they did that?"

"I'd say they took me there so I should come back soiled."

"Right," said Midwinter. "Why?"

"You shift the blame of betrayal to protect a betrayer."

"Right," said Midwinter. "Newbegin had already made a deal with the Communists but he could escape blame for a short extra period by setting you up as a patsy. You got that, eh? You suspected Newbegin?"

"That's it," I said.

"I get a blast out of you, son. You can really sort the mustangs from the broncos." He flashed me a friendly smile.

"Yes," I said. "But I don't see what you expect me to do."

"I want you to bring this guy Harvey Newbegin back here." Midwinter pointed to an empty chair by the window to tell me exactly where he wanted him put. "I don't care what it costs. Cuff the tabs for anything you want. Use any of my people, I can get you full cooperation of the police anywhere in the States . . ."

"But he's not in the States," I said patiently.

"Well, you dope it out," said Midwinter. "All I know is that you are maybe the only living person who knows Harvey New-begin as a close friend. There are plenty of people who can find him, but the guy who finds him has got to be able to talk some sense into the guy. What's more," added Midwinter archly, "I figure you've got a motive not to be too well disposed to him."

"When you hook a sucker, reel him in slowly," I said. "Being the archetype Judas is not my kind of image."

"No offense, son," said Midwinter. "Maybe you can get yourself more than half killed and still be tolerant and professional. If you can, I admire that, I admire it. There are no personality failures here either—the organization is paramount. That organization means more to me than anything else in the world. If Harvey Newbegin takes the sort of information he has to the Russians, I'll never forgive myself."

I said, "And you'll probably have the CIA squeezing you to death as a security risk."

Midwinter nodded nervously. "Yes," he said. "Expect I'll fall down and go boom." He hammered the edge of his false hand against the table like a karate expert warming up.

"There's another factor," said Midwinter. "There is this girl named . . ." He pretended to search his memory.

"Signe Laine," I supplied.

"Right," said Midwinter. "Is she reliable?"

"She's reliable for some things," I said.

"She's emotionally entangled with Harvey Newbegin," Midwinter pronounced. "The Laine girl is a member of our organization. In the ordinary way of things I would have given her the task of contacting Harvey but under the circumstances . . ." He tapped his hand again. "You are the only person. Don't let him fall into the hands of the Russians."

"He's already been in the hands of the Russians," I said.

"You know what I mean," Midwinter said. "I mean predicting, analyzing our movements and decisions. You know what I mean. They mustn't have him as an adviser."

"What you want is Harvey Newbegin dead," I said.

"Down boy," said Midwinter. "I've loved Harvey Newbegin and his wife for many years. Harvey is a vain, neurotic personality. I've already spoken to his analyst this morning. He agrees with me, Newbegin lives in a fantasy world, sexually, romantically, politically and socially. Already he's having doubts about what he's doing. Speak to him. Tell him"—the old man's soft mottled face wrinkled as though it was about to fall off—"tell him he's forgiven. We won't mention it again and he can have a year or so taking it easy in the sun. Tell him I'll even speak to Mercy. I'll tell her to take the heat off him."

"Perhaps you should have told her that a long time ago," I said.

"I should have," said Midwinter. He buttered a piece of toast with the wrist action of a swordsman and then bit a corner from it. "She just wanted the best for her husband."

"So did Lady Macbeth," I said.

Out on the gray water the harbor patrol boat had anchored while a cop in a zipper jacket stabbed at a floating bundle. Midwinter chewed at his toast. "I should have," he said again.

"I'll go now," I said. I put the hand-embroidered napkin on the table.

The cops fixed the bundle to the boat and chugged away.

"You'll bring home the groceries all right," said Midwinter.

"Perhaps," I said.

A frown passed across Midwinter's face as he wondered whether to tell me the penalty of failure. I imagine most of Midwinter's meetings ended with the penalty of failure. We stared at each other, then Midwinter said, "You'll bring home the groceries" through gritted teeth, determined to end on a note of encouragement.

"O.K.," I said. "You've been frank with me and now I'll be frank with you. First of all, you had better learn that your organization in northern Europe is pretty thin on the ground."

Midwinter said, "I'll tell you exactly—"

"Hear *me* out," I said. "Newbegin has been feeding you phantom agents for a long time. He operates a swindle with your money. He pays a package of money to one of your agents, who then passes it on to a second real agent who passes it on to a third agent who just happens to be Harvey Newbegin dressed up in fancy disguise. Harvey then puts the money in the bank for himself. He probably does that for every network to which he has access. The rest of the network is just a lot of fancy paper work."

"A month ago I wouldn't have believed it," said Midwinter.

"Well, you had better be believing now," I said, "because a lot depends on it. I know some of those phony networks and where he puts the money, but to be sure of getting Newbegin I shall have to know them all and there's no time to waste."

Midwinter said, "What are you getting at?"

I said, "I shall need to collect from the Brain the details and photos of all your agents who had access to Harvey Newbegin."

"That's Finland and Great Britain. Two key areas," said Midwinter. "Our whole pilot operation."

"Good," I said. "Just clear me to have that information and show me the telephone codes to get it."

"It's rather complex," said Midwinter, playing for time. "And what's more, you could smash our whole operation."

"It's smashed already," I said. "You couldn't use any of those agents if Harvey Newbegin is spitting blood."

"Perhaps that's true," said Midwinter, "but the normal procedure would be to keep them *abgeschaltet* * until the Russians surface Newbegin or we find him."

"That's my deal," I said. "When you first said that I was the only man who could get close to Newbegin I didn't believe you. But you're right. I'm the only person."

"You could smash up my whole scheme." He stared at me blank and unblinking. "It's too much."

"O.K.," I said, "I'll give you a bonus."

"What's that?" said Midwinter.

"Most of the money that Harvey Newbegin stole from you was paid into the Bexar County National Bank, 235 North Saint Mary's, San Antonio, to the account of Mrs. Mercy Newbegin."

The old man crumpled as if I had hit him in the face.

"O.K.," said Midwinter. "You don't have to buffalo me. You knew I had to agree."

So I let him come to terms with his betrayal by Mercy New-begin—keeper of his left hand—as slowly as he wished to. He put the binoculars over his eyes and stood immobile, staring out across the sea. When he spoke it was without looking around.

"Be here at noon, ask for the chief technical manager of Midwinter Mining. He'll be on the Midwinter Science Foundation floor waiting for you. He'll tell you everything you want to know."

"Thanks for the suit," I said. "Take it out of my wages."

"I shall," said Midwinter. He hammered his false hand against the table edge very, very gently as though exercising tremendous restraint. As I walked out, I heard the buzzer on

---

* Jargon: *Abgeschaltet* means lit., switched off, unused. To "surface" someone is to announce their capture or defection. This is often long after it happens.

Midwinter's communication box. Caroni's voice said, "There's a hawk now, General Midwinter, on the bell tower."

The foyer of Midwinter's building was crowded with neat, slim young men with short hair and faces dusted with talc. Each one was labeled with his name and rank on a conference badge. They moved through the foyer as though spilled from a tin. A uniformed guard said, "Are you with the Frozen Juice Convention?" but the man with squeaky shoes said, "It's O.K., Charlie. He's been to see the General." Outside, the morning was freezing cold and getting darker.

As I walked along the street, Midwinter's chauffeur called to me from the slow-moving Cadillac. He held up the phone that rested on the car dashboard. "The General," he explained, waving the handpiece. "He says I'm to be at your disposal."

"Thank him," I said. "And then get lost. Big black Caddies make my sort of friends nervous."

"Mine too," said the chauffeur and shot off into the Brooklyn Tunnel traffic happily. There was a backfire, and a formation of sparrows banked sharply and twittered away, unaware of the hawks watching them from above.

I got a cab to Signe's place on Eighth Street. I rang the bell and knocked at the door but there was no reply. I went down the street to the Cookery Coffee Shop, got some dimes and phoned the number I had been given as a contact. Midwinter's organization was really on its toes, because already the number had been switched through to Midwinter's personal phone.

"Keep watching him, Caroni," I heard Midwinter say. Then his voice was close. "Midwinter here."

"Dempsey. I'm going to need someone to stake out an address in the city."

"Cop?"

"A cop will do fine," I said.

"I'll have the first one there in ten minutes," said Midwinter.
"Give me the address." A cab passed the window.

"Forget it," I said, "the party I want is arriving right now."

"Newbegin?"

"It's not going to be that easy," I said. "I'll keep in touch."
Midwinter was saying "Where are you?" as I rang off. I
walked across the street and gave Signe's cab time to get clear.

When Signe saw me she hugged me and laughed and sniffed
and cried. I picked up her Braniff Airlines bag and two boxes
that said *Shoes by Frost* and carried them up to her apartment.
She went across to the mirror, "Thank God you are all right,"
she said looking in the mirror. She produced a man's handkerchief and dabbed carefully around her eyes so that the eye
makeup didn't smudge. "Harvey wanted to leave you in the
surgery. He wanted to have you arrested. I argued with him."
She turned back to me from the mirror. "I saved you," she
said.

"Thanks."

"Don't mention it. I only saved you, that's all."

"So what do you want me to do; buy you a pair of shoes?"

"He's left his wife. He wanted me to go away with him, but
I wouldn't go."

"Go where?"

"I don't know. I don't think he knows. He upset me. I
couldn't leave as suddenly as that. I have books and furniture
here, and more things in Helsinki. I couldn't just leave as suddenly as that." She helped me off with my coat and ran her
cold fingers across my face as if to reassure herself that I was
real.

"What was the final arrangement?"

"Harvey said it was now or never as far as leaving his wife
was concerned. He wanted to run away with me. I don't love
him. Well, I don't love him like that. I don't love him enough

to run off and live with him. I mean, loving someone is one thing and running off . . ." She paused in order to cry but decided against it. "I'm so mixed up. Why do men take everything so seriously? They ruin everything by taking every little thing I say seriously."

"When were you due back in Helsinki?"

"Three days' time."

"Harvey knows that?"

"Yes."

"He'll write or cable you. Do whatever he says."

"I can handle Harvey all right," Signe said. "I don't need lessons."

"I wasn't going to offer you any."

"I can handle him. He likes stories." She gave a little sob. "That's why I love him, because he likes my stories."

"You don't love him," I reminded her, but she wanted to enjoy her big scene.

"Only in a way," she said. "I love to have him around."

"Yes," I said, "but you love to have all sorts of people around." She put her arms around my waist and gripped me tight.

"Harvey isn't an ambitious man," said Signe, "and in this city that's a crime. You've got to be aggressive, pushing and making money. Harvey is good and kind." I kissed her wet eyes. She sobbed incoherently and thoroughly enjoyed it. Through the window I saw a yellow poster. The man on the poster was making a scene in a restaurant. Is THIS SOMEONE YOU KNOW? the poster said. TROUBLEMAKER. TROUBLESOME PEOPLE ARE OFTEN PEOPLE IN TROUBLE. SHOULD YOU HELP THEM? COULD YOU HELP THEM? BETTER MENTAL HEALTH, Box 3000 NY 1.

When Signe spoke again her voice was quiet and very grown-up. "Harvey knows all about that computer machinery, doesn't he?" She paused. "If he tried to go to Russia, would they want to have him killed?"

"I don't know."

"How important is that machinery? Is it as vital as they say?"

"Computers are like Scrabble games," I told her. "Unless you know how to use them, they're just a boxful of junk."

Round and round the garden
Like a teddy bear;
One step, two step,
Tickle you under there!

—NURSERY RHYME

CHAPTER 21

MARCH. London looked like the bed of a drained aquarium. Continuous rain and frost had attacked last summer's hastily applied paint. The white bones of the city were showing through its soft flesh, and lines of parked, dirty vehicles looked abandoned. At Charlotte Street the staff was rubbing its hands together to keep them warm and wearing that martyred expression that other nations keep for sieges.

"Come in," Dawlish called. He was sitting in front of a tiny coal fire and prodding at it with an old French infantry bayonet that was bent at the sharp end. Dawlish needed the daylight from his two windows: it filtered through his collection of slightly broken antiques that he had bought recklessly and then had second thoughts about. Everything smelled of moth-balls and aged dust. He had an umbrella stand made from an elephant's foot, a glass-fronted bookcase jammed with sets of Dickens, Balzac, and bright little books that told you how to recognize a Ming vase if you found one on an old barrow in the market. Unfortunately for Dawlish, most of the people with barrows had read those same books. On the walls there were cases of butterflies and moths—one of them with a badly cracked glass—and a dozen small framed photos of cricket teams. Visitors to the office played the game of deciding which was Dawlish in each team, but Jean said he had bought the whole lot cheap on a barrow. I put my six-page memo on his desk. The dispatch department—where the duty drivers sat around drinking tea—was playing gramophone records, brass band music, always brass band music.

"Want to buy an old Riley?" Dawlish said. One large flat slab of coal was giving him trouble.

"You're selling it?" He was very attached to his old car.

"I don't want to," Dawlish said, the even flow of his words distorted by the spiteful attacks he was making upon the piece of coal. "But it has just become impossible to carry on with it. Every time I drive it away from the repairers a new noise begins. I'm becoming a mechanical hypochondriac."

"Yes," I said. "I suppose it's expendable."

Dawlish abandoned the attempt to split the piece of coal. "Everything is expendable," he said. "Everything. When it gives more trouble than it's worth, no matter what the sentimental attachment might be." He waved the red-hot poker at me.

"That's right," I said. I was looking at the case of butterflies on the wall. "Wonderful colors," I said. Dawlish grunted and prodded at the coal. He still failed to break it. He built a couple of extra pieces up on it. "What are the Socialists going to do about the public schools?" he asked.

I was one of the few grammar school boys that Dawlish ever came in contact with. He considered me an authority on all aspects of left-wing politics. He levered the coal up with the bayonet and left it impaled there. The rush of air through the lifted coal made the fire spit like a kitten but it didn't catch light.

"Send their sons to them," I said.

"Really?" said Dawlish without too much interest. He clapped his hands to free them of coal dirt and wiped them on a duster. "They will make a formidable pressure group— working-class flagellants."

"Oh, I don't know, 'Down with the beer that is bitter, up with the wine that is sweet'— What's more working class than that?"

"Eton," said Dawlish, "that's not a public school; that's group therapy for congenital deviates." Dawlish was a Harrow man.

"Therapy?" I said, but Dawlish was watching the fire anxiously. A downdraught filled the room with a sudden billow of smoke. "Damn," Dawlish said but he did nothing about it, and soon the fire began to burn properly again.

He removed his spectacles and cleaned them carefully with a large handkerchief. When he was pleased with them he put them on and tucked the handkerchief into his sleeve. It was a sign that we should begin to talk business. He read the notes. At the end of each page he sniffed. When he had finished, he patted the sharp corners into alignment and stared at them as he tried to concentrate all the information known to him into one organic lump. "One good thing about the criminal activities of your friend Harvey Newbegin—by inventing personnel in order to pocket their wages he has left us with only a small number of Fact-free men to worry about." He removed one sheet of paper from my report and placed it in the very center of his desk. I expected him to quote something from it but he reamed out his pipe on it and the charred pieces fell exactly upon its center. "Sweden. Plenty there. We've been comparatively lucky." He tipped the dirt into the wastebasket and then blew on the paper before reading it. "You make penetrating the Midwinter people sound too easy," he said.

"Purposely," I said. "Since the CIA and the State Department are supporting it, I want them to know that in spite of the gloss, it's still an amateur setup and it will never be anything better."

Dawlish shook his head. "You're too ambitious, my boy, too anxious to share our secrets with the world. We've got Midwinter's johnnies taped now, why alert them? Why help them improve their security? Better a devil you know than a devil you don't know."

"I'd like to see them discredited. I'd like to see all these privately owned outfits discredited."

"Discredited?" Dawlish scoffed. "Discredit is a state of mind. Your mind works like that chap Kaarna's. How much did he finally discover, by the way?"

"He stumbled upon the network, heard their story about being British and believed it. He got his hands on some eggs but didn't know where they'd come from or where they were going. Being a journalist, he began guessing. He was still guessing when they killed him."

"Is Newbegin going to defect to the Russkies?" Dawlish wrote something on his notepad.

"Who knows what he's likely to do? He's been embezzling from Midwinter's network for ages. He must have made a fortune. Since he sent most of the same information to the Russians as well, he probably has a healthy account at the Moscow National Bank."

"Enterprising joker Newbegin," said Dawlish approvingly. "I rather liked the way he stole the virus eggs from you instead of merely receiving them from you. Terribly good that, not a likely suspect; the man who is due to take delivery."

"He's good at avoiding blame," I agreed. "He did a similar

sort of trick with Ralph Pike—after he went to all that trouble to send him off by plane—who'd suspect he tipped the Russians off to expect him?"

"And to cap it all," said Dawlish, "he asks Stok not to arrest Ralph Pike until you are there to take the blame for betraying him." Dawlish blew through his unlit pipe. "Jolly good stuff. Keeps us all on our toes, stuff like that."

"Us?" I said. "I haven't noticed you up on the points lately."

"Figuratively. I was speaking figuratively." He filled his pipe and lit it. "But why—if Stok and Harvey Newbegin are so friendly—did Stok save you from a violent end at the hands of the holdup men?"

"Stok's frightened of the paper work involved in my death. The questions from Moscow. He's frightened of the sort of retaliation his people here would get. Make no mistake. Stok is a very rough customer," I said. "The people who work with him call him Beef Stroganoff because he pours so much cream over you that you don't notice you're being cut into shreds. But Stok doesn't want a mess on his doorstep any more than we do."

Dawlish nodded and wrote a little note about it.

"So what are you doing to locate Newbegin?"

"I'm covering three angles. One, he might have one last go at getting this virus to Russia as his entrance fee. We know the eggs come from Porton MRE and we have a photo of Midwinter's agent there that I had their computer send from San Antonio. The MRE security people there are watching him closely but won't do anything except keep us informed if he tries to pinch more. Two: Newbegin might want to put his hands on some of the money he has salted away, so I have put a search through the British banks for any blocked account that has San Antonio as a base. Three: Harvey Newbegin is

madly in love with this Finnish girl Signe Laine so I have someone watching her. . . ."

"I wouldn't count too much on that line of inquiry," Dawlish
said. "A man doesn't desert his wife and two children for a
young girl that he's already had an affair with."

"Four," I continued. "I have people checking passenger lists
of aircraft destined for Leningrad, Moscow and Helsinki."

"He could slip past all that," said Dawlish. "He's an actor,
remember that. You can't apply normal standards to people
whose greatest ambition is to listen to hands smacking together."

"Possibly so," I said. "But I think we have to keep a sense
of perspective on this thing. If he does defect to the Russians,
as long as he doesn't have the virus, it's not going to be the
most terrible thing that ever happened."

"What makes you think that?"

"It's something I learned when ordered to give those gents
from the Foreign Office their airline tickets and whisk them
away from the Special Branch boys."

"Ah," said Dawlish, "but had they faced trial it was a matter
that would have embarrassed the Government. There are such
things as elections, you know."

I knew that Dawlish was just provoking me because we had
enjoyed this argument at least twice before. It wasn't that
Dawlish disagreed strongly, he liked to see me angry.

Dawlish read down the rough notes again. "This fellow in
the dentist's chair; how do you know he was dead?"

"The policeman said so."

"The policeman said so." Dawlish nodded. "And you of
course believed him. Why, you can't even be sure that he was
a policeman. He wasn't in uniform."

"He was working there with policemen all around him," I
said patiently.

Equally patiently Dawlish said, "And I am working here

with imbeciles all around me but that doesn't make me an imbecile."

"Do you want a second opinion?"

"Leave it all out of the report. If the Minister thinks I have people here who can't even recognize a corpse when they see one . . ." he tutted. It all looked so damn easy if you sat in Dawlish's chair and read the reports; it was useless to explain that there were always loose ends unless you faked the report up.

Dawlish said, "I've an official request on the teleprinter. I'm to locate Newbegin and hold him and inform the Americans. On no account, this message says, must Newbegin fall into the hands of the Russians. On no account, you know what that means?"

"Yes," I said.

"Right," said Dawlish. "Well, that's official. That's not your Freefactmen or whatever they call themselves. That's the U.S. State Department speaking through the Cabinet. That's your orders. That's official." Dawlish took off his spectacles and pinched the bridge of his nose while closing his eyes as tightly as possible. When he opened them he seemed mildly surprised that I, and the whole office, hadn't disappeared. We looked at each other deadpan for a moment or so. When he spoke again he spoke very slowly. "Speaking personally," Dawlish said, "I hope that Harvey Newbegin isn't found anywhere in my territory. I hope Newbegin stays well away from here and gets arrested somewhere like Helsinki. I'll then arrange that his playmates—Dr. Pike and company—are put into the bag by someone like the Porton Security people. All nice and quietly parochial. But if it's done the other way, with us arresting Harvey Newbegin and the story about these Pike brothers stealing viruses from Porton being told to an American interrogator, the whole thing will blow up into a big front-page sensation.

We can't serve D notices to newspapers in America, my boy."

"Your point is well taken, sir," I said.

"That's why I would like you to come off this case," said Dawlish. "At the next stage you are going to come up against all manner of problems because you are too close to the personalities involved."

"I must stay on it for exactly that reason."

"The authorities in their infinite wisdom have decreed that I run this department," Dawlish said in a good-natured way. "So don't cast me as Don Quixote to your Sancho."

I said, "Then perhaps you would stop casting me as Sam Weller to your Pickwick."

Dawlish nodded wisely. "Are you sure that you could do all that might be needed?" he asked. "It could mean a bit of brute strength and ignorance. I mean, Newbegin . . . well, you know. He can be a rough customer."

"I'll see to it," I said. "Satisfaction guaranteed."

"My satisfaction has precedence."

"Yes," I said. Dawlish picked up the shiny brown sphere that the Midwinter organization gave each of its graduates.

"Soil of Freedom," I explained.

"Yes." Dawlish shook it, sniffed it and listened to it. "I thought someone had been soiling it."

"It's American dirt," I said.

Dawlish put it back on the desk. "Well, we don't want any of that," he said. "We've got enough dirt of our own."

CHAPTER 22

I SPENT the next three days like a cat watching mouseholes. Harvey Newbegin had been at the game a long while. He ignored the instructions on his brain sequence and he kept well away from all the people we were watching. On the other hand, our people in Leningrad didn't catch a sight of him either. On the evening of the third day I left the office about six and went to Schmidt's to pick up some groceries. When I got back to the parked car and switched the phone on, the operator was putting out an urgent repeat call. "Oboe ten, oboe ten. Northern Car Hire control to oboe ten. I have an urgent message for you oboe ten come in please." At first I thought it was just going to be Dawlish trying to catch me for an extra evening on duty officer. People who live in the center of town are always getting emergency standbys because those who live in places like Guildford just say it will take them another hour to get back to Charlotte Street and by that time the crisis is over. Anyway I answered the car phone and they said that a customer named Turnstone wanted to contact me. Please phone on the landline. Turnstone was the code name for the whole business with Newbegin, so since I was only a few yards from the office I went along to the Charlotte Street control room. The building that houses the ghost phone exchange, ciphers, and a lot of overflow people from South Audley Street is a large new building right next door to one in which I worked. I went up to my own office and across into the new block, because you could spend half an hour trying to get past the doorman of the new block even if you were a relative of the Prime Minister.

Bessie was in the control room when I went in there. The communications people had arranged to have an operator on full time watch on the Turnstone operation. Bessie knew all the details.

She said, "There's a Special Branch constable watching a doctor's surgery near King's Cross."

"For a man named Pike," I said.

"That's right," said Bessie. "It's a man named Pike. This man Newbegin visited the surgery this evening—I have the times on the message sheet—and left just ten minutes ago."

"I understand," I said. "Go on."

"Well, the constable has a penceiver—that's a little thing like a fountain pen that I can make a buzzing noise on if I press that key there—I'll press it now." She pressed it with an exaggerated show of strength to make it clear to me. "Now that makes the penceiver buzz. Now the constable knows that you are ready to receive a message from him. Of course I didn't know you would actually be up here on the switchboard so I was going to switch the call through to whatever line you came in on." A white light came up on the board. "That's his acknowledgment," Bessie said. There was nothing to do then except hang around talking to Bessie until the Special Branch constable was able to get near a telephone and call us.

"Next year," said Bessie, "they are going to have some satellite receivers and we will be able to draw lines on a map to show where the penceiver is transmitting from."

"Very Dick Tracy," I said.

"No," she said. "In America they have much more advanced things than this."

"So I hear," I said. "How's Ossie?" Bessie Butterworth's husband Austin did free-lance jobs for us from time to time.

"Not too well," said Bessie. "He's not getting any younger, you know. I said to him the other day, You're not getting any younger, Austin. Now that the children have grown up and left us we can manage on my money, but he likes to work now and again. I suppose it's the same with all of us. You get to be good at your job, to take a pride in it, and then you find it's difficult to give up. He's been working since he was fifteen. Well—it's natural to him now, like breathing."

"Planned your holiday?"

"Imperial Hotel Torquay. We always go there. As Austin says, they know us and we know them. We always go there. Every year. Sometimes I'd like a change but they know us and we know them, so Austin likes it."

"Yes," I said. The buzzer went.

Bessie said, "This will be him. This number is only for him. Yes. I'll put you through. Exchange greetings. Remember this is an open line."

I said, "Rita Hayworth." The voice at the other end said, "Love Goddess," then he said, "Suspect answers to the description of Harvey Newbegin. He is now driving south."

Quite calmly I said, "And you've let him drive away."

The constable said, "Don't be alarmed, sir. This isn't a bicycle and notebook job. We have two cars with him as well as another constable with me on foot."

"I thought I was being very restrained under the circumstances."

"Yes, sir," said the constable. "It's quite a conspicuous car to follow, sir. One of those little bubble cars. A Heinkel, I think."

"Conspicuous in what way?"

"Well, in the first place, it's pillar-box red. Secondly, it had a sign in the front that says 'This is a transistorized Rolls Royce' and thirdly, someone has written 'learn how to park, you berk' in the dust on the rear window."

When I told Bessie that there was a car following it, she connected us to the Metropolitan Police information room and we heard the police car reporting Harvey's driving right through central London, over Waterloo Bridge, Waterloo Road, Elephant and Castle. Bessie wrote down the address outside which Harvey had parked.

Bessie handed it to me with a puzzled expression. "That's your . . ."

"My address," I said. "Yes, exactly where I would be right now if there hadn't been a call for me."

I got back to my flat and Harvey was still ringing the doorbell and a plainclothes constable was talking to Harvey and complaining about how late I was. As I arrived, the plainclothes policeman said something about collecting some papers but I told him they wouldn't be ready till morning.

"Good thing," said Harvey. "That guy being here to collect documents. That's how I knew you were due back any moment."

I grunted and wondered whether Harvey believed it. I fixed coffee for him while he went poking through my bookshelves. *"The Fall of Crete, Histoire de l'Armée Française. Buller's Campaign. Weapons and Tactics.* What are you—some kind of nut about soldiers?"

"Yes," I answered from the kitchen.

"Crazy stuff to read," said Harvey. "Haven't you got any books that a bum like me can understand?"

"Wouldn't have them in the house," I said and took him a cup of coffee.

"I've left my wife," Harvey said. "I'm never going back."

"I'm sorry."

"At least I won't have to worry whether I can afford to send the kids to camp." He gave a forced chuckle. "You know I've cleared out of the Midwinter setup?"

"Yes, I know."

"Would your people—" he was searching his pockets— "would your people . . ." He looked up.

"Would my people what?"

"Give me a home."

"No," I said. "English homes have American landlords."

"I'd pay rent. I'd give them details of the Midwinter Group U.K. Photos . . . everything."

I said, "I've already taken details of the Midwinter Northern Europe Group. Photos . . . everything."

"So," said Harvey. "Midwinter taught you how to collect data and pictures over a phone line from the Compuscan. I see. Well, in that case you can bust up the whole group any time you like. Are they looking for me?"

"You are a source of embarrassment to my masters, Harvey. They don't want to employ you and they don't want to arrest you. They just want you to vanish." Harvey nodded.

"But when you go," I continued, "let me arrange things. The military and the Ministry are in on the act now. One of their people gets a little overkeen and . . ." I shrugged and made a nasty noise.

"O.K.," said Harvey. "I'll let you know." He stood up. He was wearing one of those very English tweed suits that they sell only in America. He searched his pockets, sifting through keys, credit cards and screwed-up paper money and pushing it back again. He said, "Do you ever have that feeling, I have it sometimes, that all the men in the world are moving so fast that they are burning up? Thinking. All the women are standing still and you are whizzing past them at a tremendous speed, you know, burning up with thinking." He stopped and I didn't speak. Soon he began again, not caring very much if I was listening. "They will all be here, just as static, having babies and setting their hair. Still. Very still. Like grass just before a storm. Other men will be here, moving at the same sort of speeds and also burning themselves out; but the women will be still." He began to search through more junk. "What do they do with all that money?" he asked. "My wife swallows money like salted peanuts; can't get enough of it. Money money money; that's all she ever thinks about."

"What's that?" I asked.

"Rabbit's foot. It's supposed to be lucky," said Harvey. It was a poor shriveled piece of fur and bone.

"Tell that to the rabbit."

Harvey nodded. He found the wrinkled photo of Signe and looked at it to assure himself that she existed. "I've got to talk to her again," he said. He twitched the photo around to show me whom he meant. "She says she doesn't love me anymore but I know she does. I'm seeing her again in Helsinki. I'll persuade her."

I nodded unenthusiastically.

"You don't understand," said Harvey. "Something like this happens only once in a lifetime. Look at her—the texture of her hair, soft hands, her skin. She has youth."

"We all had that once," I said.

"Not like that."

"Well, I . . ."

"I'm serious," said Harvey. "Very few people have this quality, this secret quality. It frightens me. She's soft and trusting and vulnerable; like an injured animal. It was weeks after I first saw her that I ever had the nerve to speak to her. I used to go home at night and say please God make her love me. Please God I'll never ask you for anything again if you make her love me. Even now when I see her, I stand staring at her like a farm boy among the tall buildings. I first saw her coming out of a shoe shop. I followed her to the office where she worked, I hung around at lunchtime and finally one evening in a restaurant, I spoke to her. Even now I just can't believe that she loves me. I can't believe it." Harvey sipped at his coffee and I thought, So much for Dawlish's guess, and felt pleased that I was right, so far. "Innocence," said Harvey. "That's what she has, you see. To an innocent, anything in the world is possible because there's no experience programmed into the memory to tell you that things aren't possible. You see, innocence is the knowledge you can do something and experience is the knowledge that you can't."

"Experience is a method of endorsing prejudices," I said.

"No," said Harvey. "When did you last call on your experience? When you doubted your chances of success, that's when."

I said, "Have some more coffee." It was no good having a normal sort of discussion with Harvey. I said, "You are manic-depressive, upward phase, Harvey."

"That's it," said Harvey. "And I'm a little sick."

"Are you?" I said.

"You're smiling, but I have a temperature of one hundred and two."

"How do you know?"

"I carry a thermometer, that's how I know. Do you want me to take your temperature?"

"No, why the hell should I?"

"It's a good thing you are fit and well. Just in case something happens to me."

"If you are really sick I'll call a doctor."

"No, I'm fine, fine. I'm really fine." The way he said it, it meant I'd rather die in harness.

"Just as you prefer," I said.

"You can collapse with a thing like I've got. It can be nasty." He picked up a bottle of Long John and looked at me and I nodded and he poured out half a tumbler of Scotch for each of us and drank half his own in one gulp. "This girl," he began again, "you don't know what she's been through."

"Tell me," I said.

"Well," said Harvey, "although he has never had proper international recognition, Signe's father was the brains behind the invention of the atomic bomb. After the war it affected him. He felt guilty and became very morose and all he wanted to do was to listen to Sibelius. Well, they were quite a wealthy family so he could afford to have an orchestra along to this enormous house they had in Lapland and he would just sit and listen to Sibelius all day and all night. Sometimes there would be nothing to eat in the house and this orchestra would still go on playing. It must have been terrible for Signe because her mother was in an iron lung. Can you imagine that?"

"Easily," I said. "Easily."

Harvey stayed on, talking and drinking his way through my supply of whisky. At nine o'clock I suggested that we might go out and eat.

"Boil an egg," he said. "I don't want much." I fixed some steak and pizza from the freezer while Harvey tried his hand on my old Bechstein. Harvey only knew a few songs and they were a strange collection: "Two Little Girls in Blue," "The Wearing of the Green," "I'll Take You Home Again Kathleen" and "I Don't Want to Play in Your Yard." He sang and played each of them all through with care and concentration. During the difficult chord progressions his eyelids drooped and his voice sank to a whisper, rising again to a lusty bellow during the simpler parts. When I took the food into the sitting room Harvey balanced the plate on the piano and hit a few chords while talking and munching. "I want to ask you a couple of favors," he said.

"Go ahead."

"First, can I sleep on the sofa tonight? I think I was being followed today."

"You haven't brought a tail here?" I said in alarm. "You haven't led anyone right here to my flat?" I got up and walked around in neurotic agitation. The performance must have reassured Harvey. He said, "Good God, no. I got rid of them all right. Don't worry about that. I lost them O.K., but they know my hotel now. If I go back there I'm being tailed again."

"O.K.," I said grudgingly. "If you are sure you weren't followed here."

"It's probably only one of Midwinter's people anyway," said Harvey. "I mean they know where you live, so what's the difference?"

"It's a matter of principle," I said.

"Yes," said Harvey. "Well thanks."

"I'll have to go out before eleven o'clock," I said. "I'll be working all night."

"What's on?"

"Duty officer," I lied. "They put me on it while I was away. It's always us part-time people who get the worst duties. I'll be back around midday. You'll still be here?"

"I'd like to stay two or three days."

"Sure," I said. "I would like that."

Harvey hit a minor chord.

"It's about Signe," Harvey said. "She's high on you, you know." I said nothing. Harvey said, "I wish you'd come to Helsinki with me. To help me talk her into coming away with me. With you to help me I'm sure I'd make it."

It was going too well. It was too easy and I mistrusted it or perhaps I was seeing my role in a new light.

"I don't know, Harvey," I said.

"I won't ask you any more favors," Harvey said. "Not ever. And we'll make you godfather of our first child." He played the opening bars of the Wedding March.

"O.K., Harvey," I said. "We'll go to Helsinki together."

Harvey played a little trill.

CHAPTER 23

I LEFT Harvey in the flat. I felt sure he wouldn't want to go anywhere without me, but I didn't feel so sure about it that I called off the man who was still watching the flat. From the car I phoned the office. Harriman and the duty officer would meet me. Chico was the duty officer.

I phoned Dawlish and told him that I wanted to seal off the MRE thefts at once. I suggested that we let the Porton Security people grab the agent who was working inside the Experimental Establishment when he arrived next morning but I would deliver Pike into custody myself.

"Have someone who can take Pike from me between two and three A.M.," I said. "He'll have a written statement ready by then."

"What sort of story?"

"One without a beginning," I punned clumsily.

"That's exactly the sort of story one wants for a few days," Dawlish said. He laughed; he liked puns.

I went out to Pike's place in the country with Harriman and Chico. It was a cold night and the wind buffeted the car like a riot mob. Ralph Pike's house was in darkness, but the driveway of Doctor Felix Pike's mansion was crowded with motorcars of all shapes and sizes and every light in the house was on. The downstairs windows had the curtains open and yellow light fell across the lawn.

Inside, a crowd in evening dress was drinking and talking and beyond them on the far side of the room couples were dancing to the music of an elaborate gramophone with six loudspeakers. The Spanish manservant opened the door until he noticed we weren't in evening dress. He said, "It's not good where you have parked the car."

I said, "It's not good anywhere around here," and we eased our way in without further ceremony. "Where's Doctor Pike?" I said.

The manservant said, "He perhaps is busy. My master—"
"Get going," I said roughly. He spun around and headed into the smoke and noise. Harriman and Chico were sniffing at the engravings and waving away trays full of drinks. Pike appeared in a dinner suit, maroon with silk facings and shoulders padded like he'd left the hanger in. He smoothed his brocade waistcoat and held his smile tight enough to prevent the lower half of his face from falling off. "Dempsey," he exclaimed meeting my eye suddenly as though he hadn't been watching me from across the room. "To what do we owe this honor?" I said nothing.

Harriman said, "Doctor Pike, Doctor Rodney Felix Pike?"

"What's the trouble?" said Pike. He gripped the knot of his bow tie and pushed it hard against his thyroid.

"Are you Doctor Pike?" said Harriman.

"Yes," said Pike. "But you can damn well . . ."

"I think we had better go somewhere we can talk," said Harriman, speaking at the same time as Pike but slightly louder. They stared at each other in silence for a moment.

"Very well," said Pike. He turned and began to walk up the stairs. "Johnson," he called over his shoulder. "Send champagne and chicken for four up to the study." Only Pike would think of calling his Spanish servant Johnson.

The study was the sort of room that doctors keep in their private houses for tax purposes. There was just the light of the standard lamp shining on the oak paneling and on sabers and flintlock guns lined up over the fireplace. On the antique writing table there were copies of *Country Life* and three Bristol glass decanters. We all sat down in the Queen Anne chairs, except Pike, who walked across to the door to make quite sure it was closed. "Perhaps you'll tell me who the devil you are," he said finally.

"Inspector Simpson, Special Branch, sir," said Harriman. "This is Sergeant Arkwright." He indicated Chico.

"What about this fellow?" said Pike, pointing to me.

"I'll be coming to him, sir," said Harriman. There was a knock at the door and the white-jacketed man came in with a bottle of champagne, four glasses and a plateful of sandwiches. He said, "It's nicely chilled, sir. Will you be wanting the ice bucket?"

"No, that's all right," Pike said. He was standing in front of the glass-fronted bookcase twisting the key in the lock absent-mindedly.

When the waiter had gone, Harriman pointed at me. "We have this man in custody in connection with the theft of certain public stores from the Microbiological Research Establishment at Porton, said premises being a prohibited place in the meaning of the Official Secrets Act." Harriman looked at Pike. "I must caution you, sir, that anything you say may be used in evidence."

Downstairs the gramophone played mambo. Pike was looking at the books in his bookcase. "I'd like to see your warrant cards," he said. They gave them to him and I said, "They've got us, Pike. It's no good your thinking that you're going to get away with it while I go to prison for twenty years." Pike studied the cards and handed them back as though he hadn't heard me; then he walked across to the telephone. His way was blocked by Chico. Harriman said, "I wouldn't advise that yet. Not yet I wouldn't. After all, you have a lot of guests downstairs. We are being very civilized. You don't want us to go downstairs and interview your friends."

"What do you want?" said Pike. There was a knock at the door and then it burst open. The white-jacketed man said, "The house next door, sir, a chimney on fire." The woman with mauve hair was right behind him. "It's blazing, Felix," she said. "Shall I waken Nigel?" The music downstairs stopped abruptly. The white-jacketed man tried to reassure the woman. "They look worse than they are, madam. It's not dangerous." He looked around at us, awaiting instructions. "Call the fire brigade," said Pike. "That's what they're paid for." Pike turned back to the books. "Big sparks," said the woman. "Falling onto the lawn, but I've only just got Nigel to sleep." She went out. Soon the music began again. Harriman said, "This man says he collected the stolen items from you."

"What stolen items?" said Pike.

"Eggs. Fertile hens' eggs containing a live virus. These same articles being received by you knowing that they were stolen public stores." Pike turned back to his bookcase. We all looked at each other. Quiet. The tick of the clock seemed very loud. The woman's voice called, "Felix! It's getting worse and they haven't arrived yet." Pike was standing immediately behind me. It was so quiet in the room that I could hear Pike breathing even though the music still continued downstairs. The woman called again but Pike still didn't answer.

I said to Harriman, "I'll tell you about it." I turned to look up at Pike. I said, "If you want to pretend you *laid* the eggs, that's up to you."

Pike stared at me but said nothing. I turned to Harriman. "We're caught so that's all there is to it. Pike's brother . . ." I felt a stunning blow against the side of the head, my teeth clanged together and the room seemed to go soft for a moment like a movie dissolve. I shook my head, half expecting it to fall off and roll under the bookcase so we'd have to prod around with sticks to get it back. I pressed my hand against my head. There was a discordant noise in my ears and the room was rippling in waves of bright blue light. Harriman had Pike in an armlock and Chico was holding an antique pistol that was red and shiny at the muzzle end. The woman called again. The klaxon noise and blue flashes filled the room.

"For God's sake," Pike was saying to me. "Haven't you got any self-respect?"

Outside there was the hoo-haw of a fire-engine klaxon and through the window I could see a Pump Water Tender moving cautiously into the drive, its flashing blue light making a pattern on the ceiling.

"If you want to pretend you *laid* the eggs," I said to Pike again and rubbed my head. Pike made a movement but it wasn't a serious attempt to get free. The woman downstairs called, "Felix dear, you'd better come and speak to the firemen." Then I heard her say, "Perhaps he can't hear."

Harriman said, "I was hoping for a little more cooperation, Doctor."

"I'm busy, darling," Pike called. The gramophone began to play "When I Fall in Love" and there was a sound of dignified clapping as the guests continued to demonstrate the never-say-die spirit.

"I suppose you are going to deny you met me in the park and brought me here to meet your brother," I said.

Harriman said, "I'd be interested to hear your answer to that, sir."

"I've nothing to say," Pike said.

Harriman looked around the room as though checking how many of us there were. Chico was wrapping up the antique pistol in a grubby handkerchief. "Assault with firearm," I said. "That's a felony." Harriman let go of Pike and spoke very quietly to him. "Quite honestly, sir, I've no respect for people like this." He moved his head toward me. "Scum of the earth, just out for what they can get. But they know the way the law works, you've got to give them that. He knows the Public Stores Act isn't so serious and he could well have only a misdemeanor charge for receiving. I would have liked your story on paper first. I wanted to use your evidence to nail him. But he's determined to have it the other way round. He'll come out unscathed. You see—it's idealists like you that suffer. They always do." There was a brief knock at the door and it swung open. "You've got to come, Felix," said the woman's voice desperately. She pushed a red-faced fireman into the room ahead of her. "Tell him he's got to come downstairs," she said. With the door open the gramophone music was much louder and I could hear the radio-phone of the fire engine and the noise of the pump idling.

The fireman said, "I don't want to alarm your guests but it's getting a bit of a hold, sir."

"What do you expect me to do?" said Pike in a high-pitched voice.

"There's no danger, sir," the fireman said. "We've got our first-aid lines out but we'd like to get the appliances into the drive before we connect the main hose. We're blocking the street at present and your guests' cars are blocking us. There's no danger but we've got to have room to move." He ran a finger round the chin strap of his helmet.

The woman said, "They've got to have room to move, Felix."

"Wait a minute," Pike said. "Wait a minute." He pushed

Mrs. Pike and the fireman out through the door, closing it and turning the key.

Harriman continued to speak to Pike as though nothing else was happening. "Did you know these eggs were being sent to the Soviet Union, sir?"

"That's ridiculous," Pike said slowly and patiently. "We are all members of the Free Latvia movement. We have been working with the Americans. I am an American secret agent. All our planning is devoted to removing the Communists from Latvia." He explained it to Harriman as though he was becoming a new member.

"The cars," I heard the fireman shouting outside the door.

I said to Harriman, "I insist upon being allowed to write out my statement now."

"Very well," said Harriman. "Go along with him, Sergeant Arkwright," he said to Chico and the two of us made for the door.

"No," said Pike loudly. "I must go with him." He pushed past the fireman and the woman and overtook us on the stairs. Behind us I heard the fireman saying, "But I told him that he's not in any sort of danger. He's not in danger at all."

We took Doctor Felix Pike to the Ministry of Defense. Three policemen were waiting in the hall and they had cleared a couple of offices for us. Pike offered to make a statement. Harriman put a sheet of paper on the table in front of him and Pike began writing. The first paragraph gave his date and place of birth (Riga in Latvia) and the social condition of his parents. The rest of the statement was little more than a political manifesto advocating immediate armed invasion of Latvia to overthrow Communism. When Harriman told him that the immediate concern was theft of virus from the Government Research Establishment at Porton, Pike got very excited. He tore up his statement and folded his arms. He sat there gleaming in his white shirt like a man in a detergent ad.

"You can't hold me here against my will," said Pike.

"Yes, I can, sir," said Harriman patiently. "I am holding you under Section 195 of the Army Act. A person holding Army property without explanation may be arrested without warrant. You are not under arrest but you will stay here until I get an explanation."

"I want to see my lawyer," said Pike.

"And I want the explanation," said Harriman, a duologue they repeated sixteen times.

Finally Pike said, "I'm a doctor. You should show me a little respect."

"Doctoring isn't a club for supermen," Harriman said gently.

"Oh isn't it?" said Pike. "Well, sometimes I wonder. When I see some of my subhuman patients, I wonder."

One of the Ministry Police—a thin man in his middle forties—walked across to Pike and slapped him across the face with his open hand. Three smacks seemed very loud in that room. The policeman's hand moved faster than the eye could follow.

"Don't start arguing with them," the policeman said affably to Harriman. "You'll go around in circles." The policeman looked at Harriman but Harriman's face was blank. "I mean" . . . said the policeman . . . "I mean . . . We want to get home, don't we?"

Pike had gone white and his nose was bleeding. The front of his white shirt was a polka-dot pattern of blood. Pike stared at us, then down at his stains. I don't think he believed he'd been hit until the mottled shirtfront confirmed it. He dabbed at the blood with a handkerchief and carefully removed his tie. He folded it and put it into his pocket. His face was smudged with blood and he was sniffing loudly in an effort to stop the bleeding.

"Write," said the policeman. "Stop sniffing and start writing." He slapped the sheet of paper and left a tiny fingerprint of blood there. Pike took out his fountain pen and uncapped it, still sniffing; then he began to write in that crabby handwriting doctors take six years to perfect.

"Take Doctor Pike next door," Harriman said to the policeman.

I said, "And no more rough stuff."

Pike rounded on me—he still thought I was a fellow prisoner. "You look after yourself," he said angrily. "I don't need people like you to protect me. I did what I did for America and for Latvia, the land of my father and of my wife." His nose began to bleed again.

"Your nose is beginning to bleed again," I said. The policeman picked up the pen and paper and led Pike out of the room. The door closed. Harriman yawned and offered me a cigarette.

"It will be all right, I think," Harriman said. "And Chico thinks you are a genius." He smiled to indicate that he didn't agree. "No matter what I say, he's got it fixed in his head that you set a light to Pike's brother's chimney pot."

"That's marvelous," I said gloomily. "The next thing we know, Dawlish will start thinking so too."

| *Helsinki — Leningrad*

Who killed Cock Robin?
I, said the sparrow,
With my bow and arrow,
I killed Cock Robin.

—NURSERY RHYME

CHAPTER 24

I LANDED in Helsinki with an easy task. Harvey Newbegin must be arrested by the Americans without my being involved in the business. It was a simple enough problem. Any of our most junior operators fresh from the Guildford training school would have been able to do that, see a film, have dinner and still be able to catch the next plane back to London. Within five minutes of landing I knew that Dawlish was right. A new man should have taken over, someone who hadn't known Harvey for over ten years and who could deliver him to some pink-faced agent from the CIA like a parcel of groceries—sign here please, out-of-pocket expenses three hundred dollars—but I couldn't do that. I'm an optimist. In the last act of *La Bohème* I'm still thinking that Mimi will pull around. In spite of the evidence I didn't completely believe that he had tried to have me killed by the holdup men near Riga. I thought I might be able to straighten things out. Well that just goes to show that I should be in some other kind of employment. I've suspected it for years.

If the Americans were looking for Harvey they weren't doing it very well. I was half hoping that they would pick him up when we landed in Helsinki but Harvey had travel papers that said he was a Swedish national named Eriksson which meant he didn't have to show a passport at all. We took the airport bus with only three other passengers and Harvey asked the driver to let us off at a bus shelter about a mile down the road from the airport. The fields were gray with a hard carapace of frozen snow. We waited there only long enough for the bus to disappear, then Signe's VW tootled up to us. We didn't waste much time in greetings. We threw the bags behind the rear seat and then Signe drove into town, taking a long detour so that we came in on the Turku road.

"I did exactly as you asked," she said to Harvey. "I rented this apartment we're going to, by post, using a false name and not paying anything in advance. Then I went out and made a big thing of renting a place in Porvoo. I spent every spare moment in Porvoo tidying it up and dusting it and putting in a new bed. Yesterday I ordered flowers and smoked salmon and those *lasimestarin silli* that you like and extra sheets and said it must all be delivered in three days from now." The back wheels of the VW slid a little on the icy road but Signe corrected the slide effortlessly.

"You're a sensation," said Harvey and he lifted her hand from the steering wheel and kissed the back of it. "Isn't she the inside of a fresh bread-roll?" Harvey said over his shoulder to me.

"You took the words right out of my mouth," I said.

"We have a *ménage à trois*," said Signe. She turned to me. "You'll like that?"

I said, "My idea of *ménage à trois* has always been me and two girls."

Signe said, "But with two men you have a richer household."

"Man does not live by bread alone," I said. Signe kissed Harvey's ear. When it came to handling Harvey, Signe's European instinct was worth ten of Mercy's New World emancipation. Signe never tried to fight Harvey or hit him head-on; she gave way and agreed to anything for the sake of a temporary advantage, counting on her skill at making Harvey change his plans later. She was like an army poised to strike; probing and testing the disposition of the enemy. Signe was a born infiltrator; it was almost impossible not to be in love with her, but you'd need a guileless mind to believe half the things she said. When he was with her, Harvey had a guileless mind.

We stayed inside the house all the time except for a visit to an old Ingrid Bergman film and a short trip Harvey made to buy two dozen roses at 4 finnmarks each for Signe. Harvey never mentioned the fact that the Americans might be looking for him. We had a lot of fun in that apartment even though it was an ugly place where every room smelled of new paint. On the second night there I discovered what *lasimestarin silli* were. They were sweet pickled raw herring. Harvey ate six of them followed by steak, fried potatoes and apple pie; then we sat around and talked about whether Armenians are always short and dark, whether Marlboro cigarettes taste different when made in Finland, would my broken finger heal up as good as new, the sort of sour cream you put into borsch, can workers in America afford champagne, was a Rambler as fast as a Studebaker Hawk, judging a horse's age by its teeth and should America adopt the metric system. When we had exhausted Signe's search for knowledge we sank back with reading matter. I was reading an old copy of *The Economist,* Harvey was picking his way through the Finnish captions in the newspaper and Signe was holding a copy of an English woman's magazine. She wasn't reading it, she snatched items from it at random and threw them at us like hoops on a hoopla stall.

"Listen," Signe said and began reading aloud. " 'She saw Richard, his misty green eyes and smile were reserved for her alone and held a strange exciting promise. She knew that somewhere in the lonely corners of his heart he had found a place for her.' Isn't that lovely?"

"I think it's wonderful," I said.

"Do you?" said Signe.

"Of course he doesn't," said Harvey irritably. "When are you going to get it through your skull that he is a professional liar? He's a deceit artist. What iambic pentameter was to Shakespeare so lying is to him."

"Thanks, Harvey," I said.

"Don't take any notice of him," Signe said. "He gets mad because Popeye speaks in Finnish."

"Rip Kirby," said Harvey. "That's the only comic strip I read."

About midnight Signe made cocoa and we all went to bed in our various rooms. I left my door ajar and at eleven minutes past one I heard Harvey walking across the living room. There was a gurgling as he took a swig from one of the bottles on the serving cart. He let himself out of the front door as quietly as he could. I watched him from the window; he was alone. I walked to the door of Signe's room and I could hear her moving restlessly in bed. I decided that it was likely that I would foul matters up by trying to follow Harvey through the empty streets, so I went back to bed and smoked a cigarette and backed my judgment that Harvey would come back for Signe before disappearing for good. I heard footsteps across the living room and there was a tap at my door. I said, "Come in."

Signe said, "Want a cup of tea?"

"Yes," I said.

She went to the kitchen. I heard the sound of the matches and the kettle being filled. I didn't move from the bed. Soon Signe appeared with a tray crowded with teapot, milk jug, sugar, toast, butter, honey and some of the gold cups that were marked "Special" on the inventory we had signed.

"It's not even two o'clock," I protested.

Signe said, "I love eating in the middle of the night." She poured the tea. "Milk or lemon? Harvey's gone out." She was wearing Harvey's old pajamas, the jacket fastened by only two buttons. Over it she had a silk housecoat.

"I know," I said. "Milk."

"He'll be back though. He won't be long."

"How do you know? No sugar."

"He didn't take that old typewriter. He never goes anywhere without that. He wants to marry me."

"That's lovely," I said.

"Of course it isn't lurvelee," she said. "You know it isn't lovely. He doesn't love me. He's dotty about me but he doesn't love me. He said he'd wait for me. What girl would want to waste time with a man who could bear to wait for her? Anyway he's going to live in Russia."

"Yes," I said.

"Russia, do you hear that? Russia."

"I heard it," I said.

"Can you imagine a Finn going to live among the Russians?"

"I don't know," I said.

She sat down on my bed. "On the last day of the Winter War, after the armistice was signed, all shooting was to stop at noon, so during the last hour the Finnish soldiers were collecting their equipment and the ones that weren't in the fighting lines were marching back. All the roads in the rear of the armies were crowded with horses and civilians and soldiers all pleased that the war was over even if we had given the Russians our beautiful Karelia. It was fifteen minutes before noon when the Russian bombardment began. They say it was one of the most intense bombardments ever carried out; thousands of Finns were killed in that last fifteen minutes of the war, many were only crippled and hobbled back to tell us of it. The only way I want to see a Russian is through a telescopic sight."

"Perhaps you should have made your point of view clearer to Harvey instead of encouraging him in his illusions, of every kind."

"I didn't encourage him. I mean, I had an affair with him, but a girl should be able to do that without a man going dotty. I mean he's dotty, Harvey." Signe's long silk housecoat was black and gold, she got up and shook the skirt of it. "Do you think I look like a leopard in this?"

"A bit like a leopard," I said.

"I am a leopard. I shall spring on you."

"Don't do that, there's a good girl. Drink your tea before it gets cold."

"I'm a leopard. I'm cunning and ferocious." Her voice changed. "I'm not going to Russia with Harvey."

"O.K.," I said.

"Harvey said you thought it's a wonderful idea."

"Well," I said, "Harvey's very fond of you, Signe."

"Very fond," she said scornfully. "A leopard wants more than that."

"O.K.," I said. "He's madly and passionately and desperately in love with you."

"Well, you don't have to make it sound so . . . so eccentric.

You don't have to make it sound like he's got some sort of disease."

"Well, I'm sorry," I said, "but if you felt the same way about him I might be a little more enthusiastic."

"Oh so that's it. You're thinking about Harvey. All this time you're just feeling sorry for Harvey. Here I am thinking that you're jealous, thinking that you fancied me yourself and all the time you're just feeling sorry that Harvey has got himself trapped by a terrible girl like me. So that's it. That's it, I might have guessed."

"Don't start crying, Signe," I said. "Pour me some tea, there's a good girl."

"Don't you fancy me anymore?"

"Yes, I do."

"On Sunday," Signe said, "Harvey goes to Russia on Sunday. He's going on the midday train to Leningrad. When he's said good-bye and gone to Russia will things be different then?"

"In what way?"

"Will things be different between us? Well . . . you know."

"It's a lovely idea," I said. "But I'll be going to Russia with Harvey."

"You are a terrible tease," she pronounced.

"Don't spill the sugar in my bed."

Signe jumped onto the bed and punched me playfully but with a certain sexual innuendo. "I'm a leopard," she was shouting. "My claws are long and feeerooooocious."

She put her long fingernails against my spine and counted the thoracic vertebrae as far as the lumbar region. "I'm a left-handed leopard," she said. Her fingertips moved carefully like an archaeologist disinterring a fragile find. She measured four finger widths to the left and then stabbed me with her fingernail.

"Ouch," I said. "Either go to bed, Signe, or put more boiling water in the teapot."

"Do you know where Harvey has gone?" She nuzzled her head against my shoulder, her face was sticky with cold cream.

"I don't know and I don't care," I said, knowing that she was going to tell me.

"Gone to see a doctor from England," she paused. "You are listening now."

"I'm listening," I admitted.

"A Mrs. Pike—a woman doctor—brought some of those fertile hen's eggs. The woman thinks that they are going to America but Harvey has to take them to Russia with him or the Russians won't let him stay."

She must have collected them from the agent in Porton Experimental Establishment before we took him into custody Kept at the correct temperature they would be perfectly O.K. and Mrs. Pike would know all about that.

"Harvey's crazy to tell you anything," I said.

"I know," said Signe. "Leopards are cunning, merciless and untrustworthy."

She reached across me to the bedside light. That damned pajama jacket was far too loose on her. The light went out.

"As one leopard to another," I said, "remember that baboons are the only animals that can put us to flight."

CHAPTER 25

ALL my plans were made by Sunday. I had informed London, I had a visa for Leningrad, and Harvey seemed pleased that I had agreed to go with him. On Sunday morning we got up late. Harvey and I packed our suitcases slowly. Signe sipped coffee and listened to the English football results, marking her Finnish football pool coupon. She didn't win. I think Leeds United lost instead of drawing just as we finished packing. We had a late breakfast at the station. The restaurant is on the first floor and there is a view down the long central hall where the kiosks sell hamburgers, shirts, flowers, souvenir jugs, *Mechanix Illustrated* and *Playboy*.

Two fur-hatted policemen in blue mackintoshes were combing the seats for vagrants and another plainclothes cop was leaning on the 24-hour locker eating a hot dog. The shoeshine man was studying the shoes of passersby. Outside in the cold roofless terminus the trains were lined up side by side. The coaches were dark brownish-gray and made of thin vertical wooden slats. They were high and angular with a dozen big ugly ventilators along the roof. On the rear of the final train there were three red metal carriages. A yellow stripe ran beneath the large windows and on each there was a Soviet Union crest and a white sign that said HELSINKI—MOSCOW. From the chimneys of these carriages came a thin line of black smoke.

There was a Russian conductor standing at the foot of the steps to the carriage. He was a huge man in a blue overcoat and fur hat. He took our tickets and watched the embrace of Signe and Harvey with dispassionate interest. There was plenty of snow around and the steam and train whistles gave Signe a chance to play Anna Karenina. She had prepared for the part with matching fur hat and muff and a coat with a high collar. I kissed Signe in a brotherly way and she dug her finger-nails into that vulnerable place in my spine as I made way for Harvey to do his farewell scene. It was amazing how much they both enjoyed acting. She adjusted the collar of Harvey's coat like she was sending him to his first day at school. There were tears in Signe's eyes and I half expected that she would change her mind and climb aboard if only to do the same scene all over again in Leningrad.

When Harvey finally joined me in the compartment he pressed his nose to the glass and waved and waved until Signe was a tiny dot on the snowy station yard. The conductor had taken off his overcoat and was piling fuel onto a fantastic little stove that stood at the end of the corridor. He soon brought us a cup of weak lemon tea in a nickel-plated sputnik holder, and a packet of Moscow biscuits. Harvey settled back in his seat. His decision was made, he sipped his tea and watched the long trains loaded with timber, oil and paraffin clanking down the same route with us. The smoke scrawled graffiti across the slatelike sky. There was a jolt and a clang and the train stopped. The colorless northern winter lay heavy and inert on either side and across it, tiny black scratches of civili-zation—fences, wires, paths and slow trains—moved nose to tail like ants across an ashen corpse.

"This winter will never end," Harvey said and I nodded. I knew that for him it wouldn't.

There was a hiss of brakes. Some small animals—perhaps rabbits—ran out of the trees on the far side of the field, fright-ened by the sudden noise.

"You think she's a whore," Harvey said. "You can't under-stand what I see in her."

What a pair, I thought, both of them more concerned with seeming to be fools than being foolish.

"I like her very much," I said.

"But?"

I shrugged.

"But what?" Harvey demanded.

"She's a child, Harvey," I said. "She's a replacement for your children, not for your wife." Harvey, his arms folded, stared across the snow and ice. His face moved slightly, perhaps he nodded.

We looked at each other without communicating.

"It just couldn't be," said Harvey. "It was wonderful while it lasted but it was too perfect. Personal happiness must take second place when life itself is threatened."

I didn't know what he was talking about. "I'm glad you see it like that," I said.

"You knew all the time?"

I nodded.

"He wasn't an important agent. He was a courier, he'd been working for the Russians a couple of years and they didn't rate him so highly. Not until Signe killed him. Then they did. After Signe killed him with a hairpin—the Midwinter school taught her how—and stole a couple of documents from him, he suddenly became important and heroic and a martyr. I didn't know," Harvey said. "That's the funny thing, I didn't know until Signe told me yesterday." His arms were tight across his body like hoops around a barrel. "They won't do anything to her as things stand, but if she went to Russia it would be asking for trouble."

I nodded. "Asking for it," I agreed.

"She's killed four men if you include the Russian courier and Kaarna. She's the official killer for the Midwinter organization. An amazing girl."

"Yes," I said.

"She'll marry her cousin now. It will be loveless, just for appearances, he's a police official. Loveless marriage, poor devil." His folded arms relaxed.

"The husband?"

"Yes," said Harvey. "Poor devil. I wish she had told me before. I shall never marry either." He produced his cigarettes and offered them but I didn't accept one.

"But you *are* married," I reminded him.

"But not deep down," said Harvey. He shook his head in wonder. "Poor devil," he said.

"Yes," I said. "Poor devil."

The train gave a long agonizing groan of stretching metal and a *plink-plink-plink-plink-plink* ran like a shudder up through it.

I said, "We've known each other a long time, Harvey. I didn't ever try to give you advice before, did I?"

Harvey didn't say anything.

I said, "When this train gets to the station at Vainikkala we are both going to get off."

Harvey continued to look out of the window but this time his face moved enough to indicate that he wouldn't.

"What you are trying to do is impossible, Harvey," I said. "And Washington will have to keep everyone knowing it's impossible. They'll squash you like a gnat, Harvey. They might take a year to do it but they will. When an agent has the sort of knowledge you are carrying . . ." I shook my head. "Parlay your situation into a deal with Midwinter. He'll pension you off for the rest of your life."

"And he'll make sure it doesn't last too long," Harvey said.

"We can work out details to protect you if that's what you are scared of. Take a year's holiday, fish and relax. I'll work on Signe. She'll visit you—"

"She will not. It's the end. We said good-bye."

"There are other girls."

Harvey shook his head again.

"If it's girls—"

"For Christ's sake," Harvey said. "You're talking to me like I'm a cipher clerk in East Berlin. Girls and champagne, roulette and fast cars. Look, I love Signe. Are you incapable of understanding that? I'm pleased that she isn't with me. She's too wonderful to be mixed up in this stinking business." Harvey made pecking gestures with his fingers and thumb, emphasizing each word as if he were taking them and placing them upon the horizon in a long, precarious string. "That's how I love her; I talked her into staying in Helsinki. I don't want your lousy holidays around the fleshpots of Europe, but most of all I don't want girls."

I'd gone wrong. I tried again. "All right, Harvey," I said. "We'll play it any way you want. You don't have to do anything you don't want to do. You know what my orders have to be; we are both in the same business. Let's figure out something that will make Washington happy and make you happy too."

"Don't you ever give up? Can't you see that I'm not just a defector?"

"What are you then exactly—a trade commission selling extramarital sex?"

"Leave me alone." Harvey crammed himself into the corner and took the very tip of his nose between his finger and thumb as though it were another word he was trying to wrench loose.

"Just what do you think is going to happen when you get across that border?" I asked. "You think that someone is going to be waiting for you with a medal? You think you're just in time to watch the May Day Parade from Lenin's tomb? You know what happens to defectors that come to us, what makes you think you're going to be different? You'll end by teaching

English at a political school in Kiev. At best, that is; at best."

"What do you think I'm defecting for?" Harvey said scornfully. "Because Midwinter wouldn't give me a fifty-dollar raise?"

"I don't know what you're doing it for," I said. "But I know that when the train moves out of Vainikkala it's going to be too late to change your mind. It'll be good-bye to your kids, good-bye to your wife, good-bye to Signe and good-bye to your country."

"It's not my country anymore," said Harvey. "They tried to make me into an American but they couldn't do it. I don't need Walt Disney and Hollywood, Detroit and Madison Avenue to tell me how to dress and think and hope. But they write the script for the American dream. Every night America goes to bed thinking that when they wake up tomorrow there will be no Red China. They dream that the Russians will have finally seen reason. *Time, Life* and *Reader's Digest* will all have Russian language editions, and Russian housewives will be wearing stretch pants and worrying about what kind of gas stations have clean toilets and whether Odessa will buy the Mets."

"Midwinter doesn't think that."

"Sure he does. He just thinks we'll have to shake a fist at them first, that's all. Look," he said confidentially, "I don't have any strong political opinions but I'm a Russian. My old man was a Russian. I speak Russian nearly as well as Colonel Stok does. I'm just going back home, that's all."

"O.K.," I said. "But not with the eggs, Harvey. I can get away with not hauling you back feet first, but I can't let you take the eggs. I mean . . ." I opened my hand toward him. Harvey interpreted the movement as a threat.

"Just don't get rough," he said. "I have four fertilized hen's eggs inside my shirt. They are the few successful ones existing

of a batch of twelve hundred. I don't say your boys can't reproduce them, they can. But you know they won't believe any
story you tell them about their being broken."

I nodded.

"Well, those eggs are against my body. They are alive because of my body heat, those virus samples. I only have to roll
against this seat and I'll be wearing scrambled eggs. I'll tell
you what we'll do. You come to Leningrad with me and I'll
have their boys reproduce that virus and then give you four
eggs sealed in exactly the same way to take back to London.
How's that for a deal?"

"It stinks," I said. "But just for a minute I can't think of anything else."

"Atta boy," said Harvey. He drank the rest of his cold tea
and watched the countryside. "I'm really pleased you made
your pitch; I'd gotten quite tense waiting for it."

The train stopped and started many times all the way to the
border. Harvey stared moodily out of the window as a long
freight train went by.

"Trains," he said. "They used to be important once. Remember bogie-bolsters, borails, refrigerators, ventilated, low-
loaders? Remember all those reports?"

"That's going back a bit," I said.

Harvey nodded and said, "I'm glad you know about Signe
killing that Russian courier." He smiled and exhaled smoke
very slowly so that he disappeared behind a veil of it. "You
know what Signe's like."

"You thought she was inventing that story," I accused him.

"Hell no," said Harvey. He smoked his cigarette. "She was
more upset about leaving me than I was about leaving her.
Much more upset." The snow began again. Harvey said, "This
must be the most terrible winter of all time."

"It is from where you're sitting," I said. The train stopped again.

"Vainikkala." The voices called the name of the Finnish border station.

"Let's go and have coffee," I said. "We have twenty minutes here while they couple up the Russian locomotive. Last cup of real coffee for a little while."

Harvey didn't budge. I said, "Last cup of real coffee, Harvey. For a lifetime."

Harvey grinned and put on his overcoat cautiously so as not to disturb the eggs.

"No funny business," Harvey said.

I raised my hands in a gesture of surrender and led the way along the corridor.

"Too many Finns about anyway," I said.

The Russian conductor looked up from his stove and grinned. Harvey spoke to him in Russian and said something about not letting the train go without him and we will have more tea and biscuits when we come back. I said, "What do we want tea and biscuits for? We are getting off the train now to go to the buffet."

"You don't have to eat them," Harvey said. "But the old guy makes a little profit on them so that he has some spending money in Finland."

"Looks like he's doing nicely," I said. "Judging by that bottle of Gordon's gin he's clutching."

"That was a present," Harvey said. "He told me that was a present from someone he hardly knew."

Harvey was very proud of speaking Russian.

We had coffee in the large station buffet. It was clean, warm and bright and had that hygienic Scandinavian atmosphere that goes so well with the Christmas-card landscape outside. We stood in the falling snow and watched the locomotive—a huge green toy with bright red wheels and a red star on its navel. It clanked gently against the train which now had shed its Finnish coaches.

"What happens next?" Harvey asked.

"Soon Soviet customs and immigration men get aboard and process us as we go through the border zone. At Vyborg they put a diesel locomotive onto the train and add some extra coaches to take zone traffic to Leningrad."

"So once I'm back aboard I'm as good as in Russia?"

"Or as bad as in Russia," I said. I climbed up the steps and into the train.

"As bad," said Harvey. "What have you got that the people of Leningrad can't get?"

"Speaking personally, a ticket back to Helsinki."

Harvey punched me in the arm but when I went to hit him —equally playfully—he said, "Take care now, I'm a nursing mother." He thought I had forgotten that he was carrying the eggs, but I hadn't forgotten.

It was a long journey to Leningrad. The afternoon light was beginning to go. The snow was still falling and the flakes were light against the darkening sky. Harvey took off his coat and settled into the corner seat. There was a white embroidered cloth on the table and a reading lamp. The train trundled on for what seemed like hours, stopping and starting every few yards for men to do technical things with the switch levers, throw salt on the points and wave flags and lamps. We stopped in a forest. The clearing was as big as a football field and from it an unused timber siding looped off to a tumbledown shed and weighbridge. Along the firebreak between the trees came a large black Russian motorcar. It drove cautiously over the rough track, skirting piles of sleepers and heaps of brushwood. At this point the forest road was about fifty yards from the railway. It was as near as the car could get to us. It stopped.

"So this is Russia," I said to Harvey. I switched on the table lamp, the yellow light reflected our faces in the window.

Harvey said, "Are you sure there's no dining car all the way to Leningrad?"

"Ask them," I said. "You're friendly with the management."

"Aren't you going to tell me it's my last chance?" Harvey said.

"It's too late," I told him. "The MVD are here." I could see them through the half-open door, walking down the corridor as if they owned the train. They slid the door back with an abrupt crash. "Papers," said the shortest one and he saluted. They wore khaki jackets and shirts, dark trousers and green peaked hats. The sergeant who had saluted examined Harvey's passport tentatively as though he was having difficulty with the Western script. The captain reached across him and snatched it away. "Newbegin?" he asked.

"Yes," said Harvey.

"Proceeding to Leningrad?" Harvey nodded.

"Come with me, bring your baggage." The captain turned to go. The sergeant snapped his fingers at Harvey to hurry him up. They didn't seem any too friendly.

"I'll come along too," I said.

The captain turned back to the compartment and addressed me. "You will stay on the train. Mr. Newbegin will be travelling to Leningrad by car. You will stay aboard the train. My orders were especially clear about that."

The sergeant pushed me back into the compartment and closed the door. From the corridor I heard the captain tell the sergeant not to get near Newbegin. I suppose he didn't want him to crush the eggs. The train started again and ran forward a few yards. It stopped. I opened the window in time to see the man in captain's uniform drop to the ground and help Harvey with his suitcase. It was more than forty yards between the timber road and the railway and although the Volga car moved forward to stay abreast of the train it was a long walk across the deep snow. The windshield had gone gray from the snowfall but two shiny black triangles were swept clean by the wiper blades. The exhaust rose in that evil-smelling black cloud Russian gasoline gives off and I could almost smell it from where I was leaning out of the train. The three men seemed to be moving very slowly, like athletes in slow-motion films. Harvey looked back at me and smiled. I waved good-bye to him. The two Russians hustled him toward the open door of the car. Perhaps it was because they were in deep snow or perhaps because they were all wearing such thick outer clothing but they all moved with a slow choreographic grace. Harvey took his overcoat off with a twirl and the sergeant stood behind him with a small cardboard box for the eggs. The car driver was sitting well forward in his seat and I could see him staring fixedly at the train as though it was the first one he had seen and he was a little frightened of it. Harvey took off his overcoat and his jacket to get to the eggs that were under his shirt. The wind was inflating his shirt like a spinnaker and his face was pinched with the pain of the icy gusts. The captain laughed and made motions for him to hurry so that they could all get into the warm car. I don't know what happened next exactly but suddenly Harvey—still in shirt sleeves with the wind inflating him like a Michelin man—was running. He ran toward the train. His movements were curious, the deep snow made him lift his feet high in the air like one of those horses specially trained for trotting races. He scrambled across the first lot of tracks, slipping and sliding on the icy sleepers and taking his weight briefly on the fingers of his right hand. Pursuing Harvey came a column of tiny red ants. Harvey stumbled and fell forward up to the wrist in the snow but he pushed himself clear and was up and running in strange convulsive movements, weaving and twisting, falling and rolling in the air as he fell, touching the ground with a finger tip and springing up to full height like a jack-in-the-box. All of Harvey's skill was mustered in this one long choreographic routine. All of his balance, timing, and speed were tested as he jumped, slipped and slithered through the deep snow.

The sergeant had dropped the empty cardboard box and was standing in the classic stance of the pistol range, his elbow slightly bent. His arm jerked abruptly as he fired at Harvey. The driver of the car let in the clutch. The car came bouncing forward after Harvey. Harvey was trying to get to the train. The column of red ants was still following him across the snow and I realized that they were tiny drops of blood scattered by the wind. The captain was hanging out of the front door of the Volga car and also firing at Harvey with a large pistol. It seemed unlikely that he would hit him for the car was bounced up and down by the mounds of ice, old sleepers and junk frozen tight into the earth.

The train made a loud clanging and jerked forward. Harvey had been very close to the train but now it was snatched away from him. The car had stopped at the place where the forest track curved sharply away from the railway lines. The sergeant had stopped firing. He stood lonely and motionless out there in the snow, his pistol arm outstretched, his head cocked on one side like a perverted Statue of Liberty. His gun was steady and sighted on the entrance to the train. Harvey would have to climb those metal steps and when his arm reached up to grasp the handrails his body would be fully extended—a large target even for a pistol shot. Harvey reached toward the train. I watched the sergeant as he fired his gun. It jumped in his hand and there was almost no smoke.

He fired three shots in rapid succession, not waiting to see the effect of the first as he put the other into the target area.

I don't think Harvey knew what was waiting for him at the steps to the train; it was one of the few pieces of good luck that he had ever enjoyed. He slipped. He slipped on a sleeper or tripped over a rail or a spike and went down full length into the snow. I couldn't see him very clearly now but as he picked himself out of the indentation he had made in the snow I could see that one elbow was red with blood and he was wearing a yellow girdle of smashed raw egg. The sergeant took ten seconds to remove the empty pistol clip, find a fresh one in his pocket, insert it and go back to the firing position but it was long enough for Harvey to fling himself headfirst into the open door of the carriage. When I got down the corridor he was wriggling on his belly like an eel. The train jerked forward with a terrible groan, then began to pick up speed. Harvey was breathing slowly in deep noisy gulps and his whole body was shivering. He rolled over very slowly until he could see me. His heavy eyes were only half open. "Christ, I was frightened," he said. "Christ."

"I can see your yellow belly," I said.

Harvey nodded and continued to use every muscle he had to keep his lungs moving. Finally he said, "I thought the bastard was going to give me one last volley up the backside as I was lying there."

I said, "You'd better let me look at that arm of yours."

"Let *you* look at it?" said Harvey. "Do you think I don't know that they were your boys? That railway sign there, about ice on the points, is in Finnish. We're still on the Finnish side of the frontier. They were your boys dressed up as Russian border men."

"They were Americans," I said. "We would have done it better than that. Let me look at your arm."

"What do you want to do, finish the job for them?"

"Don't be bitter, Harvey. There were no recriminations when your protégés arranged a violent end for me in Riga."

"That had nothing to do with me," Harvey said.

"On your honor, Harvey?" I said. Harvey hesitated. He couldn't lie on his honor. He could cheat, steal, have Kaarna murdered and the man in the dentist's chair. He could even have his boys attempt to kill me but he couldn't tell a lie on his honor. Harvey's honor was important to him.

"O.K. Look at my arm," said Harvey. He turned his elbow toward me. "I cut it on the car door." From the conductor's room I could hear the snoring of a man in a very deep sleep and out of the corner of my eye I could see the Volga car speeding away down a narrow forest road. Harvey had sticking-plaster in his luggage. I pulled it tight across his cut. "It's only a scratch," I said. There wasn't much time before the real customs men got down to us.

CHAPTER 26

WE both stayed at the Europe Hotel that night. The next morning Harvey and I had breakfast together in the buffet—curd cakes and sour cream—and I got around to saying good-bye as gracefully as I could.

"Coming out to the airport?" I said. "I'm catching the morning flight."

"What's waiting out there for me? Twenty strong-arm men and a padded jet plane?"

"Don't be that way, Harvey."

"Don't be that way, Harvey," Harvey echoed. "What I should be doing is turning you over to the Russians right now."

"Listen, Harvey. Just because you've been playing electronic monopoly out there in Texas for too long, don't get the idea that you're in the intelligence business. Every senior-grade Russian intelligence man knows that I came into town on the train last night. They know who I am just as I know who they are. No one puts on false hairpieces and pebbles in one shoe and sketches the fortifications anymore."

"I did," said Harvey.

"You did and that's what had us fooled for a couple of weeks. I couldn't make anyone believe that there were people like you around anymore except on late-night TV."

"I could still tell them a couple of things they don't know about you."

"Don't bet on it, sonny. If you take my advice you are going to stay dumb because it's my guess that you are going to get very disenchanted with this town and when you do, you are going to need some nice friendly country to move to—and you're running short of countries to move to—especially since you are going to have no hot news or live eggs to peddle next time."

"That's what you think—"

"Don't say a word," I told him. "You may spend the rest of your life regretting it."

"All I regret is that those boys in Riga didn't knock you off." Harvey wiped some cream off his mouth and threw down his napkin. "I'll see you to your cab," he said.

We walked out. There were signs of a thaw. All along the Prospekt the huge drainpipes were groaning and rattling and emitting sudden avalanches of ice across the pavement. Sweeping machines were removing the final traces of last night's snowfall, but even as Harvey remarked on how clean the streets were, a formation of suicide flakes came spinning down preparing the way for a new snowstorm.

A few cabs went by. All hired. One of them switched out his green light when he saw us. I suppose he was heading home —all over the world taxi drivers return home the moment the weather takes a turn for the worse. Harvey got depressed because he couldn't find a cab. I suppose he felt everyone should be greeting him and thanking him for being a convert. "I've got a headache," Harvey said. "And last night I had a temperature and the cut on my arm hurt. I bet I've got a temperature right now."

"You want to go back to the hotel?"

"No, I'll be all right but everything goes black. Whenever I bend down, everything goes black. Why does it do that, I mean, is it serious?"

"That's because everything is black and you only see it properly when you're bending down."

"You don't give a damn about anybody. I'm sick." But Harvey didn't go back to the hotel. We walked slowly up the Nevsky; it was crowded like a rough sea of dull overcoats and fur. There were the wide faces of Mongolia, small pinched Armenians with little black moustaches, naval officers in black uniforms and soldiers in tall astrakhan hats.

A boy in a jazzy bow tie grabbed Harvey's arm and said, "You an American? You want to sell something . . . cameras . . ."

"No I'm not," Harvey said and wrenched free. The youth blundered into a group of naval officers and as we moved on I could hear their voices scolding him. "He hurt my arm," Harvey explained. "My bad arm." He rubbed the arm. Harvey wanted to cross the Prospekt against the red light, but I dissuaded him. "Is it man's ultimate fate to be ruled by machine?" Harvey said. He smiled. I tried to see the extent of his irony. Was that Harvey's comment upon the Billion Dollar Brain? I couldn't tell. I'll never know, for that was virtually

Harvey's last remark to me. We edged down the pavement of
Nevsky Prospekt, Harvey stroking his grazed arm and me
watching for a taxi.

"Yes," I said, still looking for a taxi.

"More cabs on the other side of the street," Harvey said.
We stood on the corner watching the fast-moving traffic.

"There," I said. "There's one."

He stepped off the pavement. There was a scream of brakes
and a man shouted, but the single-decker bus slammed into
Harvey fairly and squarely and Harvey disappeared under it.
The bus gave two jolts and then, as the brakes were applied,
the locked wheels slid on a slick of red oil. A bundle of rags
spewed out from the rear of the bus as it slewed around and
came to rest broadside to the traffic. The long puddle of oil
was streaked with blood. There were two shoes sticking out
from the bundle but they were at a strange angle. The driver
climbed stiffly down from the bus. She was in her early thirties,
her large peasant face made even rounder by the head scarf
tied tightly under her chin. She was wiping the palms of her
hands on her hips and watched while the man who had shouted
—a tiny wiry man—knelt down beside the bundle and clawed
at it gently, after first removing his fur hat.

"Dead," he called.

The bus driver was crying and wringing her hands. She intoned a short Russian prayer over and over again. Two policemen arrived on a motorcycle and sidecar. They fastened back
the flaps of their fur hats and began to question the bystanders.
One of the passengers on the bus pointed to me and as the
policeman looked around I eased my way back into the crowd.
The man immediately behind me did not stand aside. He was
still blocking my escape when one of the traffic cops reached
me. The cop began to speak to me in Russian but the man
showed them a card and they saluted and turned on their heels.

"This way," said the man, "I'll get you along to the airport." The woman bus driver's prayer was broken by her racking sobs. They had moved Harvey's body and she could see his face. I didn't want to go with this man, I wanted to comfort the driver. I wanted to tell her that it wasn't her fault. I wanted to explain that she was just a victim of circumstances which she couldn't possibly have avoided. But as I thought about it I thought that perhaps it was her fault. Maybe it was Harvey who was the victim of circumstances where the driver and a few million others do nothing to cure a mad world in which I am proud of myself for being on my side, and I despise Harvey for his code of honor and telling the truth.

"The airport?" said the man again.

One of the policemen began to scatter sand over the pool of oil and blood. "Yes please, Colonel Stok," I said. Nearby a thawing drainpipe gave a great rumble and vomited a heap of wet ice across the pavement.

Stok stepped clear of the crowd and snapped his fingers. From across the street a Zis car swung through the traffic and drew up in front of us. The driver leapt out and opened the door. Stok motioned me in. The car radio was going and there were warnings being broadcast. The ice was cracking on the river Neva, people were warned against walking across it. Stok told the driver to switch the radio off. "Ice," Stok said. "I know all about that." He pulled a small flask out of his pocket and handed it to me. "Have a drink; it's warming."

I drank a little and then coughed. It was thick and so bitter as to be almost undrinkable.

"Riga Balsam," said Stok. "It will warm you."

"Warm me? What do I have to do, set fire to it?" But I took a second swig anyway as the car pulled out onto the road for the airport. I looked back toward the bus. No matter how much sand they put down, the blood and oil showed through it.

Some of the Zis cars have a special tone of horn that warns policemen on point duty that a VIP is on his way. Stok's car had such a horn and the car roared through the intersections without pausing.

Stok said, "It's an anniversary for me today. My wound." He rubbed his shoulder. "I was wounded by a sniper during the Finnish business. If he'd had a little less vodka perhaps he would have killed me." He laughed. "It wasn't often their snipers missed—cuckoos we called them—they infiltrated miles behind the front and even killed generals. Some of them would infiltrate our lines, eat at our field kitchens and then vanish back to their own bunkers. Remarkable. It was a day a little like today. Icy, a slight snowfall. I was with a tank regiment. We saw a group of men in Red Army traffic-control uniforms, complete with armbands, waving their flags and diverting us off the road. That was not unusual, we often traveled across open country. But those men were Finns in Red Army uniform. Suddenly we came under a terrible fire. I kept the hatch open. I had to see. It was a mistake." He rubbed his shoulder and laughed. "It was my first day of front-line action."

"Bad luck."

"We have a saying here in Russia, 'The first pancake is always a lump.' " He kept hold of the shoulder. "Sometimes on a cold day I feel a twitch in the muscle. The medical men on the front line were not good with the sewing needle, and you would never believe how cold it was. The fighting went on even at forty degrees below zero. Ice formed across the open wounds. Ice is a terrible thing." Stok produced a packet of cigarettes and we both lit up. "I know something about ice," Stok said again. He exhaled a great billow of smoke. The driver hit the horn. "I fought near here during the Great Patriotic War.* On one occasion we went out on skis to take samples of local ice.

* Russian name for World War II.

We needed to know if the Lake Ilmen ice would support the weight of a KV tank—forty-three tons—so that we could take the Fascist 290th Infantry Division in flank. Forty-three tons is three hundred pounds per square centimeter. The Lake Il-men ice was fine. It was frozen almost to the bed of the lake, but do you know, at times it was possible to see the ice bending, bending under the weight. Of course the tanks had to keep well spread out across the lake as we moved. There were two rivers ahead, the movement of the water meant that the ice would never grow very thick. On our reconnaissance we put logs into the water so that the logs would freeze together to make a hard surface. We put steel cables from tank to tank—like men climbing a mountain—and the first four tanks went over the ice and logs without trouble except that there was a crack here and there. Then as the fifth tank was a little over halfway across there was noise like pistol shots. The four leading tanks revved up and as number five sank they dragged it right through the surface ice—perhaps half a meter of ice—with a tremendous noise. For perhaps three minutes the tanks were not moving, straining at . . ." He paused. Stok pressed his enormous hands together and made cracking sounds with the joints. "Then with a huge noise, through it came."

"The crew couldn't have survived that freezing water for three minutes."

Stok was puzzled. "The crew? No, there were plenty of crews." He laughed and for a moment stared past me at his youth. "There are always plenty of men," Stok said. "Plenty to follow me, plenty to follow you." We turned across the traffic at the Winter Palace. There were a dozen tourist buses and a long line of people waiting patiently to view the treasures of the Czars.

"Plenty to follow Harvey Newbegin," I said.

"Harvey Newbegin," said Stok, choosing his words with

even greater care than usual, "was a typical product of your wasteful capitalist system."

I said, "There's a man named General Midwinter who thought Harvey was a typical example of your system."

"There's only one General Winter," Stok said. "And he's on our side." The car was speeding along the bank of the Neva. On the far side I saw the Peter and Paul Fortress and the ancient cruiser *Aurora* through the veil of falling snow. In the Summer Garden the statues had been encased in wooden boxes to prevent their cracking in the cold.

The snow was getting heavier and visibility was so reduced that I wondered whether the plane would be on schedule. I wondered too whether Stok was really taking me to the airport.

"Harvey Newbegin was your friend?" Stok asked.

"To tell you truthfully," I said, "I don't know."

"He had little faith in the Western world."

"He had little faith in anything," I said. "He thought faith a luxury."

"In the Western world it *is* a luxury," Stok said. "Christianity tells you to work hard today for little or no reward, and tomorrow you will die and awake in paradise. Faith like that is a luxury."

I shrugged. "And Marxism says work hard today for little or no reward, and tomorrow you will die and your children will awake in paradise. What's the difference?"

Stok didn't answer, he tugged at his chin and watched the crowded pavements.

Finally he said, "A high official of your Christian church spoke at a conference recently. He said what they have most to fear is not a Godless world but a faithless church. This is the problem of Communism too. We do not fear the petty psychopathic hostility of your Midwinters; if anything they help

us, for our people become at once more unified when they understand the hate directed toward us. What we have to fear is
the loss of purity within ourselves—faithlessness of leadership
—an abandoning of principle for the sake of policy. In the
West all your political movements from the muddled left to
the obsessional right have learned how to compromise their
original—perhaps naïve—objectives for the sake of the reali-
ties of power. In Russia we too have compromised." He
stopped talking.

"Compromise is no pejorative word," I said. "If we choose
between compromise and war, I'll take compromise."

Stok said, "I am not talking about a compromise between
my world and the West; I am talking about a compromise between Russian socialism today—powerful, realistic and worldly
—and the Russian socialism of my youth and even my father's
youth—uncompromising, idealistic, pure."

"You are not talking about socialism," I said. "You're talking about youth. You are not regretting the passing of the
ideals of your boyhood, you're regretting the passing of your
boyhood itself."

"Perhaps you are right," said Stok.

"I am," I said. "Everything that has happened to me in the
last few weeks has been due to this sad envy and admiration
that old age has for youth."

"Oh well, we shall see," said Stok. "In a decade we shall
know which system can offer the best standard of living if
nothing else. We'll see who has an economic miracle. We'll
see who is traveling where to get luxury consumer goods."

"I'm pleased to hear you endorsing the idea of a competitive
system," I said.

Stok said "You are going too fast" to the driver. "Overtake
the lorry with care." He turned back to me and smiled a warm

smile. "Why did you push your friend * Harvey under the bus?"

We looked at each other calmly. There were cuts on his chin and the blood had dried in small shiny dark pimples. "You tried your criminal murdering activities at the frontier and failed, so you were assigned the murder of Newbegin here in the center of our beautiful Leningrad. Is that it?"

I took another swig at the Riga Balsam and said nothing.

"What are you, English, a paid assassin, a hired killer?"

"All soldiers are that," I said.

Stok looked at me thoughtfully and finally nodded. We were speeding down that incredibly long road to the airport that ends at some strange monument I have never visited. We turned off to the right, through the entrance to the airport. The driver drove up to the wire barriers and sounded the horn. A soldier swung the barrier back and we drove right on to the tarmac, bumped off the concrete and pulled up alongside an IL-18 that had the turboprops spinning. Stok reached inside his black civilian overcoat and produced my passport. He said, "I collected this from your hotel, Mr."—he peered at the passport—"Mr. Dempsey."

"Thank you," I said.

Stok made no attempt to let me out of the car. He went on chatting as though the wash of the turboprops wasn't rocking us gently on our springs. "You must imagine, English, that there are two mighty armies advancing toward each other across a vast desolate place. They have no orders, nor does either suspect that the other is there. You understand how armies move—one man a long way out in front has a pair of

---

* Stok used the word *droog*. While a *tovarich* can be anyone with whom you come into contact even if you hate him, a *droog* is someone who has a special closeness and for whom you might possibly do something against the national interest. E.g., if the police are after you, you would possibly go to a *droog* for shelter but a *tovarich* would turn you in.

binoculars, a submachine gun and a radiation counter. Behind him comes the armor and then the motors and the medical men and finally dentists and the generals and the caviar. So the very first fingertips of those armies will be two not very clever men who, when they meet, will have to decide very quickly whether to extend a hand or pull a trigger. According to what they do, either the armies will that night share an encampment, exchange stories and vodka, dance and tell lies; or those armies will be tearing each other to shreds in the most efficient way that man can devise. We are the fingertips," Stok said.

"You are an incurable romantic, Comrade-Colonel Stok," I said.

"Perhaps I am," Stok said. "But do not try that trick of dressing your men up in Soviet uniforms for a second time. Especially in my district."

"I did nothing like that."

"Then do not try it for the first time," said Stok. He opened the door on his side and clicked his fingers. His driver ran quickly around the car and held the door. I got out of the car past Stok. He looked at me with Buddha-like impassivity and cracked his knuckles. He held out an open hand as though he expected me to put something into it. I didn't shake hands. I walked up the steps and into the aircraft. There was a soldier standing in the aisle scrutinizing the passport of every passenger. I wasn't breathing easily until we were out over the sea. It was then that I found myself still holding Stok's hip flask. Outside, the snow beat around the plane like a plague of locusts. It wasn't going to thaw.

| *London*

*There was an old woman
Lived under a hill
And if she's not gone
She lives there still.*

—NURSERY RHYME

CHAPTER 27

RESPONSIBILITY is just a state of mind," said Dawlish. "Naturally Stok is going to be furious, all his work has come to nothing, but from our point of view it happened beautifully. Everyone is pleased about it. In fact, the Minister used these very words: "The Newbegin business happened beautifully," he said.

I stared at Dawlish and wondered what really went on under that distinguished graying hair.

"The operation was successful," Dawlish said as though explaining to a child.

I said, "The operation was successful but the patient died."

"You mustn't ask for too much. Success is just a state of mind. We don't get called in until there has already been a failure somewhere. The trouble with young people nowadays is that they worship success. Don't be so ambitious."

"Did it occur to you," I asked, "that Harvey Newbegin

might have been ordered to defect by the CIA or the Defense Department? He used to work for them. It's a possibility."

"It's not our job to calculate the permutations of deceit. If Newbegin were still alive at this moment we'd be sitting here worrying about him. A Newbegin dead means there is no risk." He leaned forward to tap ash into the wastebasket and stiffened as a new thought hit his mind. He swiveled his head to look at me. "You did see him dead?" I nodded. "It was his body? No chance of a substitution?" He began to tidy his desk.

What a convoluted mind Dawlish has. I said, "Don't make it even more complex. The dead body was that of Harvey Newbegin. Do you want it in writing?"

Dawlish shook his head. He screwed up a couple of memo sheets and threw them into the wastebasket. "Close the file," he said. "Check records for sub-files and give anything we hold to the morning War Office messenger for Ross. He'll probably file it under Pike. Check that by phone and mark our card accordingly." Dawlish scooped up a heap of pins, clips and ribbon from the morning's correspondence and threw it away. He picked up a blackened light bulb from his desk. "Why do electricians leave these dud bulbs lying around?"

"Because they're not allowed to take anything out of this building," I said. Dawlish knew that as well as I did. Dawlish weighed the bulb in his palm, then tossed it gently into the wastebasket. It shattered. I don't know if he intended that it should, it wasn't like him to break things, not even a used bulb. He looked at me and raised his eyebrows but I said nothing.

Of course the case wasn't over. It never will be over. It's like a laboratory experiment where some poor bloody mouse is injected and everything is normal for one hundred generations and then they start bearing offspring with two heads. Meanwhile science had pronounced it safe. That's what we did. We pronounced it safe but we weren't surprised when the two-headed monster turned up. It was first thing in the morning—9:45. I had just got to the office. I was reading a letter from my landlord that said that playing the piano and singing "Wearing of the Green" at half past midnight was breaking the terms of the lease. The landlord only mentioned that one song and it wasn't clear whether his objection was political, musical or social. Furthermore, said the letter, there was a small motor vehicle parked outside which had offensive remarks scrawled over it. Would I please clean it or remove it. Jean was saying, "It could be the steam treatment but I think it's the back-combing." The phone rang and she said "Very good" and hung up. "The car is outside. Hair is very delicate —if you continually brush it the wrong way, it begins to break."

"What car?" I said.

"Trip to Salisbury. First of all you feel the texture getting rough and stiff and then the ends divide." She twirled an end of hair around her finger.

"What car?"

"Trip to Salisbury. And of course it won't hold a wave. Stringy. I don't want that to happen."

"What for?"

"You've got to go to see Doctor Pike in prison. So I had the best man there look at it. Geraldo. He's going to reshape it so that it can grow right out."

"First I've heard about it."

"It's on the memo under your digestive biscuits. No more back-combing and certainly no more steam until it grows back into a soft texture."

"Why didn't you tell me?"

"I thought that would be the first place you would look.

Once you break the hair it can be very serious. The actual growth is impaired. Now I don't know whether that means . . ."

"All right, I'm sorry. When I said yesterday that I didn't need you to do anything except type and answer the phone I was hasty. I apologize. You have made your point so let's not carry the scheme of sabotage any further." I got up and stuffed the memo into my briefcase. "You'd better come with me. There's probably all sorts of information that I will need, and you have."

"That's right," said Jean. "If you would deal with the files in order instead of getting madly interested in half a dozen of them and neglecting the rest, you would know your day-to-day schedule. There's a limit to what I can handle."

"Yes," I said.

"And on Wednesday I would like . . ."

"To get your hair done," I said. "O.K. I get the message. You don't have to be subliminal. Now let's go." Jean went to her desk and found a sealed file with a code word—Turnstone— and a reference number on it. Penciled very lightly in the corner was the word Pike. "I wish you wouldn't do that," I said, pointing to the penciled words. "They are going dotty over at South Audley Street about two of our files that had names penciled on the outside. It's a bad breach of security. Don't ever do it again, Jean."

"I didn't do it," Jean said. "Mr. Dawlish did it."

"Let's go," I said. Jean told the switchboard where we would be, told Alice that we wouldn't be wanting morning Nescafé, locked the carbons and ribbons, etc., into the metal cabinet, renewed her lipstick, changed her shoes and we left.

"Why is Pike at Salisbury?"

"He's being held as a psychotic under treatment at a military prison. He's tightly locked up; they aren't very keen on even us seeing him but Dawlish insisted."

"Especially us, if I know Ross."

Jean shrugged.

I said, "Ross can't hold him longer than a month. Can't hold him at all if he's a voluntary patient."

"He's not a voluntary patient," Jean said. "He's protesting like mad. Ross gave him a wad of papers to sign and Pike found he had applied for a commission in the RAMC. They commissioned him and put him straight into prison. He smashed up his cell and now is held in the mental ward. Ross is holding on to him like mad. It looks as if he'll be there until Ross is certain that the Midwinter network is absolutely disintegrated. Ross, you see, got the rocket about the eggs from Porton. The cabinet was very shirty and reading between the lines told him that it was us that pulled the coals out of the fire."

"Ross must have been delighted," I said, not without some pleasure. "So what have I got to do, sign something?"

"No," Jean said. "You've got to get Pike to write his wife a letter advising her to leave the country."

"Ho-ho."

"Yes. The cabinet is desperately anxious that we don't have another big spy trial this year, the Americans are making life difficult enough already. This business—Midwinter amateur spy network—will get colossal exposure in the States and there will be even more pressure about U.S. secrets not being shared with Britain."

"So Mrs. Pike will join that great army of people spirited away to all parts east before the Special Branch boys arrive huffing and puffing with an arrest warrant, its ink still wet, in their hand. It's only a matter of time before Special Branch tumbles to what's going on."

"It's only a matter of time," Jean said, "before the *Daily Worker* tumbles to it."

We collected a file of flimsies from RAMC records at Lower

Barracks Winchester and stopped in Stockbridge for lunch. From there it's only a short journey.

The fingers of winter pressed deep into the white throat of the land. The trees showed no sign of leaf and the soil was brown and polished shiny by the damp winds. Farms were still and silent and the villages deserted as though spring was not expected to return. The prison is sited on a narrow ridge on the extreme edge of the plain. It's the only psychiatric (maximum security) prison that is run entirely by the Army. The buildings are modern and light and in the grounds there is a huge piece of abstract sculpture and two fountains that are switched on when someone important is coming. Along the drive flower beds—now brown and bare—were the size and shape of newly filled-in graves. The Governor's secretary was waiting for us in the main entrance. It was a Kafka-ish place that looked a little too big for humans and smelled of ether. The Governor's secretary brandished a large manila file at us. He was a small beautiful man who looked as though he had been assembled from a plastic kit and his fingertips were in ceaseless movement as though he had got sticky stuff on them and was trying to remove it. He extended one of the flickering little hands to me and let me shake it. Then he saluted Jean and went into an on-guard with a copy of the prison rules, which I signed. Jean parried with the RAMC documents and a straight thrust with Pike's passport. The man did a cut-at-flank with a Governor's memo that we hadn't seen. Jean lost ground initialing this but did some crisscross high-cuts with a War Office file from Ross. The man was signing it with a flourish when Jean lunged with a photostat of some cabinet minutes that had nothing to do with this case at all. She had judged her opponent well for he surrendered before reading it all through.

"Very comfortable interrogation room," the man said.

It was much too likely to be bugged.

"We'll see him in his cell," I said. "Perhaps you'd send some tea down there."

"Very well," said the man. "They said you'd have your own way of doing things." He smiled to indicate that he didn't approve. I waited a long time for him to say "It's very irregular" but he didn't say it. We walked down the main hall to the senior warder's office. Inside, a muscular warder with a key chain down to his knees looked up from his desk as if he hadn't been poised there waiting for us.

"Take these people across to Three Wing—special observation," said the man. He handed the warder the flimsy sheet of yellow paper which I had signed.

"That body's receipt must be back in my office before this lady and gentleman leave the main gate." He turned to us and twittered an explanation. "Otherwise you won't get out." He turned back to the warder. "All right, Jenkins?"

"Yes sir," said Jenkins. The Governor's secretary offered us his fidgety little hand.

I said, "It's very irregular."

"Yes," he said and went away tut-tuttering.

Jenkins went across to the filing cabinet and unlocked it. "Would you like some tea?" he asked over his shoulder.

"Yes please," Jean said. He unlocked the filing cabinet and produced a bag of sugar. "I'll bring some sugar down for you. Have to lock it up," he explained. "The night shift pinches it."

Three Wing is used for the prisoners who need constant attention, and is set apart from the other buildings. The grass was beaten into mud by winter and the grounds were silent and devoid of any sign of gardeners or guards. The psychiatric prison was like a very modern primary school from which all the breakables have been removed. The gates were designed in modern patterns to avoid the feeling of being behind bars. But the patterns weren't large enough to squeeze a man through. There was a constant clang and clatter of keys and everywhere was much too clean. As we passed each door Jenkins sang out the name of it—dining room, association room, quiet room, classroom, library, physiotherapy, electroconvulsive therapy. Obviously Jenkins was kept specially for visitors. In the highly polished corridor leading to Pike's cell there were prints by the better adjusted of the Impressionists and outside his cell in a wooden frame were slotted cards bearing his name, number, a colored one for his religion so that the chaplain could spot it and special diet (none), but I noticed that there were no cards in the space that said "sentence and classification."

Pike's cell was small but light and—oddest of all for a prison —the window was low enough to see through, although only for a distance of ten yards. The wind was howling across the yard outside but the cell wasn't cold. The paint work was a petrifying yellow and there was a narrow strip of coconut matting of the same color. On the wall was a copy of the prison rules in microscopic type. There was a hospital bed, a triangular washbasin and a flushing water closet. On the wall there was a crucifix, a photo of Pike's house, a photo of his wife and a photo of the Queen; the Queen was in color. Beside the bed there was a tiny reading lamp with a lampshade of a baroque design with red plastic tassels. Pike had been reading a copy of *I Claudius*. He placed a cigarette paper inside as a marker and put the book on the table.

The warder said, "Vis'ter f'yer, Pike, on y'er ft nat erper sission nerve tenshun." Pike obviously understood this strange language for he stood rigidly at attention. He was dressed in army fatigue uniform. The warder walked close to Pike and inspected him. There was nothing threatening in the way he did it. He did it like a mother who had cleaned a bowlful of porridge off her child and wants to be sure he is now quite tidy. The warder turned back to me and spoke in a different voice. "Two teas for you and the lady. I'll put sugar on the tray. Do you want tea for the prisoner?"

"That would be very nice," I said.

When the warder had left, Pike said, "You've done all right for yourself, haven't you?"

"I'm a busy man, Pike," I said. "If I had my way I would just deliver you to the Soviet Embassy and forget the whole thing, but providing you don't make my job more difficult than it already is I'll try to remain as unprejudiced as possible."

"Well, first of all you'd better hear——"

"When and what I want to hear from you, I'll let you know," I said. "In any case, you're one of the Army's problems at present, nothing whatsoever to do with me."

"What do you want then?" He touched his buttons to be sure they were all correctly fastened. Finding that they were, he glared at me defiantly.

"I'm here to tell you that if your wife decided to leave the country, nothing would be done to impede her."

"Very kind," said Pike huffily. He stroked his uniform in quick nervous movements.

"Don't let's be confused about this. We know that last week she took another—I might add a final—batch of stolen virus to Helsinki. She returned to England yesterday. Although she thought she was doing it for the Americans, those eggs were due to be delivered to the Russians. Luckily they didn't get there."

"Russians," said Pike scornfully. "They've told me some stories in here but that's the best one yet. I am an American agent. I work for a secret American organization called Facts for Freedom."

"It's about time you moved into the past tense," I said. "And it's about time that you got it into your thick pill-pushing head that stealing from a highly secret government establishment is a very serious criminal charge no matter if she was going to boil the eggs for three minutes and eat them with thin bread and butter."

"Threats, is it?" said Pike. He undid his pocket button as though he were getting a notebook, then he fastened it up again. "I'll have the whole lot of you in the Old Bailey. They tell me that psychiatric prisoners are not allowed to petition the Home Secretary or the Minister of Defense but I'm going to take this matter to the House, the House of Lords if necessary." The words came smooth and fluent as though he had said them to himself many times; although without believing them.

"You are not taking anything anywhere, Pike. If I let you walk out of here now to . . . well to anywhere, to the BMA, or to your MP or your mother . . . you'll spin your story about joining the Army by accident and then being held by Military Intelligence in a lunatic asylum. Do you expect anyone to believe that? They'll say you are a nut, Pike, and so will the army psychiatrist that they send along to examine you. You would feel your arms slipping into a backward overcoat before you knew what was happening to you. Then you would begin to struggle and shout and yell about your innocence and sanity and everyone would be even more convinced that you're a nut."

Pike said, "No psychiatrist would lend himself to such a thing."

I said, "You're naïve, Pike. Perhaps that's been your trouble all along. That army psychiatrist will uphold the diagnosis of his colleagues. You were a doctor, Pike; you know what doctors always do; they agree with their colleagues. Haven't you ever covered up for someone's faulty diagnosis by agreeing? Well, that's what this psychiatrist would do; especially after reading your dossier." I tapped it. "It says in here that while masquerading as a doctor you endangered the lives of fourteen persons."

"It's all a tissue of lies," Pike said desperately. "You know that. My God, it's diabolical. A man came here three days ago and insisted that I had once been an artillery officer in Kuwait. Last week they said I was an abortionist. They're trying to send me insane. You know what's true."

"I know only what's in your file," I said. "You played amateur wonder-boy spy games. Men get hurt doing that. Most of them are far more interesting than you. Now let's get down to business. Where would you like your wife to go?"

"Nowhere."

"Just as you like, but when your wife goes into custody they will probably make your child a ward of the court; he'll end up in an orphanage. Your wife will get at least seven years." I put all the documents back into my briefcase and locked it.

Pike stared at me. I could hardly recognize the man I had met in the King's Cross consulting room. The hair that had been sleek and steely was now as limp as cotton and streaked with gray. His eyes were sunk deep into his skull and his protests were not accompanied by any muscular activity. He was like a man dubbing a sound track on an action film and unable to make it convincing. He ran a finger around the neck of his uniform blouse and waved his chin about. I offered him a cigarette and while I lit it for him our eyes met. Neither of us could muster the slightest glint of kindness.

"Yes . . . well. We have relations in Milan. She could go there."

I said, "Here's some paper, write her a letter suggesting

she go to Milan. Don't date it. Make it a very strong suggestion because if she doesn't go within a couple of days I won't
be able to prevent her arrest."

"A different department," said Pike sarcastically.

"A different department," I agreed, and I let him have pen
and paper and when he had finished writing I let him have
a cup of tea with two cubes of sugar.

CHAPTER 28

JEAN was typing out our file on the Midwinter
organization. She stopped. "What a lovely name, the Loving
Trail. Why is it called that?"

"A man named Oliver Loving drove cattle from the pasture
of Texas to the railhead at Cheyenne."

"It's a lovely name, Loving Trail," Jean said. "I suppose
that's what they were all on. General Midwinter loving America strongly although not very cleverly."

"The understatement of the year."

"And Mrs. Newbegin. I know you hated her but I'm sure
that it was a distorted sort of love that drove her on to soft-
soap Midwinter and pressure Harvey into being a big success."

"Stealing. Is that your idea of success?"

"I'm trying to understand them."

"Mrs. Pike and Mrs. Newbegin are exactly the same type.
Tough, aggressive, hard-bitten, handling their husbands like a
road manager with a new pop singer. You work with these
files all day, you know that women like these almost never
think in terms of politics. They are biologically motivated and
biology being what it is, the female of the species will survive.

Drop them into Peking and in six months either of those women will have a big house, nice clothes and a husband operated by remote control."

"What happened to Harvey Newbegin? Did his control blow a fuse?"

"Harvey loved youth. Like a lot of people who covet other people's youth he really wanted to be rid of his memories. Harvey wanted to start all over again—by marriage, by defection—he didn't mind as long as he could have a new clean slate."

"I'd say that was his wife's fault; he felt trapped."

"Everyone feels trapped, it's our way of rationalizing our leaden lot in the face of our golden potential."

"That reminds me," said Jean. "I must renew your subscription to the *Reader's Digest.*"

Very funny. I fixed fifteen paper clips into a neat chain but when I pulled it, one, the third from the end, distorted and gave way.

"Why did Harvey Newbegin defect?" Jean asked. "I still don't understand."

"He was an unstable man in a high-pressure world," I said. "There's no nice glib explanation. He wasn't a Communist spy, a revolutionary or a subversive Marxist. They never are. The day of the political philosopher is over. Men no longer betray their country for an ideal; they respond to immediate problems. They do the things they do because they want a new car or they fear they'll be fired or because they love a teen-age girl or hate their wife, or just because they want to get away from it all. There was no sharp motive. There never is, I should have known that, just a ragged mess of opportunism, ambition and good intentions that go wrong. That's the path to hell. Just build an inch of it every day and it can be a painless journey."

"What does your golden potential tell you about Signe; a sex pot?"

"No," I said. "You know . . . young girls."

"No," Jean said woodenly. "You do."

"She's a young girl who suddenly discovers she's a beautiful woman. The sort of men who have been telling her not to make so much noise are suddenly waiting on her and listening to every word she says. Power. She gets a little drunk on it, it's nothing out of character. Madly in love one day, out of love the next. A lovely little game but Harvey took it seriously. But Harvey was an actor too, he relished it."

"I was looking at the medical report on Kaarna's death," Jean said. "The Helsinki police said that it was a thin pointed instrument, the wound being delivered by a right-handed assailant from behind him with a downward striking action—"

"I'm way ahead of you," I interrupted. "A hatpin used by a left-handed girl who had her arms around him while both were lying on the bed would give the same sort of wound. A Russian courier died from exactly the same type of wound five months before, so did several others. She was good at counting vertebrae.

"Cloth traces in the teeth?" said Jean in a businesslike way.

"We all have our funny little ways," I said.

"My God," said Jean. "You mean she *was* the official killer for the Midwinter organization just as Harvey Newbegin said?"

"Seems like it," I said. "That's why old man Midwinter asked me if she was emotionally entangled. He was still thinking of using her on Harvey."

"What will happen to her now?"

"Dawlish is hoping that Signe Laine and Mrs. Pike can be employed by us."

"Blackmail."

"A harsh word, but if we offer them a job they'll be in a difficult position to refuse."

So Ross at the War Office had found a way to hold Dr. Felix Pike in custody without the publicity of a public trial but even Ross couldn't pretend that Mrs. Pike had joined the Army and gone crazy. We had a tacit agreement with Ross that he would leave Mrs. Pike to us. We wanted to keep her under observation with a view to recruiting her.

Ross wouldn't break his agreement but he knew other ways of sabotaging us. Early Friday afternoon we heard that Special Branch had become interested in Mrs. Pike. We all knew it was Ross's sly hand, the artful little sod.

"The artful little sod," I said.

Jean snapped the file closed and produced a large manila envelope. Inside it there were two airline tickets and a bundle of American currency. "Dawlish wants you to put Mrs. Pike on an airplane." She looked at her watch. "Special Branch is going along there with a warrant this evening, so you'll have to use the letter from Pike after all. You should have an hour to turn her around if you hurry."

"I hate these bloody jobs."

"I know you do."

"You are very sympathetic I must say."

"I don't get paid to be sympathetic," Jean said. "I don't see why you must always be so holy about the sort of jobs you do. It's quite straightforward; get Mrs. Pike on the plane before she gets arrested. I should have thought you liked playing good Samaritan."

I took the tickets and stuffed them in my pocket. "Well, you can come too," I said. "Then you'll see how bloody enjoyable it is."

Jean shrugged and gave the driver Pike's address. Friday night in weekend cottage land. Foundations were sinking and damp rising. Stockbrokers in Daimlers and casual clothes arrived relaxed and would leave Monday morning tense and exhausted. It was a cold evening. Toasted tea cakes, kettles singing on the hob, hansom cabs and deerstalker hats almost visible through the light fog. Besterton Village was a clutter of architectural styles from timber frame with brick nogging to the phony Georgian of the Pike residence.

The converted barn that Ralph Pike had lived in had burn marks on two of the upstairs windows. There were no cars in the drive now, no music or signs of life anywhere. I rang the bell. The Spanish manservant came to the door.

"Yes?"

"Let's see Mrs. Pike."

"Not here," he said and began to close the door.

"You'd better find out where she is," I said, "before I find myself checking your work permit."

He grudgingly admitted us. We sat down on the long-buttoned Chesterfield among the ivory carvings, antique snuff-boxes with funny rhymes, silver pen sets and letter openers. In the hearth a dachshund was curled like a pretzel among the carefully polished fire irons. The manservant came back. "Mrs. Pike is here," he said and gave me a bright orange paper.

> Besterton Village Junior Private School invites parents and friends to a grand performance. *Ting-a-ling-a-ling.* Performances by children of Besterton Junior Private School. Doors open 6:30. Performance begins at 7 P.M. Admission free. Silver collection in aid of local charities. Come early. Coffee and light refreshments available at popular prices. Teachers will be happy to answer parents' questions.

"Come on, Jean," I said.

A cold wind howled through the telephone lines, the last molecule of daylight gone. A great amber traffic-light moon urged caution upon the reckless universe. Toads croaked in the ditch. Somewhere nearby a little owl was making its *kiu-kiu-kiu* call.

Jean took my arm and said,

> *"The owl shrieked at thy birth, an evil sign;*
> *The night-owl cried, aboding luckless time;*
> *Dogs howled, and hideous tempests shook down trees."*

I said, "My sole excursion into Shakespearean drama was playing the ghost of Hamlet's father. My cue was Marcellus saying, " 'Look where it comes again.' Enter ghost; stand around haunting until someone said, 'Stay! speak, speak! I charge thee, speak!' then exit ghost, without a word."

Jean said, "You were forming the behavior patterns of later years."

I said, "The ghost does have lines, 'My hour is almost come when I to sulphurous and tormenting flames must render up myself.' And there were some about 'lust, though to a radiant angel link'd, will sate itself in a celestial bed, and prey on garbage' but they didn't like the way I said them and they finally had a boy backstage speak them through a metal funnel."

The school was a large house that was once called The Grange. Its grounds had been divided into rectangles upon each of which a modern house stood. A large signboard— BESTERTON JUNIOR PRIVATE SCHOOL—had been hammered into the front garden to attract juvenile residents of the village who declined to mix with lower-income groups.

A lady in a fur coat sat on a chair in the doorway. "Are you a father?" she asked, as Jean and I entered.

"We're working on it," I said. She smiled grimly and allowed us in. A large hand-drawn arrow pointed down a corridor that smelled of exercise books and chalky dusters. We went through the door marked ASSEMBLY HALL PLATFORM. The monotonous sound of a carefully played piano came from the body of the hall. Mrs. Philippa Pike was behind the scenes. I gave her the note from her husband and she looked at me a long time before unfolding it. When she had read it she looked unsurprised.

"I'm going nowhere," she said. There was only just enough light to see her face but beyond her a little girl on the stage was caught in the crisscross green beams of the spotlights. She wore sequin-covered wings and they flapped as she moved, twinkling in the hard green light.

"You'd be wise to take your husband's advice," I said. "He's probably in a better position to judge the situation."

The little girl was saying:

> *"The north wind doth blow*
> *And we shall have snow,*
> *And what will poor Robin do then?*
> *Poor thing."*

"No, I don't think so," said Mrs. Pike. "You tell me he's in prison. That's not a good place from which to judge any situation except your own."

"I didn't say where he was, I said I had a message from him."

The little girl said:

> *"He'll sit in a barn,*
> *And keep himself warm,*
> *And hide his head under his wing,*
> *Poor thing."*

The spotlight changed to pink as she hid her head under her nylon wing.

"It's simple enough," I said. "Here's an airline ticket for you and your son to Milan. If you catch this next plane I will pay your expenses and there will be plenty for clothes, et cetera, to save your going back to the house, which may already be under observation. If you don't do that we will accompany you back to the house when you leave here. You will be taken into custody."

"I suppose you are just obeying your orders," she said.

"But not unthinkingly, Mrs. Pike," I said. "And that's the difference."

The little girl on the stage twirled around with her head under her wing. I could see her lips move as she counted the twirls. Mrs. Pike said, "I don't trust you."

A little boy dressed as a toy soldier with huge white buttons and two disks of red on his cheeks came up to Mrs. Pike and touched her hand. "I'm on next, Mummy," he said.

"That's right, dear," said Mrs. Pike. The little girl on the stage was waving a large papier-mâché lantern about the stage and there was now only one blue spotlight.

She said:

> *"How many miles to Babylon?*
> *Three score miles and ten.*
> *Can I get there by candlelight?*
> *Yes, and back again."*

All the lights came on. Mrs. Pike's face was suddenly revealed clearly. The little girl curtsied and there was a noise of clapping. The audience had been so quiet that I hadn't realized there were about sixty people just a few inches behind the hardboard.

"Do you have a clean handkerchief, dear?" Mrs. Pike said.

"Yes," said little Nigel Pike, the toy soldier. The little girl came flushed and laughing to the side of the stage where her father lifted her down. A man said, "In position the toy soldiers. Where's the unicorn?" He climbed onto the stage and arranged Nigel and his friends in formation and scrambled out of sight behind a pile of dwarf-size desks.

"And I don't trust you," I said to Mrs. Pike. "I also was in Helsinki last week."

The toy soldiers, a lion with sticking plaster on its knee, and a unicorn with a horn that was coming unraveled had formed up on the stage. The piano began. One of the toy soldiers waved a sword and the others began to recite in unison:

> *"The lion and the unicorn*
> *Were fighting for the crown;*
> *The lion beat the unicorn*
> *All round about the town."*

The lion and the unicorn tapped wooden swords and made growling noises like TV wrestlers.

Mrs. Pike was watching the brightly lighted children with unseeing eyes.

"You'd better make up your mind quickly," I said. "But let me just make it as clear as I can. By now"—I looked at my watch; it was 7:45—"a warrant has probably been issued, but because this is Buckinghamshire there will probably be a bit of telephoning going on to appease the Chief Constable. I'd say you have two hours before they block ports and airfields. These tickets won't be worth a damn once Special Branch at London Airport gets its orders."

One of the toy soldiers was singing,

> *"Some gave them white bread,*
> *Some gave them brown;*
> *Some gave them plum cake*
> *And drummed them out of town."*

Mrs. Pike was watching her son. The man at the other side of the stage was whispering very loudly, "Go on, unicorn. Go on, unicorn, run round the tree."

"The unicorn has taken too long eating the plum cake," I said.

"Yes," said Mrs. Pike. "He did at rehearsals too."

"It beats me," Dawlish said. He had the office fire piled precariously high with coal and had borrowed a fan heater from the dispatch department, but still the office was cold. Dawlish leaned down to the fire and warmed his hands. "You walked through London Airport with this child dressed as a toy soldier? I don't know how you can be so foolish. Passport control noted it of course. When the alert came through they remembered."

"Yes," I said patiently, "but Mrs. Pike and the kid had left the country by then."

"Dressed as a toy soldier," said Dawlish. "Can you think of anything more conspicuous? Couldn't you have put an overcoat on him?"

"Where would I get an overcoat to fit a small child between Buckingham and Slough at eight o'clock at night?"

"One improvises," said Dawlish. "Use your initiative."

I said, "I used up so much initiative on this case that it was wearing thin."

"You do think of some things," said Dawlish. "Dressed as a toy soldier. I said that to Ross the other day when he was objecting to you going down to Salisbury. I said he may be a little captious, he certainly has a chip on his shoulder and he is liable to get hold of the wrong end of the stick, but he does keep the Department lively. What were you thinking of, walking up to the Alitalia desk with a toy soldier?"

"I was thinking how lucky I was not to be there with a unicorn."

"A unicorn," said Dawlish humoring me, "I see."

Behind him I could see a tiny blue patch through the gray cloud. Perhaps spring would be coming soon.

Appendix 1

SOVIET MILITARY DISTRICTS

There are twenty-three military districts. The most important are: Moscow, Leningrad, Baltic, Belorussian, Kiev and Maritime (which includes Far Eastern). As well as these there are Army Groups Germany and also the Polish Army which is still largely officered by Russians, some of whom don't speak Polish.

A Military Council commands each Military District under the direct orders of the Ministry of Defense. The Military District is remarkably self-sufficient, commanding even tactical air forces.

Naval units and long-range air force units have their own systems of districts and are under Moscow's orders but, like Stok's KGB, their food, lodging, vehicles, fuel, etc., are supplied by the local Military District.

Appendix 2

SOVIET INTELLIGENCE

Soviet units are not only very complex and overlapping but constantly change their names and their relative power. For instance, the MVD (formerly the NKVD) was at one time the most powerful of all such organizations and a visit from a sergeant could intimidate an ordinary army colonel. It had its own air force, tank force, supply service and communications. Nowadays the MVD sergeant will be the man looking under your seat for stowaways when you cross the Soviet border, and even then he is likely to have an officer watching him to see that he does it right. Among the many other intelligence units in the USSR there are those of the Foreign Ministry, the Party, the Air Force, Army and Rocket Forces. The major units however can be divided into three.

1. The MVD. It has been called the Cheka, GPU, OGPU and NKVD, but after Stalin's death the Ministry of Internal Affairs (MVD) became mostly concerned with intelligence only at a tactical level. Its present duties include highway patrols, traffic services, fire services and militiamen. It also handles all registration, e.g., marriage, birth, driving license, visa and passport, including those of foreigners. Each Border District H.Q. has an Intelligence Unit to report about the foreign territory facing them. At present its most important unit—GUVV—is responsible for internal security units.

2. All military intelligence of the General Staff comes under the Chief Intelligence Administration (Directorate) and this is the GRU. Each army division has a GRU unit commanded via its military council GRU. At the top of the GRU tree there are GRU networks in Western countries. Famous old boys include Colonel Zabotin of the Gouzenko affair in Ottawa, Alexander Foote (au-

thor of the famous *Handbook for Spies*), and Richard Sorge of Tokyo. The GRU also control the specialized "Study Department" which studies documents published in the West which will provide information—especially technical information—of use to Russia. Over the past decade this particular department—in spite of its lack of glamour—has provided more and better information than all the other departments put together.

3. The most important unit of intelligence is the KGB. Under Beria this was the Ministry of State Security—MGB—but was re-formed as a mere committee of State Security KGB and had certain devices built into the chain of command to prevent another Beria—or even a Hoover—taking it over as a personal force. The top-ranking Foreign section—INU—is calculated to operate about 75 percent of all Soviet espionage overseas. Rosenberg and Colonel Abel were employees of the INU section of KGB, so were Petrov, Khokhlov, Rastvorov, etc. There are many sections of the KGB: the KRU—counterintelligence—and SPU Special Political are next in order of importance after INU. There is a special part of the KGB which is devoted to watching the army. This is called the GUKR, which is often translated as Senior Counterintelligence and its duties are thereby confused with the KRU mentioned earlier. The GUKR however *watches the Soviet Army*. Before 1946, GUKR was sometimes called SMERSH and was a part of the Defense Ministry.

The function and power of each of these organizations is subject to change. Although there is just as much backbiting among Soviet intelligence as among Western intelligence there is one difference: it is not unusual for one department to relinquish its network to a rival command. A man this week working for the GRU might next week be working for the KGB whether he knows it or not. In any case, as I have pointed out, he probably thinks he is working for America or France. So if you are indulging in a little extracurricular espionage, remember that you might be working for your ideological enemies. Take a tip from the professionals; do it just for the money.

Appendix 3

PRIVATELY OWNED INTELLIGENCE UNITS

There are quite a few of all shapes and sizes. Most of them are émigré formations like the Ukrainian Socialist Party which is an anti-Communist Russian group based in Munich. There also is the Natsionalno Trudovi Soyuz (NTS) or National Labor Alliance, which has been going since the early thirties. It has Whites and all sorts of Soviet Army deserters mixed up with the ex-Vlassov men (a Nazi puppet army). It is especially interested in putting men into the USSR to spread propaganda because it feels that the USSR is on the verge of revolt. It is said to have links with the Gehlen Bureau and the CIA. NTS men were parachuted into Soviet territory in April 1953 but their trial didn't come until much later because Soviet Intelligence didn't want to endanger a man named Georg Müller who had penetrated the NTS in 1948. The trial said the men were trained at Starnberg School in shooting, radio, forging, sabotage and parachuting. They publish news sheets *Za Rossiou* (*For Russia*) and *Nacy Dni* (*Our Days*). NTS also controls International Research on Communist Techniques.

When this book was in galley-proof stage Mr. Gerald Brooke, a London lecturer, was brought from the Lubyanka Prison to the Moscow City Court and tried for subversive activities and propaganda in connection with the NTS. He was sentenced to one year in jail and four years in a strict-regime labor colony. Mr. Anthony Bishop, a British diplomat, was expelled from Moscow because— the Soviet authorities allege—he was also connected with the NTS.

The most famous private organization is the Crusade for Freedom headed by Eugene Holman (Standard Oil-Esso, New Jersey) which runs Radio Free Europe and Radio Free Europe Press. The RFE has 28 transmitters and employs well over one thousand persons. Some people think that RFE was too provocative in its broadcasts to Hungary during the revolt.

Another organization is the International Service of Information Foundation Inc., which is run by Air Force Reserve Colonel Amoss on a grant from a millionaire businessman. Information Bureau West is a private news agency which concentrates upon building a minutely detailed picture of the DDR (East Germany) from press, radio, visitors and government sources.

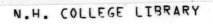